By Lex Chase

Loving and Loathing Vegas
With Bru Baker: Some Assembly Required

Screw Up Princess and Skillful Huntsman Trilogy
Fairy Tales of the Open Road
Americana Fairy Tale
Bayou Fairy Tale

Published by Dreamspinner Press
www.dreamspinnerpress.com

By Bru Baker

All in a Day's Work (Anthology)
Branded
The Buyout
Campfire Confessions
Diving In
Dr. Feelgood (Dreamspinner Anthology)
King of the Kitchen
Late Bloomer
With Lex Chase: Some Assembly Required
The Magic of Weihnachten
Talk Turkey
Traditions from the Heart

DROPPING ANCHOR
Island House
Finding Home
Playing House

Published by DREAMSPINNER PRESS
www.dreamspinnerpress.com

SOME ASSEMBLY REQUIRED

LEX CHASE
and
BRU BAKER

Published by

DREAMSPINNER PRESS

5032 Capital Circle SW, Suite 2, PMB# 279, Tallahassee, FL 32305-7886 USA
www.dreamspinnerpress.com

Some Assembly Required
© 2016 Lex Chase and Bru Baker.

Cover Art
© 2016 Reese Dante.
http://www.reesedante.com
Cover content is for illustrative purposes only and any person depicted on the cover is a model.

ISBN: 978-1-63476-809-2
Digital ISBN: 978-1-63476-810-8
Library of Congress Control Number: 2015952692
Published February 2016
v. 1.0

Printed in the United States of America
∞
This paper meets the requirements of
ANSI/NISO Z39.48-1992 (Permanence of Paper).

To Damon Suede, this is all your fault.

Chapter One:
DEL TORO

BENJI SERIOUSLY considered not answering when his phone rang, but he knew that would just delay the inevitable. He scowled at his mother's face on the display and swiped to answer.

"Hey, Ma."

"Is this a good time? I can call back if you're busy."

She sounded so hopeful.

Benji sighed. "No, you're not interrupting anything. I was just cleaning."

"Benjamin Goss, you're thirty-two years old! This is the prime of your life. You should not be home cleaning on a Saturday night." Somehow his mother managed to put the full weight of her disappointment in her voice. It wasn't a surprise. She'd been long-distance shaming him for years.

Benji shifted the phone, sandwiching it between his ear and his shoulder so he could keep scrubbing at the spot Mr. Whiskers had marked while he'd been out grocery shopping earlier.

"Dating's a whole new ballgame now, Ma. It's not just Saturday night anymore. People go out all week long."

Not that he'd been out on a date lately. But he was well aware that, theoretically, people went out for midweek drinks or dinners to take some of the pressure off. A Saturday-night date came with expectations. That was some serious shit. A low-pressure Tuesday or Wednesday was much more his speed. Not that he was going on any midweek coffee dates, either. But he could, if he were so inclined.

"Benjamin, you have to get out there. Date someone your own age this time. I know you miss Charles, but—"

"Nope," Benji said, stopping that before it got dangerous.

His mom had never liked his ex, Charles. For starters, Charles was ten years older, and Benji knew his mom blamed the age gap for how set in his ways Charles had been. But Benji knew the truth. It hadn't been Charles's age. It had been Benji's own inability to say no to anything. Benji desperately wanted to please people, and as a result he'd let Charles walk all over him. In the end it had landed him in an apartment he didn't want with a cat he was allergic to—and who peed on the carpet.

"At least tell me you're looking. Didn't Alyssa offer to set you up with one of her friends last week?"

His sister had indeed offered to match him up with a friend of a friend. Benji had even gotten as far as googling the guy, and he'd been pretty hot. Definitely Benji's type. A little older, strikingly handsome, smart. But they'd never gotten past the texting stage. The guy had suggested a Saturday-morning farmer's market outing as their first meeting, and that had sent alarm bells ringing like klaxons in Benji's head.

Saturdays with Charles had always been reserved for farmer's markets and lazy meals that took hours to cook and almost as long to consume. They'd load up their canvas bags and ride their quaint vintage bicycles down to the market to stock up on all manner of organic vegetables Benji couldn't afford now that he was living solely on his meager teacher's salary.

It wasn't a hardship, though. He didn't miss kale. Or rutabagas. Or the bitter-hot arugula Charles had always insisted they get, since putting spinach in salad was pedestrian. Benji was a hot dog and potato salad kind of guy. He'd branched out and gotten the Italian meatballs when he'd been furniture shopping at CASA a few weeks ago, and those had been pretty damn tasty too. Nothing free-range or organic about them. He'd savored every last preservative.

"It didn't work out," he said diplomatically.

"Oh, Benjamin."

He rolled his eyes and poured his frustration into scrubbing the carpet. What would Charles say if he could see him now? He'd probably gasp in horror at the sight of Benji using heavy-duty chemicals on their carpet. Charles was a firm believer in natural remedies and nontoxic cleaners, but that wasn't going to cut it with Mr. Whiskers's tireless war against the carpet. Benji had tried vinegar and then baking soda up until he realized that Charles wasn't there anymore, so why the hell should he suffer through that when big agro business made wonderful chemical compounds that would clean the mess much more effectively?

It was a pointless endeavor anyway, since the damn cat would simply circle back and mark the spot again as soon as it was dry, but it had to be done. He'd long since kissed his apartment deposit good-bye, but trying to maintain some general level of cleanliness made him feel like he was at least putting up a valiant fight.

Benji could see Mr. Whiskers out of the corner of his eye. He was sitting on the couch, grooming himself and watching Benji clean with a judgmental look.

"It's not a big deal, Ma. I'm fine."

She sighed heavily, and Benji sat back on his heels and braced for the big guns.

"I'm not getting any younger, Benjamin, and neither are you. You need to be settling down and thinking about having children. I want my grandchildren to know me and your father before we die."

Benji looked over at the newest addition to the apartment. He'd put the DEL TORO bookcases together last weekend, and they took up the entire wall. He'd filled them with the book collection he'd kept in storage for the last two years because Charles had thought paperbacks were tacky, interspersed with knickknacks and his absolute favorite part—almost a dozen frames that held pieces of art his students had given him. It was chaotic and mismatched and 100 percent him, and he loved it.

"I spend my entire day with twenty-three six-year-olds. Trust me when I say my biological clock isn't ticking."

That wasn't entirely true. He'd love to have kids someday. It was a huge part of the reason he and Charles had broken up—Benji wanted kids and Charles adamantly said he didn't. But right now the thought of taking care of anyone other than himself and the cantankerous Mr. Whiskers was overwhelming. He'd never lived on his own before, thanks to roommates and then moving in with Charles, and it took some getting used to. He was a full-fledged adult now. He deserved some time to enjoy that before complicating his life again with a boyfriend, let alone a child.

He'd even splurged a bit and recklessly spent his meager savings on a living room suite that didn't look like it came straight out of a frat house or college dorm when he'd replaced all the furniture Charles had taken with him when he moved out. His CASA SICILY sofa wasn't as nice as Charles's hand-upholstered settee, but it was more comfortable. And he didn't have to feel bad about eating pizza on it, which was another plus.

His mother clucked her tongue, and Benji could picture her shaking her head as she leaned against the counter in the kitchen he'd eaten countless meals in back home. He knew she'd be there because she had a phone with an actual cord. She was convinced that cordless phones caused cancer, so she had to be leaning up against the avocado-green countertop right now.

"Well, you still need to put yourself out there. I don't like the thought of you all alone," his mother said with a sniff.

Benji stashed the cleaner under the sink and washed his hands, then dried them on his pants because he never remembered to buy paper towels. Maybe he needed to go back to CASA and get some dish towels. It would give him an excuse to have the meatballs again.

"I'm not alone, Ma. I have dinner with Alyssa once a month, and I talk to Mrs. Jiminez in 3A every day when I take her the newspaper and her mail. And I have colleagues at school. The other kindergarten teachers and I go out for dinner at least once a week. I have people. You don't have to worry about me."

He was careful not to say friends because those were in short supply these days. He and Charles had been dating exclusively for a while when Charles had been offered an assistant professorship in Atlanta. They'd seen it as a sign that it was time to take their relationship to the next level and start over in a new city together. Getting a place with Charles had been fabulous. They'd been wrapped up in each other, ridiculously in love… or at least Benji had thought they were. Life had been great. They'd made friends and settled in comfortably. But after their split a few years later, he'd realized that all the friends he'd made had been Charles's coworkers. Not surprisingly, they'd stopped calling and coming by after Charles left him, probably for some PhD candidate he'd been seeing on the side who could promise him that he would never want kids.

So yes, Benji could use some more friends. But he was getting there. And in the meantime, he had Mrs. Jiminez and Mr. Whiskers.

"You could move back to Boston," his mother said, and Benji grimaced at the hope in her voice.

He had four brothers who still lived within a mile radius of their childhood home, and Benji had no desire to join them. His sister Alyssa had escaped a few years ago and now lived only an hour away from Benji, and their mother was constantly begging them to move back east.

"I have a job here, Ma. I'm settled."

It wasn't strictly true, but it didn't matter. He liked it where he was well enough, but there wasn't much keeping him here. He could teach kindergarten anywhere. But leaving felt like letting Charles win, and Benji wasn't going to do that. For once in his life he was going to take a stand, even if it meant living in a place he didn't love with a cat he frankly hated.

"Are you at least checking the online dating site Alyssa set up for you?"

Benji rubbed at his temples, wondering how soon he could get away with ushering his mother off the phone. These weekly calls were killing him.

"I wish she hadn't told you about that," he muttered. "Yes, I still get the e-mails. No, there hasn't been anyone worth following up with."

Mostly it had been spam and inquiries about the size of his penis. He didn't think of himself as a very private person, but some things just weren't necessary to talk about before the third or fourth date, if ever.

"You're too young to live like an old man," his mother said. "You need to live a little. Go out with someone even if they don't look like the perfect match. You don't have to approach every man like he's the One, Benjamin. There's something to be said for having a little fun. God knows, before I met your father, I—"

And there it was: his limit.

"Ma, I've gotta go. I forgot I promised I'd take 2B's dog for a walk tonight. I'll talk to you next week, okay?"

"Ben—"

He hung up before she could protest. He knew from experience that once his mother started down the nostalgia road, there was no getting her back, and he did not need to hear about her sowing her wild oats again. Once had been traumatic enough.

Besides, he really did need to take 2B's dog out. They were out of town for the weekend, and even though he didn't know them well, he'd volunteered when they'd mentioned needing to find a pet-sitter.

Good Deed Goss strikes again, he thought as he grabbed his keys. That had been his high school nickname. There had even been a pretty well-done caricature on one of the bathroom stalls of him wearing a Canadian Mountie uniform à la Dudley Do-Right.

Mr. Whiskers hopped off the couch and stalked over to the spot Benji had just cleaned, full of swagger and ill intent.

"I could always take you to the pound, you know. I'll do it, if you keep peeing on the carpet." Benji pointed his keys at him, but Mr. Whiskers didn't even blink. Benji sighed. "Sure, call my bluff. It's not like I'm allergic to you or anything, right? Because it would be crazy to keep a cat I don't even like around, especially if he made me sneeze uncontrollably and ruined my carpet."

Benji sneezed right on cue. "You'll be the death of me, Mr. W," he muttered as he rubbed his nose against his sleeve. He'd started taking heavy-duty antihistamines when Charles had adopted the cat three years ago, but they weren't cutting it anymore.

He could take Mr. Whiskers to the animal shelter. True, he was technically Charles's cat, but Charles was gone. He hadn't taken Mr. Whiskers with him when he'd moved out six months ago because his new place didn't allow pets. Benji was under no obligation to keep the damn cat.

But Mr. Whiskers was old, which meant he'd be euthanized instead of put up for adoption if Benji surrendered him. And as much as he hated the cat, he couldn't do that to another living creature.

"If you pee on that while I'm gone, you'll regret it," he said menacingly, giving the cat one last glare before letting himself out.

THE LANCASTERS in 2B were pretty new to the building. The bonus was they didn't know Charles, so Benji's interactions with them never included stilted inquiries about how his ex was doing or pep talks like the ones he got from 4C about how he was better off without "the old guy with the hipster glasses."

The downside was that they weren't in the building directory, which meant when Benji managed to lock himself and Patches out of their apartment, he didn't have a way to call them. He could kick himself for not getting their numbers before they left. What kind of pet-sitter was he, anyway? Way to be responsible. Maybe this becoming a full-fledged independent adult thing wasn't as far along as he'd thought.

Not that it would have mattered—they were visiting Betta's sister in Florida until tomorrow night, so it wasn't like they could just pop back by. Benji didn't even know the husband's name, but he'd heard all about his difficulty keeping a job and a laundry list of his other faults from Betta. Not that he enjoyed the gossip. He frankly didn't care, but it was impossible to shake Betta once she'd sunk her claws in. Plus, it would be rude not to take her up on her offer to come in for a cup of tea when she saw him in the hallway, right?

Patches jumped up on Benji's leg, spreading mud from outside all over his pant leg. At least, Benji hoped it was mud. Was it even raining? He looked outside, grimacing when he saw it was bone dry. So probably not mud. Perfect.

Benji crouched down and scratched behind the border collie's ears. "Hey, bud, I don't suppose you know where your owners hide a spare key, do you?"

The dog stared back, its tongue lolling out for a second before swiping across Benji's cheek. Ugh.

Benji wiped his sleeve against his face and stood up. He doubted the Lancasters would hide a key outside their door, and he knew from Betta's bitchfests that she hated her neighbors in 2A and 2C, so there wasn't much chance she'd have given one of them a key for safekeeping. The guy in 2D was a possibility, but he worked third shift so he wouldn't be home till the morning.

"Guess you're coming for a sleepover, Patches."

Luckily he'd already fed the dog earlier, so he wouldn't have to worry about going out to get him food tonight. He could figure that out in the morning after he had a chat with 2D to make sure he didn't have a key. The Lancasters would be back tomorrow night anyway, so it wasn't a huge deal.

The dog trotted along behind him, following the leash without a moment's hesitation as Benji ran up a flight of stairs to his own apartment. *If only Mr. Whiskers could be half this obedient,* Benji thought as he opened his door.

"Sit," he said firmly to Patches.

The dog plopped down on the new TUSCANY area rug Benji had brought home from his last pilgrimage to CASA. It looked perfect under the new TRENTO coffee table, and so far Mr. Whiskers had left it alone.

Maybe he found the vibrant red pattern as offensive as his previous owner would have.

Patches bolted as soon as Benji unhooked his leash from the collar, which left Benji muttering about the utter uselessness of *all* pets. At least this confirmed he didn't want a dog. He just wasn't much of an animal person. When Mr. Whiskers went to the big scratching post in the sky, there was no way Benji would be replacing him with another pet.

That might be sooner than anticipated, given the way the dog went straight for him. Mr. Whiskers let out a howl the likes of which Benji had never heard before and lunged toward the bookcases, which were full of fragile glass knickknacks and irreplaceable art.

"Dammit, Patches," Benji growled as the dog tried to scale the bookshelves as well in pursuit of the cat. He dove forward and managed to get a good hold on Patches's collar, pulling him back.

"We don't eat the cat," he said sternly. "He's old. That means he's probably too stringy to taste good, even if you could catch him."

He didn't let Mr. Whiskers in his bedroom, which was one huge improvement he'd made after Charles moved out. It was a cat-free zone, which meant he no longer woke up with his eyes half-swollen shut thanks to his allergies.

Patches could stay in there with him until he figured out what to do with him in the morning. The dog seemed a bit ashamed of himself, since he didn't fight Benji as he dragged him over to the closed door.

"Don't get on the bed," he said as he pushed Patches inside and shut him in.

Mr. Whiskers had knocked over a vase and a picture frame in his frantic ascent, but other than that, the bookcase looked relatively unharmed. Benji could leave him there, but Mr. Whiskers wasn't declawed, and he'd probably scratch up the finish if left to his own devices to get down.

"You're a royal pain in my ass, you know that?" Benji said as he tried to grab him.

Not surprisingly, Mr. Whiskers wasn't in the mood to come sedately. A whip of his tail sent Benji's collection of Avengers figurines spiraling to the floor before the cat scurried to the far end of the shelf, just out of Benji's reach.

Benji stood on his toes and managed to grab a bit of Mr. Whiskers's fur before all hell broke loose. Patches ran into the room, probably thanks to the loose bedroom door latch that Benji hadn't wanted to bother the building super about, and jumped up, nipping at Benji's elbow.

Instead of climbing up higher, Mr. Whiskers apparently decided his best hope of survival was on Benji's head. He made a flying leap and connected with a painful scrabbling of claws against Benji's scalp.

It was enough of a surprise to send Benji stumbling into the bookcase. He heard the sound of shattering glass as something hit the floor, and his stomach swooped with the familiar sensation of falling as he started to go down.

Chapter Two: MILAN

A WARNING hum vibrated low and deep inside Patrick's ears. The metallic scent of ozone followed. He rolled over in his MILAN bed, savoring the MODENA memory-foam mattress. *Five more minutes. C'mon, just five more minutes. The CASA shoppers can hold their horses.* The would-be Martha Stewarts and Nate Berkuses were the worst with obsessing about color coordination and feng shui. Because they saw it in a magazine, they were all of a sudden the next HGTV Design Star.

He tucked the black-and-gray duvet up under his chin and kicked it off his legs. Optimal for regulating body temperature, though never logical.

Click-click-hmmmmm. The overhead fluorescent lights announced their unwelcome luminosity into Patrick's darkened sanctuary.

"Goddammit," he groaned and buried his face in his pillow. He had at least ten minutes before the shoppers arrived. Fifteen at best. It always took them ten minutes minimum before they trickled into his showroom.

The fluorescent light wasn't as kind in letting Patrick have his blessed ten minutes more of solace to relish the happy ending of his dream about the cute guy in the café he'd seen for all of three seconds last week. His gut clenched with the last bits of recollection of the dream. The cutie had been a screamer, for sure. It was always the innocent-looking ones.

He was dancing on the edge of drifting off once again when he had an unfortunate sense of spatial relations and tumbled naked ass over teakettle onto the floor.

"Fuck," Patrick mumbled with his face planted in the thin carpet.

"What do you think of the MILAN frame?" an older woman said just over his head.

He scowled, eye-to-eye with her obnoxiously blingy and blinding Yellow Box flip-flops. It was way too early for this bullshit.

"It's on special," a young, bubbly blonde said, her neon pink Converse sneakers coming across his line of sight.

They both stood over him, dangerously close to kicking out his teeth, blissfully unaware of the crumpled pile of sleepy naked man between them. By the power of elementary-grade deduction, Patrick put together the mother-daughter connection.

"The frame color needs some tweaking, but the mattress is perfect. And the gray-and-black duvet makes a great accent," the daughter said.

Did no one notice the guy in the middle of the CASA showroom?

Out of one dream about a sexy rendezvous, and waking up naked in CASA. Terrific. Just what did he eat last night? Must have been the meatballs, and the sweet tomato jam was probably laced with opiates from that one weird guy who got fired a week ago.

Patrick pulled himself up, standing between the pair as they considered his MILAN bed. He scrutinized the mother with a myopic squint, close enough to see the stray white hairs on her chin. She didn't give him a single glance.

The mother brightened. "Let's see what the delivery fee is."

And then the daughter committed the ultimate atrocity of lying upon his bed. She rolled over to her side, her body meshing into the impression left by his.

Oh no.

Oh hell no.

"It seems a little... lived in?" The daughter wiggled on the mattress, trying to get comfortable. "I think a CASA employee has been sleeping here."

Patrick crossed his arms. "You get your happy ass out of my bed and go feel happy inside somewhere else."

Neither of them blinked. Mother. Fucker.

They went on obliviously chattering as the daughter continued to smear herself across his beloved bed. He had broken in the mattress perfectly. There was a notch at his shoulder and knee he had carefully cultivated.

The mother scrawled through thumbnails of room plans. The daughter gestured, and the mother nodded. She pointed at Patrick, and he tensed his grip on his upper arms. They made eye contact, and he counted the seconds until recognition.

"I think it's too big," the mother said regretfully.

Patrick took a quick downward glance at himself and then back at her, unamused. "For you? You bet it is."

"What do you think of the PALERMO frame over in the corner?" she asked her daughter.

He palmed his face. Seriously? This was seriously happening?

"Ooh, I do like that," the daughter said, and together they headed to the far corner of the showroom.

Patrick offered a two-finger salute as they stepped past him without so much as a thank-you, good-bye, or *holy Jesus*. CASA shoppers ebbed and flowed around him. Their voices like a dull cresting wave underscoring the Muzak drifting over the sound system. He ran his hands through his messy dark hair and sucked in a long breath.

"Can we bring back the cute guy?" he asked the fluorescent lights, as if they were distant gods. "We liked the cute guy." He pointed at the lights. "He did that thing with his tongue. You *know*, that thing."

Of course, the lights didn't answer. Ah, well. The employee showers beckoned.

For the humor and variety of it, Patrick followed the completely opposite path through the CASA showrooms. His bare feet slapped the concrete floor with a confident gait. It was like an absurd fever dream born from too many benders on fish-bowl margaritas. Every day he awoke in CASA, and every day no one ever noticed him.

At first, he'd panicked. Of all the places to wake up in every day, CASA wasn't exactly in his top five. Or top two thousand, for that matter. If he had to spend all of eternity somewhere, could it at least have been Tahiti? He'd worked out the theories hundreds of times. Too many CASA meatballs before bed seemed like the most plausible one.

It was like he was living the punchline of a joke but didn't know what the joke was supposed to be. Now, he strutted about with his dick out for all to see.

He dodged a harried mother carrying her toddler to the nearest restroom. She muttered under her breath to her husband that the poor little girl had messed herself. The husband nodded and hurried with their overfull shopping cart of items that they'd never find a use for.

Turning a corner into the living room displays, he saw little old Agnes sitting primly on the GENOA sofa. Her tiny silver bifocals sat at the proper angle on her sharp snooty nose. Her knitting needles flew fast and furious as she knitted and purled her way through yet another scarf. The woolen baby-pink scarf flowed from her needles to her feet.

He felt the scalding jab of her judgmental sideway glance.

He stopped next to her and looked out over the showroom as a young woman considered sofa coverings and her husband wilted with her unending indecision.

Agnes didn't look up from counting her stitches. "Patrick."

"Agnes." He watched the couple.

"Don't you have work to do?" She knitted another row.

"Always."

The young woman thrust the fabric samples at her husband, forcing him to act remotely enthused.

"There's someone in the café," she said and then counted the stitches again. "He's a darling."

"Darling, eh?" Patrick crossed his arms. "That code for something?"

Agnes looked up at him over the rims of her bifocals. "Meaning you better not be inappropriate." She shot a pointed glance at his crotch. "Well. More than you already are."

Patrick smirked. "Of course. I'll take a shower, at least."

"You'll need more than a shower." Agnes resumed knitting, the universal gesture of old-lady dismissal.

Patrick continued on his way. "Agnes."

"Patrick."

Over his shoulder, he extended his middle finger in the universal gesture of "screw you."

Lisa from Kitchens stepped through the entryway of the employee lounge as Patrick stepped past her, barely brushing shoulders. She shivered and recoiled from the slight touch and then hurried on without a word.

On his way to the showers, a young, freckle-faced teenager practiced his greetings in his locker mirror. "Welcome to CASA! How may I help you? Did you find everything all right?" He tried his most chipper smile.

Patrick winced. So perky it resembled Barbie's dead-eyed Cheshire grin. He checked the kid's name tag. "Tommy," he told himself, committing the name to memory. "You poor bastard. You haven't succumbed to the depravity of rabid consumerism yet."

Tommy tried smiling again in the mirror, and Patrick appraised his new effort.

"Better," Patrick said, thumbing his chin.

"I can do this." Tommy clapped his hands like a wrestler ready for a match. In the case of a skinny eighteen-year-old, it just appeared adorably dorky. "I got this."

"Totally got it, bro." Patrick waved behind him and headed into the showers.

He bit his lip as he forced the stubborn faucet to turn. Patrick was rewarded with the deliciously scalding and delightfully high-pressure water. Mist rose from the floor and banished the chill of the overworked air-conditioning.

Patrick groaned deep in his throat as the water hit just the right spot between his shoulder blades. He reached for the shampoo dispenser and took more than enough for his short hair. Eyes closed, he imagined a place in the tropics with a cabana and drinks with little paper umbrellas. He worked the suds into his hair and let himself drift into the space of a dream within a dream.

"Shit!" Tommy screamed and burst into the showers.

Patrick startled and jerked his sudsy fingers from his hair. "The fuck?"

Tommy darted for the faucet, narrowly missing the boiling stream of water, and then flicked off the tap. He sighed as if he had averted some nature of crisis.

Patrick scowled. He just wanted a shower. Couldn't he take one without getting fucked with?

He clenched his jaw and forced the faucet on again. The hot water flowed once more, and he ducked his head under the stream.

Tommy shrieked like a child confronted with a terrifying yet completely harmless insect. Perhaps a moth. Patrick had never been particularly fond of them. Tommy lunged forward to shut it off again, but Patrick growled and smacked his hand away in warning. Tommy reeled back as if brushed against by said spooky moth, and Patrick's vision went fuzzy from the touch.

They both stopped for a moment as the water ran. Their eyes met, and the suds slid from Patrick's hair, down his shoulders, and then over his chest. Tommy blinked, his lips pursed in an *O* as he stared at him.

Patrick pressed his lips together as Tommy hesitantly reached out, intending to touch him. Patrick gestured to his waist. "Either you're going to join me, or you're going to teach customers how to use Allen wrenches. Because this ain't gonna suck itself."

Tommy jerked his hand away, and his lips wiggled into an embarrassed line.

"Really?" Patrick arched a brow.

Tommy's answer came by way of his bolting from the employee lounge.

Patrick shrugged. "Whatever."

Once he was suitably clean, he scored some proper jeans from the Lost and Found. It always amazed him what people left behind at CASA, or what they did to leave them behind. He'd found a prosthetic leg once. The guy probably wouldn't be getting far on foot after that.

Tommy had left his locker open. A glaring yellow CASA shirt hung, neatly pressed, with three others. No one pressed their shirts. And no one kept that many spares.

"D'aw," Patrick said as he took one of the shirts. "Tommy has a mommy."

He pulled it over his head and then adjusted the sleeves. Right length, but a bit too small for him. Tight across the chest, and the sleeves stretched to the limit on his arms. He looked more like a bouncer with a bizarre choice of Halloween costume than an actual cashier. At least it was "proper." Agnes would be pleased. Dried-up hag.

Patrick's mood soured the moment he hit the café floor. The old man was back again, sitting in the corner all alone and lost in thought. The bastard never had anything better to do. He sat there for hours with a plate of meatballs he never ate. In front of him was the latest *Wall Street Journal* crossword puzzle and a pen. The *WSJ* crosswords were Patrick's drug of choice. He noted that the puzzle was blank and the pen new.

He snorted. "Stop trying to look smart," he said to the old man as he loomed over him.

The old man threaded his fingers together, refusing to be cowed by Patrick's intimidation.

Patrick stiffened at the sound of a chair scraping the ground. A young guy settled at a nearby table alone, looking much like a lost kitten bewildered by such a big new world. He smiled, bright and genuine, at

Patrick. Narrowing his eyes, Patrick gave a little wave in reply. The guy waved eagerly in response.

He was definitely a cute one, for sure. Even better than the guy in his dream. Maybe this day wasn't such a wash after all.

Patrick turned back to the old man and then crouched over him to whisper in his ear. "I'll deal with you later."

He stepped away and crossed the floor to the infinitely more pleasant and definitely doable guy. Uninvited to his table, Patrick took the initiative, spun a chair backward, and straddled it.

The guy didn't speak immediately but instead seemed to just be pleased to be in CASA.

No one ever came to CASA alone. CASA was a purgatory best faced with a quest companion, usually a spouse or next of kin.

Patrick saw neither a ring nor an indication of offspring. Perfect. He pointed his fingers like a gun at the guy and smiled, full of smugness. "Don't tell me. Derrick, right?"

The guy smiled crookedly, confused by the question. "Sorry? I'm Benjami—Benji." He nodded. "Benji. Only my mother calls me Benjamin."

Patrick sucked in an overdramatic sigh and snapped his fingers. "Dammit. Swore you looked like a Derrick. I'm usually so good at that."

"So, you're psychic." Benji smirked.

"No." Patrick pulled a face of mock hurt. "I'm Patrick."

"But your name tag says Tommy," Benji said, glancing at his chest.

Patrick blinked and patted the plastic tag. "So it does." He pointed a finger and pressed his lips together, assuming a stern expression. "So you're not a Derrick. But I promise I'm 100 percent psychic."

"Oh really?" Benji glanced out the tall windows. The sunny day filled the café. Robins busied themselves building a nest on the ledge. "So, what am I thinking right now?"

Patrick grinned. "You're thinking you need to try out the MILAN bed up in the bedding showroom."

Agnes was going to fucking kill him.

Chapter Three:
PROLUNGA

COULD ANYTHING compare to the smell of plastic and particleboard in the morning?

Well, lots of things probably could. Queequeg Coffee, for one. His mother's freshly baked apple pie. The Mrs. Meyer's Clean Day basil soap that he hoarded every time it was in stock at Scope.

The candy apple red circle décor motif of Scope seemed to try to take the edge off the unconscious suggestion of a military sniper's laser targeting. But it was easier ignoring the odd, checkered past involvement of the founder's political leanings. A senator of questionable morals founded Benji's favorite office supply store. It was his CASA of office supply needs. How politicians got into marketing everything from bedding to pencils was a strange tale.

But CASA had none of those torrid stories and scandals. The Italians had seen to that. CASA had its host of urban legends. From babies being born to weddings, it was all the talk of social media. CASA was definitely in the top ten of Benji's favorite places.

Benji inhaled deeply and let the scent wash over him. Everything about CASA screamed fresh start and endless opportunity. It was pretty much impossible to feel anything but optimistic when standing in a CASA. For him, at least. The couple sitting a few tables over probably didn't agree, judging by the angry way the woman was turning pages in the thick CASA catalog in front of her while the man stared off into space, balancing one of the nubby golf pencils the store provided on his knuckles.

There was a family of six against the back wall. The parents traded exhausted looks over the heads of the four kids chattering eagerly about Bambini Mondo.

Benji smiled at Patrick-Not-Tommy, and he returned it with a slow, easy grin like he'd heard a dirty joke he was eager to repeat.

"So, what do you do, Patrick-Not-Tommy?" Benji skewered a meatball and gestured with it like the pointer he used for the kids to sound out their ABCs.

He obviously didn't work in the café since he wasn't wearing the black chef's uniform. And even though he had the right shirt on to work the floor, his jeans weren't the CASA uniform kind.

God. How sad was it that he knew what the freaking CASA uniform was? He definitely spent too much time here.

"Patrick," he said as he picked at his thumbnail. "You need to stick with me here, Derrick."

"Benji."

Patrick waved a dismissive hand as if he were swatting away flies. "Benji's a terrier with a series of kid movies. Derrick is a guy I could get behind."

Benji coughed and concentrated on his knuckles. How could this guy just waltz in here and make everything drip with innuendo? He'd never keep a straight face in front of the kids tomorrow.

"I said," Benji said, trying to get things back on track, "what do you do?"

"Work."

"You're helpful."

Patrick's grin broadened. "Always."

"Patrick…," Benji started, surprised when a young woman with a dour expression spoke. When had she walked up? Christ. He needed to sleep more.

"Karin." Patrick sat up straighter. "Meet my new charge. Derrick, this is Karin. Karin, Derrick."

"Benji," Benji said again with a grunt.

Patrick waved him off. "Derrick's just a little confused right now. Bonked his head on the cart return, you know."

Karin clasped a hand onto Patrick's broad shoulder and then dug in her nails. "May I have a word with you?"

"Anthropomorphic," Patrick said without a blink.

Benji drew his brows together. "…what?"

Patrick winked at him. "Jeopardy! Clue of the Day."

Karin gnashed her teeth. "We need help with assembly."

The way she enunciated every syllable told Benji that Patrick had shirked his duty to sit here in the café and harangue him. Not that he wasn't interesting, if not exactly welcome, company. But he didn't want Patrick to get in trouble on his account.

"Ah." Patrick sighed but didn't seem the slightest bit exasperated. "The Divorce Maker sample again, huh?"

"Divorce… maker?" Benji asked. What kind of CASA product is that? CASA was a place of happiness, Italian Muzak, and affordable, delightful furniture.

Patrick popped up from his chair and then spun it back around, tucking it into its proper place under the table. He knocked the table with two knuckles and nodded to Benji. "Be careful what you touch here in CASA. Can't have you getting sucked into the black hole of rabid consumerism."

"Do you ever stop?" Karin asked as she pulled on Patrick's wrist.

Patrick relented and followed Karin's lead. He made a sloppy two-finger salute behind him. "Be cool, soda pop. Don't wander too far, Benji."

Looking down at his meatballs, Benji flushed. Even his name sounded like a thick innuendo in Patrick's mouth. Benji swallowed. He was going to be a flustered mess in class tomorrow. He could only hope for some classroom drama to take his mind off the way Patrick's faded jeans hung low on his hips and molded to his ass like a dream. Perhaps Kevin would stick bubblegum in Brittany's hair again. A screaming five-year-old would be the perfect distraction.

The few sentences they'd exchanged had been the best conversation Benji had had in weeks. Despite it being incredibly odd, he'd been energized just by talking with him. And it had nothing to do with Patrick's ass. Or mostly nothing. Okay, maybe a little. But it had been significantly longer than weeks since Benji had been in the presence of something that delectable, and no one could blame a man for noticing.

Benji watched the family of six gather up their trays and leave before he turned his attention back to his own table. There was a mostly empty plate of meatballs and a coffee that had long gone cold sitting in front of him. He didn't remember ordering either of them, let alone eating.

Come to think of it, he didn't remember coming to CASA this morning, either. His restless sleep had caused him no shortage of weekday morning pain getting up for school, but this was the first time he'd found himself somewhere he had no recollection of going.

God, hopefully he had driven safely.

He looked down and wrinkled his nose when he saw something staining his pants. Benji brushed at it, but it was stuck on pretty well. He could get a napkin and clean it up later. Clearly he'd had a busy morning. Stained clothes and a shopping outing he didn't remember?

It must be Sunday. He'd planned to spend it at home catching up on some very important teacher work, aka cutting shapes out of construction paper and tidying supplies. Kindergarten teachers might not have a lot of grading to bring home, but that didn't mean they had tons of downtime, either. He'd spent an increasing amount of time in his classroom during the evenings and weekends. One positive of his breakup with Charles was a spotlessly appointed craft wall. His Pinterest account was practically smoking from all the use it got these days.

Maybe he'd come in today to get some more of those SCATOLA stacking boxes. He'd noticed he was out of the small ones when he organized his classroom art supplies Friday night. Most teachers booked it out of the building as fast as they could on Friday afternoons, which made it an optimal time to stick around and get stuff done without interruptions. At least, that was his story about why he worked most Friday nights, and he was sticking to it. But he wasn't a total stick-in-the-mud. He'd skipped the paints and markers and spent most of the night cataloging his glitter supply in honor of it being Friday. Never let it be said that Benjamin Goss didn't let loose on the weekend.

The sauce on his plate had long since congealed into an unappetizing mess, and Benji was about to take his tray to the trash can when a CASA employee swooped in and took it for him. He thanked her, but she stared right past him, muttering about lazy people leaving messes for others to clean up.

Apparently even CASA employees could have bad days. He didn't see how, since it was one of the happiest places on earth, but Benji conceded he might feel differently if he worked here.

He didn't bother getting a cart, since that would only give him an excuse to stock up on more ridiculous things he didn't need. He'd learned long ago that CASA was like a gas: it would expand to fit any space, so you had to limit how much opportunity you gave it. Going in with just a yellow shopping bag meant you could only buy what you could carry. Going in with a cart meant coming out with more things than a person could conceivably use in a lifetime. It was kind of like Costless in that respect.

BENJI STRETCHED, moving his shoulders up and down and rotating his neck back and forth. There was definitely something off about him today, and not just that he couldn't remember how he'd gotten to CASA in the first place. He hadn't felt this stiff since the time he'd taken a drunken dare to climb the gigantic rock wall in the college rec center. He'd gotten up and down it without problem—a minor miracle—but when he'd woken up the next morning, he hadn't been able to open his hands or lift his arms above his shoulders. He'd had to have his roommate help him wash his hair.

Curiously, there wasn't any pain. The stiffness in his joints and muscles was troubling, but he couldn't have done anything too terrible to himself. He'd downed Advil like candy for the first few days after his rock-climbing fiasco, but the gentle stretches seemed to be working out the kinks this time. He rolled his shoulders again, luxuriating in the stretch. He sat up straighter, the aching soreness between his shoulder blades that had kept him hunched over fading. Maybe Patches was to blame. He wasn't exactly tiny, and he pulled at his leash something awful. Benji indulged in one last shoulder stretch and stood up. If walking a dog could make him this sore, he really needed to work out more. The tiny gym in his apartment's basement was damp and creepy, but he clearly needed to stop making excuses and get down there.

He nearly ran into four people on the short walk from his table to the escalator, so he decided not to head downstairs to pick up a bag. The place seemed crowded, even considering it was a Sunday, and people were obviously harried and distracted. He'd just grab a bag from one of the displays around the showroom floor.

An arm settled around his shoulders before he'd made it more than a few feet, startling him so much he stopped dead in the middle of the crowded aisle. People flowed like water around him, not even looking up to glare at him for his rudeness. It was bizarre.

Benji craned his neck, scowling when he saw that the person who'd assaulted him was familiar. Sure, he'd spent a few minutes thinking about what it would be like to get Patrick's hands on him, but not in the middle of a busy store where stopping unexpectedly could get you rammed with a cart at best, and taken out by a sale-crazed soccer mom at the worst.

Patrick released him and offered him a shark-like smile. "What are you shopping for today?"

Benji swallowed. What had he decided he'd come in for again? Storage boxes. Right.

"Organizational stuff for my classroom," he managed after a hard swallow to wet his dry throat. He glanced over at Patrick's arm, torn between missing the heat and heft of having it around him and irritation that Patrick had accosted him like that. Irritation won out. "Do you commit felony assault on all of your customers, or am I just special?"

Patrick's grin didn't dim in the slightest. "That was a misdemeanor at best," he purred in a tone that had Benji blushing. Patrick let out a delighted laugh. "Oh, you're such an innocent one. This is going to be fun."

Benji swallowed again, not because of a dry throat this time but to make sure his voice didn't break when he answered. Patrick was the most inappropriate person he'd ever met, and it was both terrifying and more than a little arousing. Benji definitely needed to get out more.

"What's going to be fun?" he asked, wary.

"Why, being your personal shopper for the day, of course," Patrick drawled. "Whatever did you *think* I meant?"

Patrick's gaze flicked up and down Benji's body, and Benji's cheeks flared hot again. He'd never been so blatantly checked out before. He couldn't help but wonder what standard Patrick was using for comparison and whether he measured up.

Benji shifted uncomfortably but didn't back down. "I don't need a personal shopper. I'm only here for some boxes, and then I'm heading home."

Patrick flinched but covered it up with a stretch. "That's what they all say," he muttered.

Benji had no clue what he'd said that had upset Patrick. He felt a twinge of guilt at knowing that someone was hurting and not trying to help, but part of the new four-point plan for a happier life that he'd come up with while staring at his meatballs this morning was not getting involved in other peoples' drama. And as cute as he was, Patrick had drama written all over him.

Patrick's sadness was fleeting, just like Benji suspected most of Patrick's moods were.

"Right. Well, first things first, let's find you some new pants."

Benji frowned at him. "Why? Wait, CASA sells pants?"

"No."

Patrick's eyes were sparkling again, and Benji took a deep breath, figuring that overreacting was exactly what Patrick was hoping for. Instead, Benji sidestepped out of the main aisle to get away from the crowd of shoppers who seemed to be paying them no mind and held Patrick's gaze, refusing to give Patrick the satisfaction of asking what he meant.

It took a few seconds longer than Benji expected, but Patrick eventually caved.

"We have a huge Lost and Found, which is where we'll go get you some pants." He looked Benji up and down and wrinkled his nose. "As to the why—because you smell like you rolled around in dog shit."

Benji looked down, a blush flaring up his neck. He'd noticed the stain earlier, but he hadn't picked up on the odor until Patrick said something. Now it was all he could smell, mixing in the most putrid way with the perfumes and other scents wafting off the people walking by. His stomach rolled.

He should just go home. But something was keeping him here— and it wasn't just his growing attraction to the mercurial and mysterious Patrick. When Benji thought about leaving the CASA, he felt vaguely nauseated and panicky.

Patrick was still watching him, his lips curved into a bit of a smirk like he was following along with Benji's internal monologue. Benji shook his head, trying to dispel the wave of unease he'd felt when he'd thought about going home.

"Fine," he said shortly. "Show me this vast utopia of forgotten pants."

Patrick snorted and put his arm around Benji's shoulders again. The skin of his forearm brushed against Benji's neck, and a small sigh escaped his lips at the sensation. Patrick felt warm, and Benji realized he'd been shivering. The panicky feeling disappeared too, and his head felt clearer and less muddled.

Patrick leaned in and pressed his lips close to Benji's ear. "Easier to steer you this way," he murmured.

Walking against the arrows in the aisles was always a bad idea, but to Benji's surprise no one snarled at them as they squeezed past, walking the wrong direction. Probably because he was being forcibly escorted by an employee, Benji reasoned.

Patrick didn't talk again until he'd ushered Benji into the employee locker room.

"Sit," he said, pushing Benji down onto a bench between two banks of lockers. He pointed at Benji, a stern look on his face. "Stay."

Benji huffed out a laugh. "I'm not a—" His throat closed, cutting him off with a choke. He shivered again, his head throbbing and his vision dimming for a second. There was some reason he couldn't say the word, and it was a good one, he knew that somehow. But it floated at the edge of his consciousness, tantalizingly close but too far away for him to remember exactly what had happened to make him fear it.

He blinked hard and the locker room swam back into focus, as did a concerned Patrick bent over in front of him, his hands a welcome, grounding heat on Benji's forearms.

"—dog," Benji finished lamely. He swallowed, his throat still feeling a little constricted.

Patrick reached up and tweaked him on the nose. "No, I can see that. No canines here, just us dudes. But you know, I'm not confirming or denying the rumor that there's a schnauzer running around the warehouse."

He massaged Benji's forearms with his large, warm hands, and Benji melted into the soothing contact. Patrick coughed and pulled away suddenly. Benji took it for what it was—the sound of someone trying to will away awkwardness. It was something he was intimately acquainted with himself. Patrick stood up and coughed again. Well. Maybe he was under the weather.

"I'm going to run to the Lost and Found and get you some pants."

Benji didn't bother to respond, since Patrick was already out the door. He'd been on the verge of saying he could go with him, but he was suddenly grateful to be sitting. A huge wave of exhaustion swept over him as soon as Patrick was out of sight. Benji wasn't out of it enough to forget where he was, but he was tired enough not to care that curling up into a ball on a bench in the CASA employee locker room was outside his usual bounds of propriety.

He felt a little better once he was prone, but the nausea had returned in full force. He breathed carefully through his mouth, even though the smell of his pants didn't seem to be as strong anymore. He didn't know how much time passed, but it couldn't have been too long because no one else came in or out of the locker room while Benji waited for Patrick to return.

Patrick bounded over to him, a pair of jeans and a familiar-looking striped yellow shirt slung over his arm. He wrapped his hand around the back of Benji's neck, fingers gentle as they cupped around the curve. Benji instantly felt better, the dull thrum in his head easing and his vision clearing again. The nausea made it uncomfortable to sit up, but after Patrick guided him through a few deep breaths—while not letting go of his loose hold on Benji's neck—Benji felt infinitely better.

"I went ahead and brought you a shirt too, since yours is a bit worse for the wear. Get changed and we'll head back up to the showroom. It's busy today, lots to do."

Benji's gaze flickered over Patrick's matching yellow shirt. Shit. Benji kept forgetting that Patrick was at work.

"You can head back up. I don't want to get you in trouble."

Patrick snorted dismissively. "Don't worry about it."

"But you'll make Karin mad."

"Pfft!" Patrick gave a dismissive toss of the head. "Karin's always mad. That thing she does, where she curls her nose up like she's smelled some bad fish? That's normal." He shook a finger. "Now, it's Agnes you need to watch out for."

"Agnes?"

He nodded. "Agnes."

"O… kay."

Nothing out of Patrick's mouth seemed to make sense, but Benji was used to straying behind a bit. And Patrick's hard-to-follow tangents were infinitely preferable to Charles's long rants about the lax rules of organic certification. Patrick was a quirky one. And more than a little confusing. Benji wasn't sure if he should give in to the way his pulse sped up every time Patrick smiled or if he should be running for the nearest exit....

Benji stood up carefully, pleased when the movement didn't bring back his headache. Patrick had the decency to look away while Benji pulled his pants off and slipped on the borrowed jeans, trying hard not to think about the fact that they were very likely unwashed.

"How does someone lose pants at a CASA, anyway?" he asked once he was dressed.

"Well, Benji, when a man loves a woman—or another man, for that matter—very much...."

Benji slapped his hands over his ears, laughing. "Never mind, never mind. I don't want to know. I'd rather not think about these jeans having jizz stains on them somewhere."

Patrick grinned at him. "Those are new. I raided the uniform closet. They fit okay?"

Benji looked down, surprised to find that they did actually fit very well. Patrick must have an eye for that sort of thing.

"They're great, thanks."

"Don't mention it. I was tempted to grab you the pair of sweatpants Karin had to remove from one of the chandeliers in a display bedroom last week, but I decided to take the high road."

His smirk gave Benji the impression that Patrick wasn't too familiar with the high road. "I appreciate your beneficence."

"Ooh, I bet you're a Sunday *New York Times* crossword kind of guy with a vocabulary like that."

They were back on the showroom floor by now, and even though there were people flocking around the two other employees Benji could see, everyone was still leaving Patrick alone.

"How's this for a crossword clue? Five letters, iconic phrase from Lewis Carroll's classic."

Patrick put a finger to his lips, considering. "Eat me? My dear Benjamin, I don't think I've known you long enough for you to come on so strong. I'm not that kind of man, dear sir."

They wandered through the store, Benji listening raptly while Patrick regaled him with tales of the shenanigans he'd seen over his years at the CASA. Patrick made it sound like he'd been there forever, which made Benji wonder if his estimation of Patrick's age was off or if Patrick had just started working there at a really young age. He couldn't be more than early to midthirties, just like Benji. If he was, he'd aged incredibly well.

Benji did a double take when he passed a kitchen display with a gorgeous subway tile backsplash and a starkly modern clock on the wall. "What time is it, anyway? Is that right?"

It couldn't be. There was no way it was that late. How could it be eight in the evening already?

Patrick lounged against the austere stainless-steel counter and shrugged. "Depends. It would be wrong in Rio, since it's nine in Brazil. And it's already tomorrow in both Paris and Jakarta."

Benji was getting irritated with Patrick's inability to be serious. They'd joked around all day, and any time Benji had tried to break away to pick up his storage boxes and leave, Patrick had found a reason to keep him there. "Here," he said flatly.

Patrick spread his hands wide and gave Benji an indolent smile. "Well, why didn't you say so? It most certainly is 8:07 in the evening here in our wonderful little corner of the good old US of A."

An older woman who looked more than a little frazzled interrupted before Benji could think of an appropriately scathing retort.

"You'd think the lightbulbs would be with the lamps," she muttered rudely, stepping right in between Benji and Patrick.

Then again, maybe *he* was the rude one, monopolizing all of a CASA employee's time. He'd hardly seen Patrick do any work today. Hell, he'd hardly noticed the entire day passing at all.

Patrick gave Benji one last smirk before turning a megawatt smile on the lady. "They're on the other side of this divider, ma'am," he said politely.

The woman shook her head, a look of confusion flitting across her face. "Oh, they are?" she asked.

Patrick made a cordial nod. "Are you picking them up for someone?"

Benji pursed his lips as Patrick switched subjects in a blink from entertaining him to being the model employee....

"I'm really taking up too much of your time...," Benji muttered shyly and inched away.

He didn't get far before Patrick laced his warm fingers with his own. Benji shivered at the heat of Patrick's skin. His energy was practically sparking off him.

"You need to stick with me, buttercup," Patrick said out of the corner of his mouth. Without missing a beat, he acknowledged the woman again. "You were decorating your daughter's room, correct?"

The old woman brightened. "Yes. Yes." She smiled broadly as if finding her train of thought. "I was looking for something bright. The wiring shorted out when I plugged the dang thing in. Shocked me so bad. Right up my arm and into my chest."

Patrick nodded and thumbed his chin. He kept silent and considered her words.

Benji swallowed, enthralled by the way Patrick was acting toward the woman. It was nothing like the brusque manner he'd shown with Karin or even the teasing, sometimes mean-spirited banter he'd kept up with Benji all day. This Patrick was attentive and kind. Benji was over men who acted one way in public and another in private—Charles had been a prime example of that, being a doting boyfriend when it suited his image and an absolute jackass when it didn't—but this was different. It wasn't like Patrick had flipped a switch and become someone different. It was more like he'd just become… more. Benji shook his head. Jesus, he was hard up and on the rebound faster than one of his students could upend a pot of tempera paint all over himself if he could fancy himself falling for a guy just because he was being nice to a confused old lady.

"It's just so dim in there," the woman continued. "I needed something bright for my daughter to do her studying. She always complained it was too dark for her." The woman looked up, her lower lip trembling. "That young woman over there looks so much like her. I tried to tell her that the lamp she was getting had a cord that was too short. She was going to plug it into an old extension cord and start a fire, but she wouldn't listen." She stopped and swallowed hard. "I don't know how I know that, but I do."

Patrick nodded. "Yes, yes. We have a lovely floor lamp selection. And some wonderful color-coordinated extension cords too. We'll help you get a much safer power unit for her. Can't have a lawsuit on our hands." He gave her an impish wink, and she tossed her head back with a laugh.

"Oh you!" she said. "You are quite possibly the most delightful employee I've come across. Everyone seems to walk away from me."

Patrick raised his brows and made a concerned and sympathetic noise. A breath hitched in Benji's throat, and he eased back a bit, stopped again when Patrick grabbed his hand, gently stroking his thumb across Benji's palm in a soothing gesture. The absent thoughtfulness made

Benji's heart pound in a slow thump. He looked to his feet, his cheeks burning. God. He really had it bad if he was hot for the first available guy with broad shoulders and hands that could crush a whole carton of Charles's certified organic ostrich eggs.

"I'll have a word with the management," Patrick said firmly. "Now, if you'll excuse me, I'll just grab one of those surge protectors for that other customer. I'm sure she'll be so happy you pointed out that she needed one." He let go of Benji's hands and took one of hers in both of his, patting it reassuringly. "There is a young lady named Karin waiting by the registers. She'll be happy to assist you. We won't keep you here any longer. I know you have somewhere you need to be."

The old woman's expression went oddly blank as her eyes glazed over. "I do," she said distractedly. She wandered away toward the vastness of the registers without so much as a thank-you.

Benji arched a brow. "Is she okay?"

"Perfectly." Patrick nodded. He picked up a brightly colored PROLUNGA extension cord from the large bin on the end cap and lobbed it overhand across the aisle. It fell neatly into the other shopper's cart. She looked down at it and furrowed her brow, but a moment later she shook her head and continued on like nothing had happened. Strange.

Patrick turned back toward Benji with a manic grin as he clapped his hands together. "Now. Where were we?"

Benji struggled as he tried to recall what they'd been doing before the old woman had stopped them. It wasn't like him to be this forgetful. "I'm not sure…."

"Excellent."

The more he tried to make sense of Patrick, the more his mind went blank in the fuzzy, cottony way that came with sleep deprivation. His mother scolded him constantly for not taking the time for himself. His time revolved around his students, and he hadn't been on a proper vacation in years since he only had summers off and Charles had taught summer classes at the university every year, being the low man on the tenure totem pole.

Benji frowned at Patrick. No one had thanked Patrick for his help today. Or Karin, who Benji had seen offer advice to several customers. They'd almost always taken her suggestion, but not a single one of them had acknowledged her at all. That was weird. Maybe it was the stress of being in a crowded store on a Sunday.

"As I was saying, yes, it is indeed that late," Patrick said, shifting back into their conversation as if they'd never been interrupted. He looked a bit paler and more drawn, which made sense if it really was that late. He'd already had a long day if he'd been here since opening, like Karin had said. "Or I suppose one could say it's that early. It's all a matter of perspective."

"Shit. I have to get home," Benji said, the now familiar prickly, panicky feeling overtaking him as soon as he got the words out. He swallowed hard. "I have to be at school at six tomorrow morning."

He jumped when someone touched his back gently, whirling around to see that Karin had crept up, ninja-like and silent. She and Patrick needed to learn to make more noise when they walked, because Benji was pretty sure someday they'd give some poor unsuspecting customer a coronary.

Even though she was looking directly into his eyes, she spoke to Patrick. "It's time."

The overhead speakers blared out a reminder that closing was in half an hour, and how had that happened? Hadn't it only been a little after eight just a second ago? Benji's breath started coming faster as he searched for the wall clock again, his heart thumping hard when he saw it was now a quarter till nine, just like the announcement had said. What was going on?

Patrick sighed. "We were having fun."

Karin squeezed Benji's shoulder before letting him go. "Take a walk to the exit with Patrick, okay? I'd take you, but I think it'll be better coming from him." She gave Patrick a sour look. "Which, trust me, isn't something I say often. But you two did seem to have a lot of fun today."

Benji narrowed his eyes at Patrick, who looked more somber than he had all day. "What is she talking about? Karin…?"

Benji turned around, but she was gone. Not just walking away, but gone. Which shouldn't be possible in the open floor plan of a warehouse store like CASA.

"Let's go," Patrick said with a resigned sigh. He wrapped his arm around Benji's shoulders just like he had earlier that afternoon, guiding him out with the herd of shoppers who were heading for the exits. "Listen, this is going to suck. And I'm sorry."

What was going to suck? Heading out to the enormous parking lot that he had no memory of parking in and trying to find his car? Wait, his pants. They were in the trash in the locker room.

"My keys," he said, turning to Patrick in horror.

"You didn't have any keys," Patrick said, his voice almost painfully gentle.

"What? Of course I did," Benji spluttered. They'd come up to the doors, but he wasn't going to leave without his keys. He'd have no way to get home or get into his apartment even if he could get there. Shoppers flowed out around them, not paying them the slightest bit of attention. Oh God. His keys. His apartment. The dog. He'd been dog-sitting, and he'd left the dog in his apartment all day long. Jesus, the mess was going to be apocalyptic.

"You didn't," Patrick said carefully. "Look outside, Benji."

Benji shook his head. "This has been the weirdest day ever, and I'm ready to go home. You can give me your number if you want. I mean, if this is some sort of ploy to get me to go home with you, it's not going to work, but I'd definitely be interested in seeing you again."

Instead of replying, he shook his head and turned Benji toward the glass doors so he could see the twilight glow of the parking lot.

Benji was about to yell at him when a group of shoppers approached the automatic doors, which hissed open, revealing the emptiness of space.

Not space as in an empty parking lot. Space as in *space*. When the doors parted, customers vanished into the starry vastness of the universe.

Benji stumbled back, his knees weak. Patrick supported him with a gentle rub to the upper arms. The doors opened, and Benji got a bigger picture of the great beyond. Constellations danced across the dark void. Green, blue, and red nebula clouds twinkled with sprinkles of stars.

The customers passed through, checking their receipts and asking their spouses what they'd like for dinner. They didn't pay attention to the blackness swallowing them into the great nothing. But when the door closed, Benji could see those same customers through the windows, walking through the parking lot.

He broke away from Patrick and ran up to the doors. They slammed shut. He stood there banging on them until a woman with a cart approached, but instead of seeing the parking lot when it opened, Benji saw the same terrifying void. The woman vanished into the rift of the Milky Way, and then the doors slid shut and outside, the same woman pushed on to her Subaru in the parking lot.

Cold sweat prickled over Benji's skin when he tried to walk through the doors the next time they swung open, and his stomach turned violently. His vision was graying out when he felt Patrick yank him from behind so hard that the two of them tumbled into a rack of yellow shopping bags.

"I have to get home," Benji said weakly.

Patrick laughed humorlessly, rubbing his hands up and down Benji's arms to soothe the gooseflesh there.

"You are home, kiddo."

What the *fuck*.

Benji blinked once, and the world filled with the same darkness of the consuming void. His head fell back and he leaned into Patrick, falling into the nothing.

Chapter Four: SPÖL

BENJI'S CLAWED hand shot through the surface of the Bambini Mondo ball pit. A wave of red plastic balls surged over the lip of the enclosure, spilling onto the brightly colored floor and rolling in a hundred different directions.

Patrick crouched at the edge and waited for Benji to emerge. He ran his teeth over his bottom lip. It was part delight and part of that prickly bothersome thing called concern.

Agnes balanced herself on the lip of the ball pit slide, her lips pressed in a tight line between intense concentration and a disapproving frown. She held out her hand over the pit, waiting for Benji's hand to come into range. Heaven forbid Agnes fall into the cesspit of grubby fingerprints, boogers, and piss. No. That was for Patrick and everyone else.

Benji's other hand clamored to the surface, and Patrick held the breath he no longer had any need for.

Agnes snatched Benji's wrist, and Patrick latched onto her opposite forearm and wrist, providing leverage.

"Pull!" Agnes commanded, and together they yanked Benji from the plastic hellmouth.

Patrick released Agnes, and she tottered on her feet. Once she'd righted herself, she adjusted her snooty bifocals and turned up her nose.

At their feet, Benji writhed like a dying carp. He gulped in air, his eyes wide and wild and his chest heaving.

Agnes's gaze softened. "The poor dear. He'll eventually get used to it."

Patrick crossed his arms as he took his sweet time studying Benji going through the stages of thinking he'd just drowned. "Nothing like a baptism from a children's ball pit. God's clearly a comedian."

Benji coughed and rolled to his side.

Agnes buttoned her cardigan. "He does have a plan for all of us."

"I can't tell if a baptism by fire is worse," Patrick said as he shifted slightly to the left to avoid Benji possibly puking on his Nikes. He brightened. "Do you think they do that at Wallville?"

Agnes shot Patrick a chilling glare. "Are you going to tend to him, or are you going to further affirm my utter disappointment in you?"

He crouched over Benji, watching his eyes roll. Hmm. Patrick had always had a soft spot for brown-eyed boys. He also had a soft spot for his MILAN bed, which had better not be sold by now to some CASA hacker planning to make a fish tank out of the frame.

"Now that that nasty business if over, I have a sweater to finish," she said and smoothed down her cardigan. "Patrick."

"Agnes." He nodded and then slapped Benji's sweaty cheek. "Rise and shine, cupcake."

Benji blinked, the first welcoming sign of cognizant thought.

Patrick slapped again. "Hey, hey, Benji. You need to stay with me, big boy." He extended his middle finger. "How many fingers am I holding up?"

"Where...?" Benji croaked and then coughed.

"Ah, yeah." Patrick smirked. "CASA. Bambini Mondo, in fact."

"What?" Benji's lashes fluttered and his head fell back.

"C'mon, shake it off." Patrick slapped his cheek, and Benji's head bounced before he drifted off to sleep. Patrick set his jaw. The gentle approach sometimes seemed hit or miss. Time to haul out the big guns. Patrick smacked him with a hard crack to the jaw. Benji gasped with the jolt to his system. "Wake up!"

Benji blinked back to the present and swallowed. He felt over his chest, and Patrick nodded as he predicted Benji's thoughts.

"When you come back, you're always in what you came in with," Patrick said.

"I smell like dog crap," Benji responded, his voice thick, like he didn't have full command over his tongue yet.

"And that damned funk will never come out of the pit."

"I smell like dog crap."

Well, at least he was forming sentences. It was a start. Patrick hooked his hands under Benji's arms and hauled him to his feet. Benji flopped against him and curled his fingers into Patrick's borrowed shirt. The close contact sparked up Patrick's spine. The fresh ones always had the strongest energy. But it definitely wasn't spiritual energy that Patrick was feeling. He swallowed and tried to cough out the tightness in his throat.

Thank God the smell of dog shit ruined the moment.

"Son of a bitch…," Patrick growled to himself, his own inconvenient needs getting in the way. He pushed Benji away and held him at arm's length. "C'mon, cupcake. Time to hit the showers and have a chat."

IT WAS difficult to have a staring contest when only one participant was aware of the competition.

Patrick sat in the café at his favorite table with the old man. He had no idea how long the guy had been coming in. But he was the one that always brought in the *New York Times*, Patrick's only lifeline to the outside world. He also brought the crossword books. The old man left them behind, and Patrick had collected them in his greed for entertainment. But as the days went by, Patrick grew unsure if they truly were forgotten. Were they an offering?

The old man had a name. Henry. Patrick once caught it on his credit card when he bought his usual plate of meatballs with extra sweet tomato jam.

Patrick narrowed his eyes, his nose millimeters from Henry's, but Henry seemed lost in some thought or another.

Two could play that game.

Patrick reached out and snapped his fingers against Henry's ear.

Nothing.

Patrick hummed in thought. He'd crack into this puzzle yet.

"Karin told me I'd find you here," Benji said as he entered the café.

Trying to play damage control for being caught, Patrick shoved his chair back from Henry's table and cast a beaming smile at Benji.

"Hey, cupcake," he drawled as he gave Benji a once-over. The hipster skinny jeans definitely fit well. Really well.

"We've moved on to cupcake?"

"Well, you do have a sweet, creamy center," Patrick said without a blink.

Benji coughed into his fist and averted his gaze.

"You should get that checked out," Patrick said as he stood.

Henry sipped his tea, still blissfully unaware.

"Know of any doctors in CASA?" Benji asked, rising to the challenge.

Patrick thumbed his chin. "Well, funny you should ask…."

"Him?" Benji asked and nodded to Henry.

Patrick's gut clenched as Henry pulled out the *Times* and ran his fingers over the front page. "Him?" Patrick tried to keep his smile intact as Benji denied him his desperate moment for news. "Naw. He's a—" Patrick snapped his fingers next to Henry's ear, only to be rewarded with no response. "—pet project."

Benji narrowed his eyes. The skepticism was strong with this one. "Then, who?"

"Me." Patrick counted the seconds until Benji's gaping reaction.

"You." Benji didn't take the bait. Dammit.

Patrick stretched with a long arch of the back. "Well… if you want to get specific, not medical. Particle physics. You know,"—he flicked his fingers dismissively—"superboring stuff about two bodies colliding together, creating a passionate explosion."

Benji coughed again. "Passionate?"

Patrick feigned innocence. "Do you find my vocabulary intimidating? I could use alternatives. How about concupiscent?"

"Wha—"

"Or would you prefer something that rolls off the tongue? How about lascivious?"

"Do you ever stop?"

"But my dear Benji, we were just reaching the climax of our verbal copulation."

"Oh God!"

Patrick licked his finger and hissed, mimicking a sizzle as he drew a one through the air. "Gotta be faster, pussycat."

Benji looked away, his jaw set in a stubborn way that made it obvious he was doing his best to deny Patrick a reaction. But his red cheeks and ears were more than enough.

"So, do you know what happened?" Patrick asked. "How you got here?"

Benji shook his head. "I drove, of course."

Oh boy. It was going to be a long day.

Patrick led Benji two tables away and gently brushed his elbow. His fingers twitched at the shock darting up his arm. He had to be mindful of that. He'd had a rule against casual touches for years, but Benji was somehow making him forget that. It made Patrick worry about what other rules might be next. "You're going to need to sit down for this."

Benji clucked his tongue. "You're really going for that trope? Are you going to ask how my heart is next?"

"You don't have one anymore," Patrick said as he plopped into the chair next to him.

"What?"

"You're dead."

The silence swallowed them. Overhead the fine musical stylings of Italian pop filtered through the showroom.

"I'm what?" Benji asked, his voice soft.

"Was I mumbling?" Patrick folded his arms behind his head and leaned his chair back on two legs. "I could have mumbled. Did you hear me say you're dead?"

"I got that."

"Awesome." Patrick let the chair slam back into place. He patted Benji on the shoulder. "Good chatting with you." He pushed up from the chair and turned to go, his good deed done for the day. That sob story in the entertainment showroom was a more pressing matter.

"Wait," Benji ordered him.

Patrick grunted under his breath as he slowly turned with a pivot of the heel. His Nike squeaked on the tiles. "May I help you?"

"You tell me I'm dead and you leave it at that?" The words were resigned and barely audible. It cut through Patrick's defenses much easier than anger or accusations would. He had a feeling Benji's angry face would be about as threatening as a fluffy kitten after his first bath. But right now he just looked confused and more than a little betrayed, and it came off as impossibly charming. Patrick wanted to cuddle him. What the hell.

Patrick shrugged. "Well. Yeah."

"There's more."

"What do you mean more? There isn't any more," Patrick said, bewildered by Benji's resistance.

"Of course there's more." Benji scowled, and his adorable factor skyrocketed. "We're in Hell, right?"

Patrick clapped his hands in laughter but more in an effort to silence all argument. "Hell? Fuck no. That's Wallville."

"So, this is heaven."

"Nope."

"What, then? We're just ghosts? There is no afterlife?" Benji swallowed. "Wait. That can't be—you said there was a hell."

Patrick kept his lips sealed, enjoying watching Benji puzzle it out.

"CASA is purgatory?"

Patrick pointed at him with a nod. "We've got a winner."

Benji blew out a breath and shook his head. "Unbelievable. How is this my life?" He barked out a short, harsh laugh. "Or I guess the point is that it *isn't* my life, right? Good to know my afterlife is going to suck as much as my real life did."

Patrick put a hand to his heart. "I'm wounded. Are you saying spending the rest of eternity here with me is a hardship?"

Benji glared at him. "I'm saying that I don't even know how I died, let alone what I did to deserve to be here. If there's a hell and a purgatory, that must mean there's a heaven, right? So why am I here? What did I do to deserve this?"

This? This was why Patrick usually left the heavy stuff to Karin. It was a huge adjustment, he got that. Hell, he'd lived it himself. Or not-lived it himself. Whatever. The point was he understood, but that didn't mean he wanted to stand here while Benji had an existential crisis. He had shit to do.

"I don't know, sunshine. Serial jaywalking? Not sorting your recyclables before you put them out to the curb? The point is you *are* here, no matter what happened to get you here."

Benji's face crumpled, going from indignant to wounded in the blink of an eye. And that should not make Patrick feel guilty. It shouldn't. He didn't *do* guilt. Maybe the swooping feeling in his stomach was indigestion.

"But—"

Patrick held up a hand. "I'm going to stop you right there. You think you shouldn't be here? Fine. That's a staffing issue, and you're going to have to take it up with Karin in HR."

For a second he didn't think Benji was going to fall for the dismissal, but he did. "Fine," he said, his lower lip trembling ever so slightly.

Ah, hell. Benji didn't strike him as a crier, but it looked like maybe things were headed that way. Time to push onward.

"Now that we've established that you're the newest employee here at purgatory CASA—"

"But CASA is such a happy place."

Patrick snorted. "Obviously you've never shopped here with your wife."

"I don't have a wife," Benji said, glancing out the window.

"Ouch. Tough break," Patrick said and followed Benji's line of sight. The robins were building a new nest on the windowsill. He took a slow breath and took comfort that spring had come around once again.

"My…," Benji muttered and turned his attention to the sugar packet container. "My boyfriend dumped me."

Patrick blinked and rubbed the back of his head. He scratched at the short fuzz at the nape of his neck. "You don't say," he said absently.

Sure, he was dead, but he wasn't blind. It would have been so much easier if Benji had had a wife. Damn.

Benji unfolded and refolded his hands. "Yeah…."

The attempt at small talk was as pleasant as a butter knife to the eye.

"All right." Patrick spun his chair around and straddled it. "If you're going to be stuck here, you're going to learn how to play the game."

"Game?" Benji perked up, seeming unsure.

"Gotta make it entertaining somehow." Patrick tapped the table with a knuckle. "Ground rules. This is a real CASA. The customers coming in and out are living and shopping for cheap minimalist furniture. They can't see us. Got it?"

"We're ghosts?" Benji knit his brows in confusion.

"Whatever you want to call it to get you through the day, sunshine," Patrick said. "Ready for the next part?"

"Should I be taking notes?"

"You'll catch on." Patrick reached out and clapped a hand on Benji's shoulder. The jolt of power shot up his arm and to the crown of his head. He forced his smile to stay in place. "I imagine you're a quick study." Patrick drew away and flicked his fingers, trying to work out the sting. "Next, our job is to help others move on."

"Others?" Benji asked. "Why us?"

Patrick shrugged. "Just lucky. I suppose. CASA chose us, Mr. Frodo."

"We're on Frodo, now?" Benji's slow grin triggered Patrick's own.

"Don't get used to it, cupcake."

"How do we help them move on?"

Patrick smirked. "You'll learn."

"Other ghosts are here with us. Like… Karin?"

"Yup."

"Who else?"

"Agnes. Who you sort of met." Patrick pursed his lips in thought.

Benji was like a dog with a bone now that he was getting some answers. Patrick reconsidered his openness. Maybe he should have stuck to cryptic answers. Though that was more Agnes's schtick. He probably couldn't pull it off half as well as she did. Damn.

"But *how* do we make them move on?" Benji asked.

"Excellent question," Patrick said. "People don't end up here by accident." He thought about it for a moment and laughed. "Or I guess they kind of do. Anyway, we help them and poof." He fanned his fingers to demonstrate. "Out the doors they go, another satisfied customer."

"Into the void?" Benji shivered, rubbing his arms. "That terrifying thing?"

"No, they go to heaven," Patrick said.

"Okay, if this is purgatory, what's heaven?"

Patrick pointed a finger. "You guess."

Benji shook his head. "Costless?"

"Pfft! Please. Costless is one of the seven circles. Keep up with me here." Patrick locked eyes with Benji. "You can do this."

Benji frowned. "Scope?"

"Is that a guess?" Patrick arched a brow.

"Is it?" Benji sat straighter in his chair like a petulant child.

Patrick stood and offered Benji his hand. "C'mon now. We have wrongs to right, skippy."

Benji stubbornly set his jaw. "But you didn't tell me."

"Let's go," Patrick insisted. "Lunch break's over. We're on the clock."

"Wait, does that mean we can actually eat? Patrick, wait up!"

THERE WAS something peculiar about Benji. Agnes had been right. He definitely was a cute one. Sandy mop of hair, fresh face, and dark eyes like he'd waltzed out of a Disney movie. His shirt was a bit loose on him, but the way that his skinny jeans were one size too small might have contributed just a sliver of a percentage to the cute.

But it wasn't that. And Patrick wouldn't admit it under penalty of death, as if that mattered anyway. Benji made his time in CASA seem easy and more tolerable. Maybe Agnes had been right. All Patrick had to do was to try on being a Guide for a new visitor for a while and see how that fit him.

That curious sensation of camaraderie was fascinating. Now the literal sparks between them when Patrick attempted the slightest touch, that was the intriguing stuff. One could get high, horny, or both on that business if they abused it. The temptation was there, but when Patrick acknowledged it, the self-disappointment kicked in. He'd have to wait for Benji's energy to taper off before Patrick decided to give it up and go for it.

"Hey," Benji said as they meandered through the herd of shoppers. "Hey!"

Patrick blinked, his throat clenching. He covered for it by stretching out his hands and cracking his knuckles. "Yo, what up?"

Benji smiled. "I asked about you."

"Yeah?"

The shoppers sidestepped around them, permitting them to pass like fish through water.

"How did you get here?" Benji asked.

"Same as you," Patrick said as he scanned the crowd. The howler monkey of a spirit was nearby. As soon as he got him out of the damned store, he could think without his head pounding. Even Tommy refused to go into the entertainment showroom. Poor weird, friendless kid.

"Which we've already covered is something I don't remember, so why not tell me and answer two questions in one?" Benji prodded.

Patrick shrugged. "I was popped out of my mother's womb, I grew up, drew the short straw, and *whack*, here I am? What more are you looking for, sweetheart?"

Benji coughed into his fist and then cleared his throat.

"You should really get that checked out."

"By you, good doctor? Open my mouth and say *ah*?"

It was Patrick's turn to flush as he sharply turned away and faked a sneeze. Dammit. Benji was definitely stepping up to the plate. Patrick came to a halt and shut out the noise of customers chatting among themselves. The howler's voice, carried over the expanse of the floor, was harder to ignore. Benji didn't seem to notice, but his mind wasn't fully wrapped around not being on a different plane as everything else.

"Am I going to move on?" Benji asked as he stood at Patrick's side.

The customers slipped around them, unconsciously shifting just out of the way as they wandered the aisles. A woman stopped next to Benji as she checked the price on a ARDERE nightlight. She turned over the rubbery turquoise cat-shaped light and flicked the switch. She gasped at the changing colors and then dropped two boxes in her cart.

Patrick arched a brow at Benji's question and then sighed. "Couldn't tell you, cupcake. CASA is a harsh mistress. She decides who leaves and who stays."

"But you said you help people leave."

Patrick pointed a finger. "Ah! Now you're catching on."

"But you just said CASA decides. And… that CASA is a she?" Benji knitted his brows. The brow-knitting thing was quickly becoming Patrick's kryptonite.

"You just said it," Patrick said and then headed off again toward entertainment.

"Do you know how unhelpful you are?"

"Unhelpful?" Patrick asked over his shoulder. "I'll have you know I'm employee of the decade." He patted his hip and snapped his fingers. "C'mon, pup. Let's go."

Benji frowned and kept in step. "Unfortunately, I liked cupcake better." He jogged to keep the pace. "Why don't you move on?"

It was an innocent question that crashed Patrick's mood as easily as his interest in Benji had risen.

"I don't." Patrick didn't need to elaborate.

"But you said everyone does."

Benji's innocence was very quickly becoming Patrick's least favorite quality. They had to find the howler and fast. Patrick's good night's sleep depended on it.

"Some people are different." Patrick clenched his fists at his sides, and he stepped up the pace.

"What's so different about you?" Benji asked, hurrying behind.

And now Benji was rapidly becoming less attractive.

"This way," Patrick commanded him and snatched Benji by his shirt.

Benji yipped as they took a sharp right through office furniture. Patrick crouched low behind a dividing wall and peered through the network of table legs. Benji stood over him, not getting with the program as quickly as Patrick had hoped.

The howler had claimed the SPÖL TV stand and shambled around it drunkenly. He was a disheveled mess of an older guy with a potbelly and broken glasses. At least he hadn't shown up covered in dog shit.

"Have you seen my wife?" he asked a customer who passed him by. "Have you seen her? Gray hair? Flowery dress? Her name's Mary. Have you seen Mary?" Another customer pushed along with her cart. Her beeper sounded that she was needed in Bambini Mondo. "Mary! *Mary*!" he screamed as he burst into tears.

Benji's lip trembled as he stood out in plain view. "He's so sa—"

"*Get down.*" Patrick yanked him by the waistband of his jeans.

Benji flopped like a marionette to the floor next to him.

"Welcome to your crash course in showing someone the exit," Patrick whispered out of the corner of his mouth.

"Did you have to nearly rip off my pants?" Benji said as he awkwardly readjusted.

Patrick didn't pay him any mind. "You need a smaller size. I'll get Karin on it." He pointed toward the sobbing old man. "Here's how it's gonna go. You're my trainee, so it's your job to observe on this one. Got it?"

"I'm not a kindergartener. I teach them, you know," Benji whispered.

"Well, this isn't painting pine cones time." Patrick snapped his fingers. "Stick with me."

Benji nodded. Finally, no witty comebacks. At last he was regaining his attractiveness. Maybe halfway yanking off his jeans had something to do with it. The situation necessitated the chance to cop a feel. That was Patrick's story, and he was sticking to it—for the time being.

"Okay, the short and sweet of it," Patrick whispered. "It's like they said in *Ghostbusters,* we're made of spiritual energy. But the more we interact with the living world, the more we deplete it. Also, helping other spirits along requires using quite a bit of energy. So we ration it so we don't dissipate right away."

Benji thumbed his chin. "And if we dissipate?"

"It's off to the ball pit." Patrick turned back to the howler. "Okay. Ready?" He popped up out of hiding and pasted on his best smile.

"Wait, wha—" Benji squeaked.

Patrick toed him with his Nike, trying to urge him into following his lead.

The howler turned, eyeing Patrick with hunger and panic in his eyes. Patrick relaxed his stance and drooped his shoulders, portraying a nonthreatening posture.

"May I help you find something, sir?" Patrick asked sweetly.

Benji peeked out from behind the divider, and Patrick nodded to him.

The howler, thankfully, stopped howling. "I'm… I'm looking for Mary," he said, confused.

"Mary?" Patrick repeated, feigning committing the name to memory. "I'm sure I can help you find her. Now, tell me where you saw her last."

The howler looked down at the SPÖL and ran his fingers over the surface of the walnut particleboard. "We were building the TV stand. And we were missing a screw. I came back to see if I could get an extra. I think? And that man over there, he's going to buy the same thing. But there aren't enough screws."

Patrick snapped his fingers. "Ah! Yes! I have seen just the screws you're looking for. If you head out to the exit, I'll have them delivered, all right? And I'll make sure the gentleman across the way picks up a pack of extra hardware. You should get going. Mary is probably getting dinner ready."

The howler nodded. "Dinner. Yes, dinner."

Patrick rubbed his stomach. "Mashed potatoes with extra butter, am I right or what?"

The howler brightened. "Oh yes! Definitely. Mary makes the best roast. Just like my grandmother." He stepped back into the aisle, flowing with living customers. "You've been most helpful, young man. What's your name?"

Patrick offered a bright grin and tapped two fingers to his forehead in salute. "Patrick, sir. Have a good dinner. Bring me the recipe some time."

The howler nodded and turned one last time. He vanished into the crowd, leaving only a trail of smoke.

Patrick took a breath and then coughed. The cold of the overactive air-conditioning seeped into his skin. Nothing a hot shower wouldn't cure. Patrick flicked his fingers and watched his hands, noting the graying of his fingertips. He concentrated and flexed his fingers into fists and then unfurled them. The pink of fictional blood flow returned.

Benji whistled a low note. "That was awesome."

Patrick crossed his arms and nodded. "And that, my dear Benji, is why I'm employee of the decade." He stalked over to the customer who'd been looking at the TV stand and reached into his own pocket, fishing around until he found a small packet of screws. He tucked them into the customer's pocket unobtrusively. "Ten thousand saved…." Distantly the entryway bell sounded over the showroom. He nodded with satisfaction. "Ten thousand and one."

Benji chuckled. "I gotta admit, you're pretty helpful."

Patrick pulled a long stretch of the shoulders and yawned. "Yeah, y'know. Some things just come naturally." He reached to pat Benji on the back and then rethought it. He grunted with another fake stretch. "Now you give it a go." He pointed across the floor to the living room section. Agnes sat on her usual pristine white couch, knitting away. She paused to count stitches and then nodded at her findings.

"Her?" Benji asked.

"Ten bucks says she's not here waiting on family."

"But money doesn't matter here."

"Eh. Semantics," Patrick said and shooed Benji forward. "Go on. It's an easy one."

Patrick would feel guilty later, but right now he refrained from pissing himself with giggles.

Benji nodded and straightened his shirt, then readjusted his jeans. The way they hung on his hips was definitely a nice touch. Patrick tilted his head as Benji took the lead across the floor.

"Remember what I said about expending energy!" Patrick called as he hung back.

Later, he would think back on sending Benji into Agnes's domain and marvel at the fact that he hadn't laughed himself silly, giving away the joke. Benji strolled by her, trying to play it cool. Patrick scratched his chin. The oddball strategy was a touch charming. Patrick would work that out of Benji's system soon. As Benji pretended to straighten items, Agnes caught on and shot Patrick a warning look. He shrugged in mock innocence.

"I hope you know how much of a shit you are," Karin said just behind him.

"The newbie's gotta learn, y'know," Patrick said.

"You need to stop being so willfully oblivious. He's more than just a newbie." She laughed softly. "Cupcake? Honestly?"

"Get off it," Patrick warned her.

"You're going soft."

"Just need something to pass the time."

"Uh-huh."

"Don't you have kitchens to take care of?" Patrick scowled.

Across the floor, Agnes glared at them both as Benji approached her.

Karin whispered to Patrick. "Here we go. Three... two...."

Patrick flicked his attention to Benji just at the right second. Like an idiot, Benji reached out to touch Agnes....

And then the poor schmuck promptly dispersed in a puff of spiritual smoke.

Agnes threw down her knitting needles in a huff. "*Patrick Harrison Bryant*!" she bellowed.

Karin chuckled. "Ooh. You got Harrison."

Patrick waved her off. "C'mon now, wanna come along as we fish Benji out of the ball pit?"

Karin stepped back and held up her hands. "That's all you, big guy. I don't tread on Agnes's turf."

"But it's fun." Patrick batted his lashes.

"Until Agnes decides to throw you in and not pull you out." She slapped his shoulder. "Now, go get your precious sweet cupcake."

Patrick happily gave her the customary salute of the middle finger.

Chapter Five:
BRESIA

BENJI FELT weightless. But also like he was lying in bed, if bed was a cloud that smelled like plastic. He shifted, his stomach swooping like he was falling as the small movement dipped him lower.

His eyes shot open. The darkness around him felt like it had weight. He moved again, managing a breathless shriek when he sank deeper into the nothingness.

"Welcome to drama queen, population one," he heard from somewhere above him.

"You have no business here. Don't you have someone to haunt in the café?"

That voice was unfamiliar, but the first one—Benji racked his brain, trying to figure out how he knew it. It gave him something to focus on aside from the blinding terror he'd felt a moment ago, which was nice.

"I'm not bringing him up until you're gone. Go," the second voice said. Benji recognized the tone. She had to be a teacher. No one could nail disappointed condescension quite as well as a teacher.

"He needs—"

The woman snorted. "What he needs to do is accomplish what he was put here to do so he can move on."

"I'm wounded, Agnes. That feels like a dig at me, not a statement about our dear Benjamin."

"We hear what we want to hear, Patrick," the woman said.

Patrick! Benji took another breath, grimacing when the inhalation brought more plastic-scented air into his lungs. He was in the ball pit at CASA. Because he was dead.

Jesus.

Benji went limp, letting himself sink deeper into the balls. He didn't want to see Patrick. He didn't particularly want to see this Agnes woman either, but needs must. He'd rather the devil he didn't know than the one he did in this instance.

Though Patrick had been adamant that this wasn't hell. Were there devils in purgatory? Probably. And Patrick, with his sinful good looks and screw-everything attitude, was definitely a prime candidate to be one.

He stayed under a few more minutes until a bejeweled and wrinkled hand thrust down into the balls.

"Patrick's gone. It's time to come out," Agnes said.

Benji put his hand in hers, wincing at her surprisingly tight grip as she pulled him up. He gasped when his head broke the surface, the open air tasting sweet and light on his tongue after the heavy, fetid atmosphere at the bottom of the pit.

There wasn't any accompanying relief in his lungs, though. He took another cautious breath, alarm spiking through him when he realized his chest wasn't moving.

"We don't need to breathe. Most of us do, just because it's familiar. But that's a corporeal need, son, and we're most certainly not corporeal anymore."

He'd only met Agnes briefly before everything had gone dark, but she sounded much kinder than she had when she'd been dressing Patrick down a few minutes ago.

Benji swallowed hard. There was saliva in his mouth, but he probably didn't need that anymore, either. If they didn't need to breathe, he doubted they needed to eat or drink. That revelation made Patrick's obsession with sitting in the café even more curious.

"New Guides are usually paired with Karin, but Patrick got to you first, I'm afraid," Agnes continued, her expression dour. "We used to have someone else who—" She shook her head. "The past is the past. Karin should have been the one to greet you, but we didn't want to get between you two. You're the first person he's shown any interest in meeting in a long time."

Patrick didn't give off the loner vibe at all. He was so—loud. But that did shed some light on his general ineptitude at actually explaining anything at all about their situation. Not that things would have been any less traumatic with Karin, but at least he'd be better informed. He still had no idea what was going on, aside from the fact that he was somehow dead.

"I wouldn't call it interest as much as amusement," Benji said dryly.

"Well, that's been lacking too." Her smile managed to be fond and disappointed all at once. "At any rate, I'm sorry you were the one to suffer for it. Patrick's a good man, but he's… conflicted."

Conflicted wasn't the word Benji would have chosen, but he let it slide. Agnes obviously knew Patrick much better than he did.

Agnes tugged on their joined hands again, and Benji took the hint and sat up. He sighed when he realized he was back in his old clothes.

Agnes chuckled. "Occupational hazard," she said, winking at him. She patted his hand, sandwiching his between both of hers. Her skin was translucent and wrinkled just like he'd expect for a woman her age, but it seemed to almost crackle with energy. Holding her hand wasn't unlike getting a static shock on a dry winter day. Not enough to feel painful, but enough that the current was obvious.

She gave him a squeeze before letting go so he could make his way out of the ball pit. He felt much better than he had when he'd woken up. His head was clear, and his skin still felt like it was buzzing where it had come into contact with hers. He was usually muzzy for a bit after he woke, something that made facing a classroom full of five-year-olds excruciating for the first hour or so, but right now he felt like he'd been awake for hours downing Red Bull nonstop.

Agnes let out another low laugh when he looked from his hands to hers. "Patrick thinks it's the ball pit that recharges auras, but I think you've already figured out he's wrong, haven't you?"

Benji flexed his hand, surprised to find it looked perfectly normal. "I didn't feel like this before you touched me. I was tired and confused." He looked over his shoulder at the ball bit. "So why do we end up there if it isn't to recharge?"

Agnes's eyes lit up, and for a moment there was a timeless quality to her appearance, a luminescence that was there and gone so fast Benji could have imagined it. He didn't think he had, though. He was still learning the ropes, but Agnes was definitely more than she seemed. How could someone as smart at Patrick not have picked up on that? Especially if he'd been around as long as Agnes seemed to be hinting.

"Honestly? Because it's a goddamn hassle for me, so it's sure as hell going to be a hassle for *you*." She snickered when he gaped at her.

"Don't look so shocked. I may spend most of my time knitting, but I'm not a delicate flower."

He had a clear memory of her now that she'd done her mojo on him. She'd been knitting on a couch in one of the display houses, and Patrick had tricked him into touching her.

"But before, you didn't recharge me. Everything went blank."

She clucked her tongue. "That was Patrick's fault. You can't touch me."

"But—"

Agnes cut him off with an unimpressed stare. "I said *you* can't touch *me*. I can touch you. In fact, it's necessary when your aura gets so depleted that you dematerialize. You were well on your way to that. Touching me just jump-started the process."

Benji looked down at himself. He could feel the texture of his jeans against his thighs, including the uncomfortable stiffness of the stained fabric. He clenched his fist, focusing on the sharp bite of his fingernails into his palm. He felt solid. He felt *real*. But Agnes had said earlier they weren't corporeal anymore. So what were they?

"You said Patrick haunts the café. So that's what our lives are? We're what, spirits? Ghosts?"

"You aren't a ghost. I said 'haunt' because he won't move on. Over the years I've wondered if he was called to be a permanent Guide, like Karin, but I think I just didn't have all of the pieces. It makes more sense now."

Benji was glad it made sense to her, because things were rapidly making *less* sense to him the more they spoke.

"Patrick's problem has always been his inability to take anything on blind faith. You want to know what you are, son? You're exactly what you were when you were human. Energy and matter and grace. Patrick talks about plasma states and harmonic frequencies and atom vibrations, but at the heart of it, that's just denial."

She pinned him with an intense stare that made Benji feel uncomfortably exposed and like she wasn't seeing him, exactly. Or at least not just him. It wasn't lost on him that she'd never once said "we" when answering his questions. *You aren't a ghost. You're made of energy.* Not we. Benji shivered under the force of her gaze. Maybe he didn't want to know what Agnes was.

Her expression softened. "You're whatever you want to be, Benjamin. You didn't get the chance to figure that out when you were alive, and it's a lesson you're going to learn here before you can move on. But you won't be here long. You aren't a stranger to stepping out in faith."

He had no idea what that meant. His mother was religious, but once he'd flown the nest he'd become a Christmas and Easter kind of guy, the kind of lapsed Catholic that made his mother suck her teeth in disapproval when they clumsily knelt on the risers, out of practice and bored during the interminable holiday masses.

Agnes smiled. "Faith is a broad term, son," she said, and Benji wondered if she could read his mind. "Think of it as trust in the unknown. And Patrick? That's too raw for him. At least, until now."

Benji didn't know how he factored into that, but the significant look she gave him left no question as to what had changed. The air between them felt charged, like Agnes was about to give him another energy whammy. The hairs on the back of his neck prickled, and Benji shivered. He wasn't scared of Agnes, per se, but he felt the need to put some distance between them, however meager that was when they were both trapped inside the confines of CASA.

Agnes nodded even though he hadn't said anything and started walking briskly toward the door. They were in Bambini Mondo, a place that had always appealed to his inner child but now seemed cloyingly bright and claustrophobic.

Karin was waiting for them at the elevators, a tense expression on her face. She'd traded her CASA uniform for a trim navy blue dress that looked like the ones his mother had worn back in the sixties when she'd been a stewardess. He blinked, wondering if Karin was just into retro clothes or if that was the outfit she'd died in. It was a damn sight better than stained jeans and a ratty T-shirt.

He turned to thank Agnes for her help, confusing though it had been, but she'd disappeared. He whirled around. Bambini Mondo was empty, and Agnes wasn't walking up the stopped escalator, either. She was just gone.

Karin offered him a wry smile and then disappeared as well. He blinked hard, jumping when a second later she was standing in front of him again, this time in the familiar yellow polo shirt and jeans he'd seen her wearing before.

She leaned against the elevator doors, and Benji had to bite back a warning that it wasn't a safe place. No one else was in the CASA, though he didn't know if it was late at night or early in the morning. Or if the other ghosts—or whatever the hell they were—could operate the thing. But Karin didn't look concerned that the doors might open and she'd plummet to her death—probably because she was already dead.

And wasn't that a mindfuck.

"First thing to know: this isn't a punishment. Yes, it's purgatory. But you're here to help other people, not because you're atoning for anything."

Benji gave her a dubious look. "I thought purgatory—"

She shook her head ruefully. "Catholic, am I right?"

He pursed his lips. "Lapsed."

Karin laughed and clapped her hands together in delight. "So the fact that there's a purgatory isn't the hard sell for you, it's the lack of atonement thing. Think of this as a clearinghouse to the other side. A pit stop where you have the chance to make a difference before moving on to wherever you are going next."

"But where am I going next? Heaven?"

She shrugged. "Only you can decide that. I've seen atheists and agnostics move on. I've seen people who were Hindu, Jewish, Muslim—your beliefs don't matter, as long as some part of you believes there's something to move on *to*. Maybe it's reincarnation. Maybe there is a heaven. Who knows? The point is that you accept whatever it is you'll see when you walk through that door," she said, nodding toward the main entrance. The one that had opened up to a terrifying void when he'd last seen them open.

She pushed off her spot against the elevator and started leading him through the store. "Okay, so that was number one. The second thing to keep in mind is that just as what comes after is up to you, so is what happens here."

Benji bit back a snort at that. He'd had less than no control over anything since arriving at the CASA.

"No, it's true. Some people are here only long enough to do what they need to accomplish so they can move on. The howler at the SPÖL, for example."

"Howler?"

"Of course Patrick wouldn't introduce himself or bother trying to explain anything," she muttered. She was smiling again when she looked up, but it didn't quite reach her eyes. "The howler was the gentleman you and Patrick helped move on yesterday."

"I helped a... howler? Person?" Benji drew a blank.

Karin sighed and dipped her head. "Patrick likes to give things pet names, as I'm sure you've learned by now. A howler is a spirit that's highly distraught. They cry and yell. And according to Patrick, keep him from his blessed beauty sleep."

Patrick and Benji had talked to several people, but Benji definitely didn't remember helping anyone move on. He wasn't even sure what that meant. "I have no idea what you're talking about."

Karin's expression grew grimmer. "Maybe we should start with what you do know. Did Patrick tell you anything at all?"

Benji shrugged, feeling uncomfortably put on the spot. "He told me I was dead and this is purgatory, and that we can either move on to heaven or hell after we're done here. That's about it."

Her smile was sharp and brittle, like it was costing her a lot of effort to keep on her face. "There's a good deal more to it than that. Did you ask him any questions about your death?"

He nodded. At least, he'd tried to ask them. Patrick hadn't been forthcoming with answers, which Benji was learning was par for the course. He divulged amazingly little for someone who rarely shut up.

"And he didn't answer them, did he?" She groaned out loud when Benji shook his head. "It's not unusual for you not to remember your death. That will come with time. And I don't know the details," she said, holding her hand up when he started to talk. "All I know is that a product from CASA was involved. That's why you're here. And as for how you move on, well, you save someone from the same fate."

Benji puzzled that out as he followed her through the store. She walked fast, and he wondered if that was something she'd done before she'd died or a trait she'd developed after coming to CASA. It was a huge space, but why hurry? They had an eternity, didn't they? What was the point of rushing anywhere?

They finally came to a stop in front of a familiar BRESIA stepladder. "For example, a new spirit entered our part of CASA a little after three in the afternoon. He was gone before I could fit him in for orientation, which I'd planned to do as soon as the store closed."

She ran a hand up the smooth dark finish of the stepladder, and she lingered along one of the thin legs, gripping it in a manner that made Benji arch a brow.

He assumed from Karin's demeanor she didn't have any flirtatious proclivities toward him. He hadn't known her long enough to make that judgment call. He swallowed. Patrick had left a hell of an impression on him.

"He was able to leave a little before six in the evening," she said, and Benji was thankful for her to break the awkward silence. He nodded obediently, indicating he was listening. "Patrick helped him save a young man who would have been killed by this in three years. I imagine the spirit shared his fate. The only thing I know for sure is that this was involved," she said, patting the top step of the ladder, "and that Patrick helped him by convincing the man to buy some floor grips that would prevent it from slipping out from under him."

It looked so utterly nonthreatening. Benji couldn't imagine it or anything else around them killing someone. What had the culprit been for him? He didn't own the BRESIA, but 90 percent of his apartment was furnished from CASA. Or had been. It wasn't his anymore. The dead couldn't own things, could they?

He sat heavily on a stool in the sleekly modern kitchen unit. God, did anyone know he was dead yet? Who would find his body? The school, probably. The vice principal usually went out to check on staff who didn't show up for work. The worst thing she'd ever found in Benji's tenure was the PE teacher drunk as a skunk playing croquet in his front yard. He swallowed and looked down at his hands, flexing them. There were still a few stray specks of glitter under his nails. Stuck with him for eternity, probably, just like the god-awful clothes he was wearing.

Except that he *could* do something about. "How did you do it?" he asked suddenly, his head snapping up. Karin was still leaning against the BRESIA, looking at him with obvious concern.

"Do what?"

"Change," he said, sweeping his hand in her direction. "Your clothes."

Her lips dropped open in surprise. She'd probably expected him to have a thousand questions about purgatory and moving on. And before he died, Benji would have. He also would have inquired about the new spirit and made sure he'd actually moved on and wasn't wandering around the store just as disoriented and bleary as he'd been when Benji had met him. But where had a lifetime of good deeds and compassion gotten him? He'd lived a half-life while he was alive, and now he seemed destined for a half death as well. It was bullshit. And he wasn't going to just roll over and take it.

"Well, like I said, it's your choice," she said.

"And if I decided I didn't want to be here?"

She inclined her head, her expression kind if a little stretched. "Patrick, Agnes, and I will help you figure out what you need to do to move on—"

"No. What if I decided *I didn't want to be here?*" he repeated, slower this time. "You said I could do whatever I wanted. What if what I want isn't to change my clothes, Karin? What if what I want is to leave?"

Her pasted-on smile faltered. "You can't leave, Benji."

The bar stool clattered to the floor as he stood. "I'm leaving."

He was four aisles away before Karin caught up to him, her usual long strides an outright run this time.

"You can't," she said. She reached out and grabbed his wrist when Benji steadfastly ignored her. Her fingers felt warm, but it was nothing like the jolt he got from Agnes. It wasn't quite the warm molasses feeling he got from touching Patrick, either. So Karin must be something else. Not that it mattered, because he was done. He wasn't going to stick around and classify the types of dead wandering CASA. He'd wasted his life, and he wasn't going to waste his afterlife. He had shit to do, and everything he'd ever put off because it was selfish or too expensive was at the top of the list. Ghosts didn't exactly get charged museum entrance fees or have to pay top dollar for seats at all the concerts he'd skipped.

Benji shook her off. She wasn't as strong as Agnes. "Thank you for your time, Karin, but I've decided *not* to drink the Kool-Aid. I'm out of here."

He made it down to the first floor before a slow clap startled him into turning around. Patrick was perched on top of the cart return, watching him with obvious glee. "As far as storm-offs go, I'll give you a 3.0 for form and a 4.5 for flair for the Kool-Aid line. Inspired, especially since you don't know how to drink in this form."

Benji scowled at him and turned back to the doors. "Have a fun afterlife, Patrick," he muttered. The store wasn't open yet, and the doors remained stalwartly closed, and Benji cursed himself for not timing things better. Not that he could do much about that, since he had no idea what time it actually was. Or what day it was. Goddammit.

He heard feet hit the floor, and a second later Patrick slung an arm around his shoulders and leaned their heads together. "Karin's upstairs ferociously reorganizing kitchenwares, and Agnes was so amused that she skipped a stitch a few rows ago and had to unravel and go back to fix it. Impressive, because hardly anyone can throw Agnes off her knitting game," Patrick said conspiratorially. "So come on, share with the class. Tell Uncle Patrick what you said to Karin. All I got out of her was a demand that I keep you inside."

Benji slithered out of Patrick's loose grip. "That! That's exactly it! You people don't actually tell me anything! It's like being stuck in a fortune cookie. 'You control your destiny, Benji,'" he mimicked. "'Ultimately only you can decide what you're wearing, or where you go when you move on, or how long you stay here,'" he continued bitterly.

Patrick nodded knowingly. "You got the open-source speech."

"The what?"

Patrick made an absent gesture. "Like computer programming. Some things are closed source. You can't see what makes them tick so you can't add to them. But open source, everything is out there. 'In real open source, you have the right to control your destiny.' Linus Torvalds said that, but it assumes you have access to the code itself. I like to call Karin's talk about being in control of your destiny and being able to mold things around you her open source speech."

Benji frowned. "I don't—"

"Torvalds invented Linux. Do keep up, young Benjamin. And if you don't know what that is, don't tell me. I don't want to live in a world where there are no alternatives to Microsoft."

Benji managed an almost soundless growl but didn't respond to Patrick's nattering. He'd gone from violent anger to despair like he'd never felt before in about two point one seconds. He grabbed the nearest thing he could reach, a stand holding an array of bright yellow bags, and threw it. The bags scattered across the floor, fanning out like flat yellow peacocks. Some sort of two-dimensional, bastardized version of Big Bird.

Did they make *Sesame Street* episodes about teachers dying? Would his kids be huddled around the TV right now, watching a giant yellow bird singing songs about grief?

His throat was tight with unshed tears, and he hated it. He'd always been taught to keep a stiff upper lip and not give in to big shows of emotion, and it had worked in the past. He'd pack away his disappointment or depression, and later, after he'd had some time to think about it, he'd find that the emotion wasn't as strong anymore. His hurt over Charles leaving him had been bad, but he'd had a life to keep living. Kids to teach, bills to pay. Mr. Whiskers to feed. Life.

And now he didn't. There weren't any mundane tasks to turn to when his emotions got the best of him. There weren't any more mundane tasks at all, because he was dead and being held hostage in CASA. The thought was so ridiculous that Benji hung his head and started laughing. He was a ghost hostage in what had been one of his favorite places on earth.

Patrick put a hand lightly on his back, and even though he didn't want to, Benji leaned into it. The heat from Patrick's palm seemed to fill some of the gaping emptiness in Benji's chest. He didn't have any idea how long they stood there, but for once Patrick was silent. They didn't move as employees started swarming around them. Someone cleaned up the bags Benji had thrown, and he felt guilty about making more work for them.

Patrick didn't drop his hand until the front doors were unlocked. People must have been lined up outside, because as soon as the store opened, people started flowing in like water, swerving around them with unblinking, unconcerned eyes, like they weren't even there.

Because they weren't, Benji realized. It hadn't really hit home until now that none of the shoppers or employees could see them. They really were ghosts.

The doors opened again, and Benji watched the latest batch of shoppers walk in, their bright shorts and flip-flops a strange counter to the gaping void behind them.

"If you're really thinking of making a run for it, the basement parking garage is where it's at," Patrick said, a wicked smile on his face.

Benji knew better than to trust anything that came out of Patrick's mouth, but he dutifully followed him down to the garage anyway. He was more than a little shocked when the elevator doors opened onto an actual parking lot and not the starry mass of infinity he'd seen upstairs.

Before he could take a step outside, though, Patrick caught his hand. He nodded toward a far corner, where an old woman sat on a motorized scooter. At first she looked just like a normal customer, but as she came closer Benji realized her skin had a sickly pallor and her eyes were pools of fathomless black.

"Benji, meet the Weople. Weople," he said, gesturing toward the growing mass of blank-faced people shuffling toward the open elevator, "meet Benji."

Benji took an instinctive step back, and the doors closed, cutting off the view of the parking lot.

"What the hell is a Weople?"

"Weople are a who, not a what," Patrick said. He hit the button for the lobby, and Benji braced himself against the wall as the elevator started moving. "They're wraiths. Wallville People. Weople. They snatch up souls who stray too far from purgatory and take them to hell."

"Wallville is hell?"

Patrick rolled his eyes. "Didn't we already go over that forever ago? Keep up, sweetheart. You're not just here to be ornamental."

"So, what do we do now?" Benji shivered as he pressed his back to the elevator wall. He hoped to never see those things again. He probably would, which was the bitch of it all.

Patrick clapped his hands, and Benji startled from the sharp echo too deep inside his ears. "You can either sit in a corner and have your little pity party—"

"Or?" Benji asked.

Patrick's bright smile resembled a hungry shark. "Or you can learn to start living again."

"Living." Benji watched Patrick, his amusement waning. "In case you missed it—"

"In case you missed it, we are all matter, mass, and energy. The living are the same matter, mass, and energy." He waved a hand, as if dismissing the thought. "That's a lesson for later. Right now the question is, 'Jasmine, do you trust me?'"

"You're... serious?" Benji couldn't help but smirk.

"Wanna ride my magic carpet?"

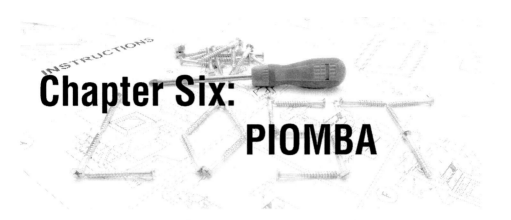

Chapter Six:
PIOMBA

THE ELEVATOR seemed to ascend slower than usual. The Weople's pull of dark energy must have been at its peak today. Maybe taking Benji down to the parking garage had not been the wisest of ideas. Patrick shoved his fingers in his pockets and relaxed his shoulders, playing casual.

"How do you do that?" Benji asked as his cheeks flushed to a red not found in nature.

Patrick arched his brows in the most poor pitiful kitten face. "Quote movies?"

"You need to stop that," Benji squeaked and then cleared his throat. He stood straighter, and Patrick stood straighter in response. Benji wasn't that much shorter; what he lacked in brawn, he made up for in height. Slight, nonthreatening. A nurturer type.

The flesh on the back of Patrick's neck tingled, and he felt his lips start to pull into a frown. He cleared his throat to cover it. Benji was right—he did need to stop.

But, unable to resist the verbal banter, Patrick went there anyway. "Stop what?"

The elevator dinged and the doors parted onto the second floor. Saved by the fucking bell. Patrick stepped out, metaphorically and physically dodging Benji's follow-up comments. He surveyed his surroundings. The office showroom seemed to be a good place to start. It seemed it was shaping up to be a quiet day.

"C'mon." Patrick gestured for him to follow and started off before Benji could respond, making sure to kill any rejoinder. He knew very well what words would come out of Benji's mouth. And he knew very well he needed to watch his own. As much as Patrick enjoyed Benji's companionship, he had no desire to travel down the path that led to feeling and expectations. He clenched his fist as he quickened his pace. Office was waiting, and with it stress relief.

The *clop-clop-skip* of Benji's sneakers on the linoleum scurried in a quickened rhythm, and Patrick hurried faster, pulling away.

"Are you guys always in a hurry?" Benji said as he puffed into existence in front of Patrick.

Blinking widely, Patrick leaned back on his heel. He cracked a lopsided grin. "Well done, grasshopper."

"What?" Benji shook his head. "I didn't do anything."

"How are you here?" Patrick asked.

Benji snorted, frustrated. "Are we doing the metaphysical thing again? That's getting old."

Patrick chuckled. "No Descartes this time. How are you here? In front of me?"

Benji pointed in the direction of the elevator. "I was trying to catch up. This isn't a hard question."

"But you were a good twenty feet away." Patrick said. He reached out, gripping both sides of Benji's head. Benji's lashes fluttered at the contact; Patrick ignored the energy transference. "Think, Benji. Think."

He broke the contact the next second and then cracked his knuckles. He shouldn't have touched Benji, even in jest.

"I wanted you to stop," Benji said.

If that wasn't a loaded statement.

Patrick grinned. "And you teleported to do it."

Benji crossed his arms and arched a dubious brow. "Like in the comic books?"

Patrick wagged a finger and brightened. "Exactly."

"Did you do drugs before you died?" Benji asked as Patrick stepped away. "You can tell me. I'm not judging. Because I can't tell if you dropped too much acid in your day or if you're just genuinely insane."

Patrick turned on his heel and then hopped up on the glass PIOMBA desktop. A pair of young women ran their fingers along the glass and through Patrick's incorporeal thighs.

"You'd have to clean it every day," one woman said to the other. "And you'd get fingerprints all over it."

Her shopping companion rolled her eyes. "You're so obsessed with fingerprints."

"Don't buy the desk," said an older man as he loomed next to Patrick.

Rolling his shoulders and trying to play off the annoyance, Patrick cast a casual glance to the disheveled older man fighting to get the customers' attention.

"Don't buy the desk," the man urgently warned them. "The glass can't support body weight."

Patrick tilted his head back as he asked the fluorescent lights to send him patience.

Benji shook his head and took a hesitant step back. "Where did he come from?"

"That guy?" Patrick asked as he cracked his knuckles. "That's an Impression. And right now he's infringing upon your tutelage." He held up a hand toward Benji. "Watch and learn."

Benji nodded, looking from him to the old man and back again.

Patrick tapped the old man on the elbow. "Can I help you, sir?"

The old man stiffened in surprise. "Oh, yes." He pointed to one of the young women, her hair a bright Day-Glo green and a ring in her nose. She seemed pretty tame, all things considered. Patrick had seen all types in his day.

"Her," the old man said with venom.

"Hey, now," Patrick warned him. "All customers are afforded equal opportunities here."

"But she's going to buy the desk," he said.

Patrick and Benji shared a glance. Patrick nodded to him, trying to puzzle out if Benji knew where the exchange was going.

Benji gave a mute nod in response, and Patrick's nonexistent heart swelled. Lassie can be taught!

"And what else?" Patrick asked, prying for more information from the old man.

The old man shivered. "They're going to do crude things on it. It'll break and she'll sever an artery in her thigh."

"So you're just trying to help," Patrick explained as he watched him for understanding.

"Yes. Help. Help that girl do something with her life instead of going down the road of depravity," the old man grumbled.

Patrick gave an overdramatic shrug. "Eh. To each their own."

Benji knitted his brows, and Patrick officially determined that was his most charming trait. "We were born with free will," Benji said. "We can make our own decisions."

Patrick internally cringed but forced his grimace into a fake, bright CASA employee smile and aimed it at the old man. "Please excuse him. He's shadowing me."

The old man nodded. "Of course."

Benji's adorable knitted brows were back, now joined by a pout. Patrick licked his lips. That was a mighty fine distracting pout.

Patrick slipped from the PIOMBA desk. "Let me take care of this." He smirked and then whispered to Benji, "Watch this."

He headed to the yellow intercom phone on a nearby column. He gestured to the handset like Vanna White ready to turn letters.

"It's a phone?" Benji asked in a half question. "You really did do drugs, didn't you?"

Patrick slipped the handset off the cradle and then hit the broadcast switch.

"Attention, CASA shoppers. All linens, towels, and washcloths are two for one for the next hour," he said into the phone and then glanced at the two women. "Perfect for cleaning those fingerprints on the PIOMBA desktop you're so obsessed about."

Both women jolted, eyes wide, seeking the source. Patrick watched Benji, who looked like he was choking on a meatball.

Patrick growled in a throaty purr into the phone, "That means you lovely ladies fondling the PIOMBA."

Both women blushed hotly and then quickly scuttled off farther into the store.

The old man gave Patrick and Benji a broad grin. "Thank you, young man. Those girls needed to learn."

Patrick reached out and shook his hand. The old man's sickly energy put a heaviness on his shoulders. Patrick pulled away before his own energy completely left him.

"You need to see Karin in Kitchens. She's also Guest Relations. She'll make sure you're well taken care of," he said confidently, trying to shake off the aura drain.

"Thank you, son—" Before the old man could finish, he vanished into long trails of colored smoke. He wasted no time heading out the doors. They chirped with a happy tune, and Benji whistled.

"That was amazing," Benji whispered in awe. "You really help people."

Satisfied, Patrick passed the phone from hand to hand as if playing with a ball and then clicked it back into place. "Part of the job, cupcake. It never ends."

"How did you do that?" Benji asked in an awestruck whisper.

Around them customers chittered their excitement about the linen sale. Patrick stepped through them, and they slipped past like water around a stone in a brook. Benji narrowed his eyes as he scrutinized Patrick.

"Voice transference," Patrick said and expected that to explain everything. "Sending your voice from our world into theirs."

"But why wouldn't you use it to say something meaningful? Like 'I love you.' Or 'I forgive you.'" Benji's innocent word choice stung like whiskey on a fresh root canal.

Patrick took a breath, working out the tension in his shoulders. Instead, he plastered a grin on his face. His trademark. Impervious. A force to be reckoned with.

"Because where's the fun in that?" Patrick asked. He nodded conspiratorially. "Do you wanna learn how to do it?"

Benji nodded once and held up his fist. Patrick responded with a fist bump of agreement.

CUSTOMERS SWARMED the kitchenware showroom, dumping silverware by the armful into their carts. Patrick had taken his vantage point away from the fray by kicking back on an endcap stack of FIDUCIA power strip boxes. Benji stood by, and Patrick caught his expression. Benji was trying not to laugh, aiming for sympathetic instead.

Patrick sighed and crossed his legs as he leaned back onto the boxes as if they were a well-loved recliner. "One day I'll know what guilt feels like," he said sleepily as customers dug through the silverware, filling their carts to the brim. "Today is not that day."

"Announcing a fifteen-minute giveaway on silverware?" Benji asked. "That's a bit much."

"You know you like it." Patrick winked at him, and Benji burst into giggles.

Patrick snorted and then broke into cackles. "Dude, that giggle is ridiculous."

Benji wheezed and tried to compose himself. "You think?"

"It's cute," Patrick said, putting his hands behind his head. "Like lying in a valley of marshmallows while fat baby unicorns frolic." Benji laughed harder, and Patrick swatted him in the arm. "C'mon. We gotta get a move on before Karin catches us. We have more havoc to cause."

"More havoc?" Benji wiped tears from his eyes.

"We're going after the big guns," Patrick said, pausing for dramatic effect. "Agnes."

"Agnes will kill us!"

Patrick shrugged. "Good thing we're already dead."

"THIS IS so not going to work," Benji murmured.

Patrick licked his bottom lip. The taste of impending victory was as sweet as the tiramisu in the café.

"Trust me. It works every time," he said.

"How many times have you done it?" Benji asked.

"Just once." Patrick rubbed his hands together. His stomach rumbled eagerly for Agnes's reaction.

"How did it go last time?"

Patrick blinked and sat back on his ankles. "Last time?" He glanced at Benji, confused. "This is the first time. Hence my answer of once."

Benji pressed his lips together and furrowed his brows. "Do you ever get any less confusing?"

"Annnd… there," Patrick said as he pushed the final red plastic ball under the corner of his MILAN bed. "That's the last of them."

He flopped onto the mattress and sighed dramatically at a job well done. He laced his hands behind his head and settled in. "You have no idea how long I've had this in the works."

Benji smiled down at him. "Hiding every ball in the ball pit like Easter eggs is a bit cruel, don't you think? The kids will have nothing to play in."

"Kids?" Patrick arched a brow.

"I suppose it's cool of you to stage an Easter egg hunt instead."

Patrick laughed and reached out to clap his hands. He wheezed and then broke into cackles.

Benji shook his head. "What's so funny?"

"It's not for the kids." Patrick wiped a humored tear. "It's for Agnes. Now we wait."

Benji blinked and pursed his lips in the most adorably kissable fashion.

Flinching at the thought, Patrick sat up just as Benji took a seat next to him. He froze, and Benji didn't notice as he looked out over the showroom rather than at him. Patrick swallowed and rested his elbows on his knees.

"So, you live here?" Benji said, his tone whimsical.

Patrick chuckled. "Living is subjective. But if we want to be normal about it, sure."

"I'm starting to see the charm." Benji's smile was infectious. Genuine. No hidden agenda.

Patrick flexed his fingers, cracking the knuckles on each hand. He remained silent. Agnes was late. Surely she'd catch on in less than a second. The quiet bonding time with Benji was something he hadn't planned on. His mouth went dry and the hair on the back of his neck prickled.

Benji continued the conversation. "It's like that dream you have as a kid about being left behind in a shopping mall. Which area would you go for first?"

Patrick clenched his fists. Benji had asked him a question. He mustered a contented smile, "Always the café."

"You seem to like it there." Benji turned back to him. Patrick had never noticed the faint freckles on his nose before. Not that he was paying attention. Nope.

Patrick leaned away, lacing his fingers together. "I go for the ambiance. I live vicariously through the customers who order tiramisu."

"Tiramisu?" Benji asked. "I'd think you'd be a meatballs guy."

"The meatballs are such a pedestrian choice." Patrick popped his neck. Where was Agnes? Or Karin? He went along with it anyway. "The sweet cream and the espresso. Damn, I miss espresso."

"Espresso?" Benji leaned back on the bed.

"Not a day goes by that I don't think about espresso." Patrick looked back at him over his shoulder. "What do you miss?"

Benji lay on the mattress and sighed dreamily.

Patrick's blood pressure rose. There Benji was, on his bed, lying there like he belonged. Patrick discreetly clenched his teeth and curled his toes in his Nikes.

"I don't think I've been here long enough to miss anything," Benji said as he flopped his arms back over his head.

Even in the most innocent of gestures, Benji proved how infinitely tempting he was. Patrick turned away, pressing his hands to his face and catching a breath. Bringing Benji to his bed had been a bad idea. And he hadn't even brought him to his bed in the biblical sense.

Either Agnes needed to bust them soon or Patrick would have to admit his prank had failed and she had won.

He would never admit defeat to Agnes.

Never.

"Sure you have," Patrick said, keeping the mood light. "I'm sure you miss a lot of things."

"Coffee," Benji said. "God, I miss coffee, too."

Patrick smirked. "I can teach you how to experience coffee again."

"Really?" Benji brightened, his eyes alight in wonder.

"It's a mind game," Patrick said and pointed to his temple. "All of your experiences are up here. If you concentrate hard enough, not only can you smell it, you can taste it. Not only that, you can change it into tasting like anything else."

"Water to wine," Benji said.

"Water to wine to coffee to margaritas." Patrick nodded. "But butter. Dammit. I can never get the taste of butter quite right. Either comes out like tasteless lard or rock salt."

Benji narrowed his eyes into merry crescents. "How did you get so good at harnessing the energy here?"

"Well, it's all particle physics. Once you realize you're just one particle in the scheme of things, you know where to push one and grab another and make it into something else. It's science."

"Says the ghost," Benji said. He crossed his legs and bounced an ankle like a teenager contemplating the supermodel poster on his ceiling.

"We're not ghosts," Patrick said. "We're just in an altered state of existence. It's like radio frequencies." He held up his hand as if turning a dial. "Between us and the customers, we're on two planes, like two different stations on a radio. And if you turn the dial, there's another plane, and then another, and another, and so on."

"And what about outside CASA?" Benji asked. "The customers go somewhere, right?"

Patrick rubbed his chin and nibbled on his bottom lip. "And that's the mystery of the day."

"I assume they go home?" Benji didn't seem sure of his question.

"But where's home? What is *home*? And why can't we *go* there?" Patrick challenged him, more at ease in his intellectual element instead of trying to fight every ounce of attraction. If he could see Benji as a colleague, it would take the edge off.

"Home is how you feel," Benji said and pointed to the overhanging sign. "Happy inside," he read from the CASA advertisement.

Patrick smirked. "Funny."

When Benji didn't move from his place on the bed, Patrick lay down next to him. He sighed a long breath, and their eyes met. There was an unexpected glimmer of mischief in Benji's.

"I thought you'd never lie down."

Patrick kept his expression even as he held his breath.

"Gotcha," Benji purred and pointed overhead.

Rolling to his back, Patrick gasped to find Agnes looming, glaring down upon him over the tip of her nose. And above her head, every last ball from the ball pit hovered in a red plastic cloud.

"Patrick." It was Agnes's only warning.

With a snap of her fingers, the balls dispersed into a shower of red plastic hail over them.

Patrick shielded Benji on instinct, rolling over him. Benji cackled as the balls harmlessly bounced over both of them. His infectious laughter caught on, and Patrick found himself lost in the moment. When the final ball bounced off the back of Patrick's head, they remained in the silence, buried in balls and close enough to breathe each other's nonexistent breath.

Agnes was gone, and Patrick let the tension in his shoulders go as he lay atop Benji. The energy seeped off Benji into Patrick, and Benji uttered a soft moan from the aura transfer between them. Patrick gasped as he watched Benji's pupils dilate and his mouth drop open in a fresh-fucked expression. Benji slid his fingers over Patrick's forearms, and the hard, pleasant shock to his system made him jerk away.

The balls scattered across the floor as Patrick shot to his feet. "Well, I guess we need to clean this up somehow," he said, followed by clearing his throat. He swallowed and cleared it again.

"Yeah," Benji said as he pushed his way from the pile. "I'd have to say in my history of dates, this is certainly the most memorable."

The words hit Patrick in the back of the head like the DEL TORO bookcase that had killed him.

"W-what?"

Chapter Seven:
SICUREZZA

THE SHARP-SALTY tang of tears that tickled Benji's nose wasn't exactly out of place in CASA. He'd learned that sometimes even the toughest men cry, and it seemed like those times were especially likely to occur the longer they were inside CASA, following around harried partners with overfilled carts. He wasn't going to generalize. While most of them seemed to be straight, he'd seen more than a few bears reduced to manfully sobbing in Housewares.

Hell, he'd practically reduced Patrick to tears when he'd joked about them being on a date during Patrick's prank. Had that been last week? Last month? Benji wasn't sure. He was hopeless at keeping track of the date without his iPhone, and the days here blended together anyway. The point was, he'd thought Patrick would laugh at the self-deprecating joke, but instead he'd looked at Benji in horror and actually *stuttered.*

That had been the last indication he'd gotten that Patrick might be into him before he'd walled himself off, becoming even more aloof than usual. Not that Benji was a good judge of what Patrick's usual was, but Karin had been very helpful in that regard. And according to her, Patrick was acting squirrelly.

It was terrible, but Benji was a little relieved to smell the tears. The only time he'd really seen Patrick lately was on their pranking missions and times like these.

Because these tears were special. This wasn't the lone tear of a man (or woman, let's be honest, there were plenty of them too) pushed past the brink of boredom and frustration. It wasn't the happy tears of a giggling coed who'd found *just the right fuchsia faux-fur rug for the dorm room, OMG*! The tears he could taste on his tongue were those of a frightened child, and they drew him in like a beacon.

Karin had told him she'd never seen anything like it. No one who'd come before him had ever been able to interact with the living the way Benji could—not through the usual means Patrick employed when he was trying to influence someone, but *actual interaction*.

And Patrick was equally entranced by it. He said it was because he was studying the phenomenon for science, but Benji was pretty sure he just actually wanted to be there to help. Who could resist a lost kid?

So far it had only worked with kids under six, which was perfect because kids under six and Benji were like peas in a pod.

Sure enough, Patrick materialized a second later.

"What is it, Lassie? Did Timmy fall down the well again?" Patrick asked when Benji lifted his head and took a deep breath.

Upstairs. Close enough to the café that the scent of meatballs and marinara made it hard to pinpoint, but that hardly mattered. That in and of itself was enough of a clue to tell Benji exactly where the kid was. He'd stopped doubting his instincts after the second lost child.

"It wasn't funny the first time you said it, and it hasn't been funny the last ten, either," Benji muttered, barely able to hide his grin. He liked that Patrick cared enough to make the joke, stale and ridiculous as it was.

He didn't need to look over at Patrick to know he was scowling at their location. They were perched on top of the display dressers bolted to the wall on the bottom floor, which was the perfect place for watching customers as they came and went since it gave a good view of both the escalator and the doors. Patrick had told him his fascination with the void was morbid, but Benji couldn't help it. He could sit and watch people pass through it all day and never get bored. Every single time the door opened, his stomach swooped with the same sick thrill. It was a lot like that moment just before a roller-coaster car reached the top of the drop. But instead of the ominous clicking of the car being pulled up the tracks, the soundtrack to his own personal spine-tingling instant was the slap of feet against the concrete.

He held his breath, pausing just long enough to watch another set of people disappear into the void—wearing flip-flops, which was crazy, since it had to be winter. In any given week, he'd see flip-flops and winter boots, with their outfits ranging just as wildly. He wondered how he'd never noticed how messed up fashion was before.

The last of the flip-flop–clad brigade stepped through the doors, and Benji hopped down off the dresser and made the death-defying—ha, wasn't literally *everything* he did death-defying now?—leap from the shelf he'd been on to the rail of the escalator. It was a lot easier to do when the escalator wasn't in motion, but where was the fun in that?

The man he'd landed next to took an unconscious step to the side, leaving plenty of room for Benji to heave himself upright and begin his sprint up the rail. He was already nearly to the top, holding his arms out for balance because he knew people would instinctively duck or move so he didn't hit them. It was weird as hell, but definitely one of the perks of being whatever he was. He was used to being invisible in crowds, but now crowds moved around *him* instead of making him accommodate them. It was kind of nice.

The scent of tears got stronger, and he hopped off the top of the rail and ran toward the café. He'd lost track of the days, but it must be a weekend. Crowds were always heavier on a weekend, and today's was insane. Benji had never been all that great at keeping track of the date when he'd had school five days a week to anchor him, so he had no chance of it now. There was probably a calendar or two in the employee breakroom if he got really curious, but he hadn't been that bored yet. Besides, what did it matter? Weekday or weekend, his routine was the same. Though maybe he'd put some effort into tracking down a newspaper after he found this missing child—the variety of clothes he'd seen lately had been crazy, which meant there had to be some seriously whacked weather going on out there.

He could see Patrick following along if he looked out of the corner of his eye, but he didn't give him the satisfaction of turning around to actually look at him. In addition to observing him "for science," Patrick liked to tease him about being a spectacle—"You're like a circus sideshow! Watch Benji the adorable floppy-haired ghost find a needle in a haystack!"—but Benji knew Patrick actually came along because he wanted to make sure the missing child got back to its parents. He hadn't known him long, but Benji felt like he'd made some progress into worming his way past the angry, sarcastic façade Patrick wore around himself like a shroud. Inside he was actually a really nice, caring guy.

"Ugh, it's all snotty."

Benji snorted. Well, a caring guy. Maybe not nice. But nice was overrated. Nice got you killed at age thirty-two with nothing to show for yourself but a foster cat that hated you and a weekly phone call from your mom.

The kid couldn't have been more than five. She might even be four. It was hard to tell with the way she was curled up. Fat teardrops rolled down her cheeks, and her T-shirt was wet enough that he could tell she'd been at it for a while. Usually when kids got this worked up, they outright bawled, but this one was silent as a grave, her eyes huge with fear and her tiny fists clenched around a well-loved blue dog that had lost most of its fur long before its trip to CASA.

She'd wedged herself under a display. Benji knelt down in front of her so he wouldn't look so big and imposing. He squared his shoulders and waited for the familiar jolt of excitement and unease that had startled him so much the first time he'd yelped from the shock of the energy transfer. The child he'd been with at the time—a six-year-old boy who'd wandered off while his mom was looking at kitchen cabinets—cried even louder in surprise and fear.

He could manage it now. It was easy to get used to people seeing through him, so having a living person actually meet his eyes and look at him was uncomfortable. It felt a lot like a rush of cold water down his spine. Eerie. Which was ironic, considering the fact that *he* was the ghost.

After a few beats of simply squatting there, not talking to the distraught child but watching her carefully, liquid brown eyes met his own. He suppressed a shiver, making himself smile instead. Kids could pick up on the smallest shift in emotions, and he'd gotten good at pushing his own down in his classroom.

"What's your friend's name?" he asked once he was sure he had the girl's attention. It was safer than asking hers. Parents often drilled safety into their kids, with good reason. But awareness of stranger danger made getting lost even scarier for a kid. The result was children hiding instead of trying to find help.

Her bottom lip quivered, but she managed to stem the flow of tears with a wet sniffle. "Sam."

Benji grinned. "Nice strong name. Bet he's pretty brave."

She swallowed, rubbed a fist across her eyes, and nodded. She clutched the dog tightly to her chest, her gaze darting from Benji to the aisle behind him. She visibly recoiled when a crowd of people went by, laughing and talking loudly.

"Did he get lost? And you had to find him?"

She nodded again, her body uncurling just a fraction. Another group passed behind him, but this time her eyes didn't leave his face.

"Can you come out, sweetheart? I know it's scary out here, but I can help you and Sam find your parents. Did you come with your parents today?"

Another hesitant nod. "Mommy and Aunt Ellen."

Benji released a breath he didn't realize he'd been holding. Sometimes kids wouldn't give him their parents' names, and that made things so much harder. He looked over his shoulder at Patrick, who was lounging nearby, looking bored. "What's your mommy's name? Do you know?"

"Sarah."

Benji smiled. "That's one of my very favorite names! Do you know your last name?"

"Grant, but Mommy's is Wagoner."

Benji couldn't help but laugh at that. The disdain in her voice had been clear. He'd bet this kid was a real spitfire when she wasn't terrified and lost. "I see. That's my fault for asking for yours and not hers. Thanks," he said, ignoring Patrick's amused laughter. "Well, I'm Benji, and back there is my friend Patrick. He's going to go have somebody call your mom and Aunt Ellen, okay? And we're just going to wait right here. Can I stay with you?"

The girl nodded. Benji looked over his shoulder again and gave Patrick a pointed look. It was just to soothe Patrick's pretend ego—he knew Patrick would go haunt someone into paging the little girl's mother even without Benji asking him to, but this way Patrick could pretend he was only doing it to have a bargaining chip later on. He'd inevitably call it in for something stupid, like a few days ago when he'd used his last favor to make Benji set off the alarm in the freight elevator by holding the door open button down when the reedy employee Patrick liked to mess with was in it.

It was terrible, but he kind of hoped Tommy was working today. He was by far the most susceptible person on staff, and it wouldn't be hard for Patrick to whisper in his ear and have the kid hightail it over to the café to "find" the little girl. It would be a shame for Patrick to lose the rest of the day to the ball pit, which was what would happen if he had to expend too much energy getting someone to listen.

Benji settled in on the floor just outside the girl's little hideout. There wouldn't be room for him under the shelf, and he was certain he wouldn't be welcome even if there was. The kid seemed to have a pretty good head on her shoulders—she wouldn't want a stranger pressed in that close. The teacher in him approved.

"Does Sam like to play I Spy?" he asked, schooling his face into a look of utter confusion when the girl burst out laughing.

"He's not real!" she said, giggling even harder when Benji furrowed his brow.

"He's not?"

"No, silly!" She loosed her grip on the stuffed animal enough to hold it out from underneath the shelf and wave it around. Benji bent in close and examined it.

"Ah, I see. I did wonder when CASA started letting dogs in." He heaved an exaggerated sigh. "Well, do *you* like to play I Spy?"

She pulled Sam back to her chest, but not with the same death grip she'd had on him earlier. She was a lot more relaxed, which was good. "Yes."

Benji nodded thoughtfully. "Okay. I'll go first. I see a—"

"No!" she howled. "Do it right!"

He scratched his head. "Do it right?"

"It's 'I spy,'" she said, shaking her head.

"Oh, right. Well, I spy a—"

"No!" She was giggling again, and while he was happy to have been the one to soothe her, something in Benji broke a little at the knowledge that he'd never hear the kids in his class laugh like that again. "It's 'I spy, with my little eye!'"

He frowned. "But my eye is big."

Her grin lit up her entire face. "It's just a saying."

"Okay, then. I spy, with my *little* eye, something red."

She crept forward a tiny bit, peering out around her. He'd chosen a color that wasn't visible from this eye level so she'd have to come out. It would make it easier for the staff to see her. He was sure there had been a lost child alert for staff already, but no one would find her tucked away back under the shelf.

"It has polka dots," he added, scooting back himself to give her room.

She edged her way out from under the shelf. There was dust in her ponytail, and Sam was definitely going to need a bath. But other than that, she looked unharmed.

"Sarah Wagoner, please return to the café," the intercom blared, and the girl's eyes widened. She wiggled out the rest of the way and stood up.

"That was my mommy's name!"

Benji nodded, indulging in a fond smile since Patrick wasn't there to see it. "Isn't Patrick clever? Now she'll know where to find you! All we have to do is stay here and finish our game."

The girl craned her neck, searching for something red with polka dots. Benji cast around his own private search for the man in question, but he didn't see him. He'd have gone to the front to find an intercom that would broadcast to the entire store. Not that he couldn't have materialized back here in the café if he wanted to, but experience told Benji that Patrick would stay away now that he'd done what he could to help.

"It's an umbrella!"

Benji whirled around, momentarily confused. Oh, right. Red with white polka dots. The ALLEGRO umbrella. He'd given one just like it to his mom for her birthday last year.

"Wonderful!" he said, his voice shaking slightly at the memory. He hoped she still carried it. He liked the thought of his mom keeping a part of him with her, especially since it would be such a nice bright spot of color on a rainy day. "And look, I think that might be someone you know," he said, pointing past the girl's shoulder.

She turned around and let out a shriek. "Mommy!"

Benji watched both mother and daughter burst into tears as they hugged, Sam the dog squished between them. The girl was talking animatedly, gesturing back toward Benji, and he could tell from her mother's bewildered look that she was telling her about him.

He stood there for another few seconds before slipping off down one of the aisles. He knew from experience that the girl wouldn't be able to see him now. They never could, once they weren't lost anymore. It didn't bother him.

Now that she'd been reunited with her mother, though, there was no reason to stick around. He set off toward Agnes's couch. It would probably be a while before Patrick turned up. He'd be off doing something devious to make up for his good deed. The last time they'd helped a missing child, Patrick had spent the next night disassembling all the chairs in the kitchen showroom and screwing the legs back on backward.

Agnes was waiting for him, holding up a tangled skein of purple yarn. He didn't question how she'd known he was coming. If he'd learned one thing in his time here, it was that Agnes was a force of nature. And also that he hated yarn. Especially hers. He'd done this for his grandmother countless times as a child, but Agnes's yarn—he couldn't describe it. It looked like regular yarn, but there was something off about it. His grandmother had liked to knit with angora, which was soft as a cloud and glided over his fingers like a whisper. She'd also worked with wool for the thick scarves she sent to his cousins who lived in Maine, and that was rough and scratchy and made him itch. But Agnes's yarn wasn't any of those things. It was warm, for one. Not hot, but warmer than room temperature for sure. And touching it never seemed to be the same experience twice. Sometimes the warmth was comforting, enveloping him like a hug. And sometimes it seemed to pulsate, making his skin crawl. He never knew what he was going to get. Agnes's enigmatic smile stayed the same no matter what she was working with.

He plopped down next to her and steeled himself for whatever today's yarn was, relaxing a bit when no shivers of unease ran down his spine as he took it from her. Happy yarn today, then.

Agnes didn't look over, absorbed in her knitting and apparently trusting him to work through the snarled yarn himself. He started winding. "Find her parents?"

Benji didn't bother to ask how she knew. Agnes seemed to know everything that went on in the store, which made it all the more puzzling that Patrick thought he could prank her. Surely Patrick realized that Agnes was *more*, didn't he? Benji couldn't put it into words, not even in his own head, so he'd never tried to talk about it with Patrick. Besides, he kind of liked the unique bond he and Agnes had. It was certainly better than the antagonistic one she shared with Patrick.

"Her mom. Pretty sure that will be the last time she wanders off. She was shaken up."

Agnes nodded, looking up briefly from her knitting. "Something about it shook you up too."

It had, but he hadn't really noticed it until Agnes said something. He was always happy to reunite a missing kid with his or her parents, but it usually felt better than this. Today Benji just felt empty.

And really, *always* and *usually*? Benji wasn't one for melodrama, even in his own inner monologues. Why was he using words that implied he'd been here years when it had been a month or two, tops? He needed to find a hobby or something.

"I wish Patrick would decide if he was avoiding me or not," he said, because Patrick was kind of like having a hobby. If a hobby were rude and sarcastic and more often than not ended with Benji needing to regenerate in the ball pit with Agnes.

Agnes hummed. "Patrick has a lot more than that to decide," she murmured. Her lips moved soundlessly as she counted her stitches, though the mass of finished rows on her lap followed no discernible pattern. Agnes's knitting was as cryptic as her advice.

He started untangling the skein faster, since the clicking of Agnes's knitting needles was picking up pace. There were tiny knots and whorls looped around themselves, and for a while at least, he could focus on the task in front of him instead of having to think. It was nice, and it was probably exactly what Agnes had intended when she'd beckoned him over to sit with her.

"Sometimes the best way to muddle through our own problems is to be outside ourselves untangling someone else's for a while," she said.

Her voice startled him, and he blinked a few times when he looked up, shocked to see that the store had emptied out. It must be past closing, which meant he'd spent hours here with Agnes and her yarn. The skein hadn't looked very big at all, but it must have been deceptively large to have kept him busy all that time. Yet another puzzle for him to think about.

There was no sign of the piece Agnes had been working on, even though Benji still had the purple yarn in his hands. Her knitting needles had disappeared, like they always did when she wasn't actively using them. Maybe they went to the same place Benji and the other ghosts did before they regenerated. Maybe they were just a figment of his imagination and never existed at all. The only thing Benji was sure about was the fact that he wouldn't get any answers out of Agnes about it, even if he asked.

If he was lucky and caught her in an indulgent mood, she would open up a little about purgatory, and he hoped this was one of those times.

"Is whatever lets me talk to these lost kids the same thing that lets us communicate with the other ghosts?" he asked.

Agnes pursed her lips and held her hands out for the yarn. Benji gave it to her obediently and then waited patiently as she studied his face.

"To be perfectly honest, I don't know how you do that. It's rather… vexing," she said after a few long seconds. She seemed frustrated by it, which made sense. There wasn't a whole lot that happened in purgatory that Agnes *didn't* know, so he could see how this would be a point of contention.

"But to answer your question, no. I don't think it's directly related. The spirits here are different from you and Patrick. They're less aware. Impressions, we call them. They're more like memories of a person. Whereas you, and Patrick, and the others who think of themselves as ghosts, you're a complete person. Your soul is intact. You think, you reason, you exist. The Impressions just exist in a loop until something breaks the cycle. In our case here, it's saving someone from the same fate."

Karin had gone over this when they'd had their heart-to-heart. Patrick jokingly called it an employee orientation, and he wasn't all that off base. Constrained though they were to stay within the walls of CASA, Benji had learned that ghosts like them moved with a lot more freedom and autonomy than some of the other spirits in purgatory.

"Ghosts who are more sensitive to Impressions are called Guides," Agnes continued.

"Like Karin," Benji murmured.

She nodded. "Like Patrick as well."

Shock flooded through Benji, cool and unpleasant down his spine and then settling as heavy as a brick in his stomach. He'd thought Patrick was the same as him, just a ghost biding his time until the way out was shown to him. Was Patrick stuck here, like Karin and Agnes? Was that why he was so bitter and aloof?

It made sense, though. Benji could barely hear the Impressions. Most of the time their voices were whispers, fading in and out like a badly tuned radio. He could see them more often than not, but thinking back, he'd always been with Patrick when they appeared. And Patrick had always helped them.

Benji had been with him a few days ago when he'd helped one of them dissuade a woman from buying a box of SICUREZZA bandages because of an undiagnosed polyethylene allergy. Once they'd saved the customer, the impression of the man he'd been helping grew a lot stronger. He'd died of the same condition, and now that he had saved someone from the same fate, the man had been able to move on.

Benji's throat went dry. "Does that mean Patrick knows what I have to do to move on?"

Try as he might, Benji hadn't been able to remember his death. And while he wasn't in a hurry to leave purgatory, especially now that he knew it probably meant leaving Patrick, he wanted to at least know what he'd need to do to make that possible. Had Patrick known all this time and just not told him? Was this all some big joke to him? Benji's neck prickled, sweat he didn't know he could still produce sprouting across his skin. Were he and Patrick even friends? Or was he just some long-running prank to keep Patrick entertained?

Agnes's palm was cool and dry when she cupped his cheek. He felt some of the heat leach out of his angry flush, flowing out as Agnes's energies flowed in, restoring him and calming him.

"No, child. You're too tied up in his future for him to be able to see yours."

As usual, Agnes's words cleared up nothing. And also as usual, they calmed him anyway.

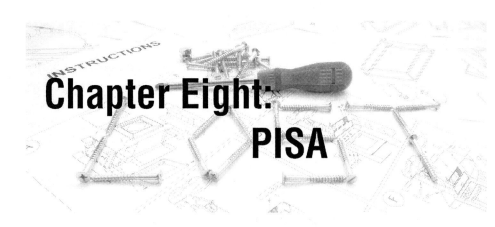

Chapter Eight: PISA

PATRICK DECIDED leaving Benji be was the best course of action for now. He had adapted well to life in CASA, easily settling into the rhythm of things. Patrick would go so far as to say Benji was having fun.

But Patrick refused to admit he was having fun too. Benji was *nice*. Nice in the way of ice-cold lemonade on a hot summer day. Patrick fought drinking the Kool-Aid.

Karin and Agnes had both taken a shine to Benji, and Patrick's gut clenched. It was fun for a while, but now he wanted off the ride.

Benji had described their pranks as a memorable date, and he didn't have an inkling of an idea how much those choice words made Patrick dig in his heels. Benji's kindness and naïveté had been a welcome escape. Now Patrick was desperate to escape *them*.

He resumed his post in the café, in his usual chair across from old man Henry. The café was his safe space, and sitting with Henry made him concentrate on something else. Henry as usual stared into space in Patrick's general direction and sipped his tea. The crossword puzzle book sat between them, a brand-new pen beside it. Henry slowly pushed the book toward Patrick's side of the table as he stared off.

Patrick leaned forward. "Do you see me?" he asked softly, waving a hand in front of Henry's blank gaze. "Work with me, Henry." He clenched his fist, trying to banish Benji from his mind. "I really need you to work with me today."

Instead, Henry scooted his mashed potatoes around his plate.

Patrick narrowed his eyes. Doubt and hesitation gave way to annoyance and then anger. "You need to let me in, Henry," he growled. "I'm trying to help you. Help me help you."

"You okay?" Benji said over his shoulder.

Patrick clenched his fists from the surprise. "Fine," he said, not smiling.

"You know, fine doesn't mean what you think it means," Benji prodded him, rolling back and forth on his heels.

Had he let himself revert to the children he taught? Patrick slowly pushed his way from his seat. "Fine means exactly what I think it means," he said tersely.

"You're no closer to solving him, are you?" Benji asked as Patrick stepped away.

"That's for me to know," Patrick said as he headed into the showrooms.

Benji appeared next to him as if they had been walking side by side the entire time. Dammit. It seemed he'd mastered teleporting. Patrick was a little bummed he'd missed that. It had probably been a pretty good show, especially since he'd convinced Benji a while back that there was a real danger of leaving part of himself behind if he wasn't completely focused. It had kept Benji from really trying, which had been amusing. Patrick wondered if Karin or Agnes had taken pity on Benji and told him the truth or if Benji had just gotten over it himself. *Ah, the things you miss when you're putting all your energy into actively avoiding someone.*

"Do you need help?" Benji asked with a bright smile.

His plan not to engage wasn't working. Benji was worse than a stray dog. Patrick pressed his lips into a line and secretly ground his teeth. "Are you always this full of questions?"

"What's eating you today?" Benji asked in a chipper tone. He was trying to be cute, trying to mimic Patrick's devil-may-care ways, but Patrick was in no mood for it. Not today. Not ever again.

"I'm fine," Patrick said firmly, hoping Benji would let it drop. "Come on. It's a busy day."

He was slipping, and he knew the only way to save himself was to grab on with both hands and let himself accept what he was feeling. Patrick's nonexistent heart thumped. No. Benji just got under his skin with his joke. Yes. That's all it was.

But why did it feel so real? Something Patrick could settle into comfortably? Such things weren't for him.

Patrick stood a little taller as a woman in Housewares screamed for help—not in the terror that sometimes comes with thinking one has gone insane, but instead….

"I need some help here!" she yelled over the crowd of oblivious shoppers. "I need some help coordinating curtain rods and lighting, preferably by someone with higher than a high-school education."

Together, Patrick and Benji halted across the aisle. Benji tilted his head like a dog hearing a high-pitched whistle. Patrick smirked.

Perfect. Just the thing to get him back into his groove.

He clapped a hand on Benji's shoulder and forced him into stillness. "I got this," Patrick commanded.

"But…," Benji said, uncertain.

"I got it." He grunted each word like a wolf defending his territory.

Tossing up his hands, Benji sighed. "Whatever."

Patrick didn't respond and slipped through the aisle as the customers shifted around him like a river current over a fallen log. They shivered and shuddered from the chill in his aura. He was expending too much from his mood alone and had to keep his cool. It was already evident to anyone in a ten-mile radius that his mood had gone to garbage.

The woman perked up as Patrick approached, and her predatory, flirtatious smile signaled he'd be in for a long day. Damned cougars that couldn't take a hint. He hadn't even liked the Mrs. Robinson act when he'd been a graduate student. The hair on his arm stood up as he shivered from the intrusive thoughts. He wasn't a graduate student anymore, and CERN would never be in his reach.

"Thank God," she said, her shoulders slumping in a piss-poor attempt at coyness. "A six-two attractive man who can lift heavy boxes to my car." She winked. "It's a Benz, by the way."

Patrick forced himself to smile. She was the perfect challenge to put him right again. Something to toughen him up and stop this self-indulgent pleasure with Benji.

"I'm sure it is, ma'am," Patrick said, smiling brighter. "How can I help?"

"You're not colorblind, are you?" She cast a dismissive glance around the showrooms. "This place is a vomit of white, black, and beige."

"Hey…," Benji said in indignation.

Patrick shot him a warning glare. Benji furrowed his brow and retreated a half step. Patrick returned his attention to the woman and flashed his cheesiest helpful-employee grin. "I'm sure we can find you a pop of color. You said you needed to color coordinate drapes? How about you check out our fine selection of carpets?"

He tossed her back a taste of her own medicine with a wink.

Her eyelashes fluttered, and Patrick internally cringed. She held out her hand in that irritatingly dainty Southern belle fashion. "I have always depended on the kindness of strangers," she said, her voice dripping saccharine in an attempt to be seductive.

"Of course, Miss DuBois," he said, taking her hand. "Right this way." Patrick swept out his arm with a graceful extension of his back.

The woman giggled like an excited schoolgirl. "Oh, call me Blanche."

Because you're two cans shy of a six pack? Patrick wanted to say, but kept it light and easygoing as they strolled to the vastness of Home Décor.

As they passed by Benji, Patrick made eye contact as he tried to mentally drill into his head to stay out of it. He'd work this one alone. He had to. Anything to make himself want to scrub down with sandpaper and bleach later. Patrick would take great delight in exfoliating off all three layers of skin—if that were possible for the deceased.

Regrettably, Benji didn't get the message and followed along.

"You okay?" he asked as he appeared next to Patrick.

"Fine," Patrick curtly replied. Benji was like a battery next to him, and he focused on opening himself to lap up the energies. Just enough to get this over with. His head was already fuzzy and full of a cottony sensation.

"You keep saying that," Benji said.

"Because it's true."

The woman calling herself Blanche brightened at Benji. "Oh! Is this your valet? He's charming. Amazing what one can do these days with educational opportunities for the disadvantaged."

Patrick jerked to a stop. "Excuse me?"

"Pardon you," Benji said, just as offended.

Blanche blinked, clearly oblivious. "Oh? Where are my manners?" She waved a hand and beckoned Patrick closer. "You know"—she jerked her chin toward Benji—"the mentally challenged."

Patrick jerked back like he had been clubbed with a VERONA table leg. "What fucking part of the devil's urethra did you fall out of and can you crawl back up in it?" he snarled.

Benji and Blanche both staggered back at Patrick's outburst.

"That's what they're called, right?" she asked primly.

Patrick flung up his hand to halt her. "Stop. Making. Words."

"Patrick…?" Benji asked with a slight shake of the head.

"You don't get to insult him like that," Patrick growled. "You don't get to waste my time with your perpetual bullshit."

"I beg your pardon?" Blanche stepped back, aghast.

"You're a disservice to the human being you once were," Patrick continued and took a challenging step toward her. "You're desecrating my sacred space. This is *my* CASA, and *I* decide if you are permitted here." He took another step, and she retreated from him. "You do not get to disrespect me, and you above all do not get to treat him like garbage. Do you know him?"

"No, of course not!" she said, flustered and with a hand to her chest.

"That's right. You don't. His name is Benjamin Goss. It's his honorable duty to escort lost children to their parents. He should get a goddamn medal for his selflessness," Patrick rumbled, like a storm on the horizon.

"Patrick…," Benji whispered, averting his eyes.

"Shut up, Benji," Patrick ordered him. His tone was purposely unkind. He turned back to Blanche. "You know what I get to deal with? Do you know?"

"No…." She took another step away.

"I get to deal with garbage like you. Day in and day out, I get to pretend I'm interested in your fucking curtain rods and window treatments." He tilted his chin, aiming a pointed glare at her chest. "You died by being impaled on a GALLEGIANTE curtain rod, by the way. Had to have sucked. I was decapitated by a DEL TORO bookcase. I think you might be a winner at what sucked more."

Benji started. His eyes rounded with worry.

Stop looking at me like that. Patrick wanted to tell him. *Stop looking at me like that!*

"Patrick," Karin said sharply in his ear as she appeared. "Is there a problem here?"

He jerked away from her. "No problem. I'm gone." He blinked once, and when he opened his eyes, he found himself in the darkness of the parking garage. Patrick crushed the heels of his palms to his eyes, trying to will the angry ball of a headache away. He took a deep breath, filling his chest, and let it go again. But nothing was helping to relax or center him.

Nothing could hide his frayed thoughts anymore. Benji was too distracting. Too kind. Too honorable. Too sensitive. Too everything. CASA had chosen Benji for something. He wasn't moving on. But Patrick hadn't tried to help him. Karin had chided him for being sweet on his "cupcake." Benji was a passing entertainment, someone he would eventually get out of his CASA uniform and into his MILAN bed. Then he'd happily send him on his way until the next guy came along.

His failure ate at his bones like a Weople dismembering its prey. He'd let himself get involved. He couldn't decide what hurt worse, the attachment or his compromised emotions. Benji had long outworn his welcome, and something had to give.

He shivered from the cold as the living customers passed him by, heading to their cars.

They could leave. Reality clung to him like the icy chains on a Dickensian ghost.

What the fuck had he been expecting? The chance to have something of a life in CASA? He and Benji settling into a routine of comfort and making the most of eternity? Playing house in simulated homes? He'd tried that once. He'd settled down. He'd fallen in love. And how had that worked out for him? He'd poured out all his devotion and love and been rewarded with the devastating truth that even in forever, nothing truly lasts forever.

He couldn't do that again.

Ever since Benji's arrival, Patrick's wandering thoughts about the would-haves and could-haves only served as a reminder CASA was a nightmare he would never wake from. A nightmare he had learned to accept. CASA became normal. His reality. Agnes, Karin, the ball pit, bugging the shit out of Tommy to break up the monotony. And Henry. His personal puzzle.

Patrick remained close to the elevators as the happy families packed their cars like Tetris masters, calling commands to one another, moving seats, taking out boxes, packing and repacking, even opening the boxes to fit the pieces into every available nook and cranny.

They were moving on, heading to their homes. Patrick didn't have to guess what they were saying. They joked about being thankful to escape CASA, what to do for dinner, and what was on TV tonight.

Patrick's knees gave out from under him, and he stumbled against the trash can. It jerked with the initial impact, but he fell through it as his corporeal form blinked out for only a second and he crashed to the concrete.

He gasped, and cold, clammy sweat ran down his back. He had to go back inside. He needed to get back to the ball pit. He had already spent too much energy in CASA, wasting it on being angry at everything and repelling the living. The longer he sat in the garage, the more his energy wicked out of him like moisture into a rag. He had to recoup his losses, but that would mean admitting his failings.

Benji had said it once: CASA was such a happy place.

Patrick chuckled bitterly. If he were a praying man, he'd hope Benji would never lose that idea. But Patrick had seen through it all too soon. All that remained now was coping.

In the darkness, the customers happily packed their cars. Finally thankful they had escaped CASA purgatory. It was insultingly laughable. The regulars would be back next week, and some as soon as tomorrow when they realized they'd forgotten a part. And the Impressions popped up in a steady stream. The afterlife side of CASA had plenty of business to keep him and the crew on their toes.

Static pricked at Patrick's skin with pins and needles before he heard the whispers.

CASA had its Impressions, which were of the pleasant variety. The Wallville had its own version, and they weren't even close to pleasant.

Patrick called them the Gloom. The Impressions had human forms, but the Gloom were mere shadows that moved like runny trails of ink. They slithered across the cars and over customers, infecting them with the temptation to go to Wallville and join the Weoples' ranks.

A husband and wife rolled by him with their cart full of gargantuan boxes. The bear of a man bounced their infant daughter in a pink flowered harness.

"She was so good." The wife smiled at their little girl. "Slept the whole time."

The husband nodded. "Did you see that little boy in the car seat?" He shuddered. "God, his wailing could have shattered glass."

The wife swatted at his shoulder. "Stop being so negative. You know Beatrice is going to hit the terrible twos and it'll be Armageddon."

"If she's a screamer like your sister's kid, I'm investing in earplugs." He frowned.

"Oh, come on."

Patrick rolled to his side as the couple strolled away, happily chatting between themselves. Their love carved a rent in Patrick's concrete heart. He'd stopped torturing himself with what-ifs after his first five years in CASA, staring at displays of happy families with their children and wondering if he would have ever been that guy. Dreams and fantasies were useless in CASA. They always ended in disappointment. It was better not to believe what else was out there. Nothing was out there.

Patrick sat up and leaned back against the glass windows of the back entrance. The dimness of the parking garage provided a soothing break from the glaring fluorescent lights. He tried to breathe. Not that he needed it, but old habits were hard to break. He wiped his forehead, but his damp hand on his skin did nothing to alleviate the clamminess. Light from inside washed over him in sunny yellow hues.

A *rat-a-tat* on the glass startled him. Patrick turned and found Karin, furious and yelling at him. Her voice was muffled, but he could make out the basics of "Get back in here, you asshole!" She tapped again and flicked her wrist, beckoning him back inside.

Patrick staggered to his feet and narrowed his eyes at her. He said nothing, and her frustration gave way to pounding on the glass.

"Okay...," he whispered and pressed his hand to the glass against hers. "Okay."

The automatic doors slid apart with a happy chime as a tween girl scampered into the parking garage. She darted toward Patrick, tears flowing down her cheeks.

"Help me! Help me!" she cried and tugged at the hem of his shirt.

Patrick stumbled back, surprised. "What?"

Lost kids were Benji's department. Unless....

"Are you lost, sweetheart?" He tried for a reassuring smile as a sickly shiver raced up his spine.

She violently shook her head and then pointed at the family casually strolling toward the outer reaches. "We have to stop them! The baby!"

Patrick's heart thumped. He'd learned the hard way not to try to connect emotionally with Impressions. They all had tragic stories—obviously, or they wouldn't be in CASA waiting to move on. But that was impossible in situations like this one. When the Impressions of children appeared in CASA, it crippled him with agony, knowing they had been ripped from their families.

He crouched to her level and gripped her tiny shoulders. "What? What about the baby? Tell me."

"She's going to swallow the dowels of the PISA!"

Karin remained on the opposite side of the glass. She pounded again, shaking her head. "Stop her!" he read on her lips.

The girl broke away from him and bolted farther into the parking garage. The Gloom perked and slithered after her.

"Fuck," Patrick growled. He glanced back at Karin. She pounded again, and he slapped the glass at her. He nodded once and sprinted off after the girl.

The Gloom screeched, attracted by Patrick's energy. He knew he'd be a more tempting morsel to them than a little girl Impression. They flanked him from behind like a rising tide, blocking his escape back to CASA.

She showed no signs of slowing down as she screamed nonsense at the living family.

Patrick gnashed his teeth. Not only had they parked in the outer reaches, their car was in the farthest row along the guard wall.

"Wait!" he yelled to her. "Fuck! Wait!"

The girl refused to slow down, booking it like she wanted to be first in line for BBMak tickets. For an Impression, she was fast. Even so, usually he'd have no problem overtaking her. But with most of his energy depleted, it was like moving through tar.

The Gloom closed in, their foul hellfire breath licking at the back of Patrick's neck.

He concentrated on moving one foot in front of the other. *Keep running. Don't stop. Don't stop.*

The Gloom shot forward, cutting him off from the little girl and the living family.

With no other option, he sprinted head-on toward a parked SUV. The Gloom might be deadly, but they were a stupid bunch. They blocked direct paths but assumed parked cars would also serve as excellent blockades. From watching them drape over the cars like a curtain of darkness, Patrick had learned the Gloom assumed the Guides of CASA would never run headlong into something that would have severely injured them in life. By staying solid, CASA Guides held on to their humanity.

Humanity was merely semantics now.

Patrick took a breath, releasing the reins of concentration that kept him corporeal. He flickered out two seconds too late as he hit the grill of the SUV straight on with his chest. His form dissolved, and the momentum carried his essence through the body of the SUV and out the other side. Flickering back into a solid shape, he crashed onto the pavement hard on one shoulder, and his vision splintered with the shock of pain.

In the distance, the girl kept to her hurried pace, screaming all the while to get the family's attention. It was useless. Clearly she didn't understand that only he could do something. She was in one piece, for now. And Patrick would see to it she stayed that way.

The Gloom regrouped, and Patrick scrambled to his feet. His breaths were heavy, and his chest burned from the impact with the grill, but determination pushed him onward. The clamminess, the cold, and the shivers of warning sickness, he pushed out of his mind. When presented with life and death, Patrick ignored his sense of self-preservation in favor of saving a little girl.

He was CASA employee of the decade, dedicated to customer satisfaction. He didn't know the meaning of sick days.

The family was in sight and, by a stroke of luck, struggling to pack their tiny car. The wife took their daughter and then maneuvered her into her car seat. Thank the almighty for new parents as she fiddled with the straps and hinges. The husband busied himself with trying to figure out how to get the titanic PISA box in the car.

"You could take it out of the box. I saw other people doing it," the wife said in an encouraging tone.

Her husband hid his frustration behind a smile that didn't reach his eyes. Patrick knew that look well. It was the same one he practiced when he looked at Benji and every nerve in his body ignited with urges he'd long denied.

Casting a glance over his shoulder, Patrick frowned. The Gloom had outfoxed him by cornering him against the guard wall.

The girl circled around the family in a panic. "You need to stop!" she yelled at the husband "The baby is going to swallow the dowels. Can't you hear me?"

Patrick swooped in and snatched her in his arms. "Shh, shh, you need to get in the car."

"W-why?" she croaked.

"If you don't want the Weople to take you away, get in the car!"

Before she could protest, he ripped open the passenger door and then shoved her inside. The wife screeched in surprise. Both of them had witnessed the door opening and slamming by itself.

Patrick's hand went numb from manipulating reality. He shook it off as next to him the husband shivered.

"Damn, did it drop out here by twenty degrees all of a sudden or what?" he asked as he shivered obliviously from Patrick's fading aura.

The Gloom hung back There was nowhere Patrick could go, and with CASA blocked off, it was only a matter of time before they took him.

But he was on the clock.

"You're in my way!" Patrick howled as he shoved the husband aside from the open PISA box. The contact of human on spirit sent Patrick tumbling back, numbing his left side. Trembling from the shock to his system, Patrick forced himself to stand.

Inside the car, the girl screamed and crawled into the backseat.

"*Stay put!*" he bellowed at her.

A warning chime and the squeaking sound of tiny wheels echoed through the garage. The scent of a burned refried bean burrito carried over the stink of gasoline and particleboard.

"Jabba," Patrick bit out, cursing roundly in his head. Perfect. He turned back to the PISA box. Patrick didn't have time to think as he concentrated on gripping the thick boards and shoving them aside. The husband had opened the damned box upside down, and the hardware packet was on the very bottom.

A menacing, gurgling chuckle made the hair on the back of Patrick's neck prickle. Jabba was close.

He had only seen the most powerful Weople once. And once was enough. He might have been slow, but he didn't need to be fast. Guides that lost enough of their energy had no fight left in them if they had gotten this far. If the Gloom was the annoying Wallville crowds as thick as a Black Friday sale, Jabba was Wallville's most valued customer.

Patrick had no chance of stopping him.

The living family grabbed their baby and danced back, pressing themselves between two neighboring cars, terrified of the paranormal happenings that they couldn't begin to understand.

Patrick struggled through the planks of the PISA. He threw the last thick plank aside and the bag of hardware went flying with it.

"Fuck!" he snapped and spun on his heel as the bag bounced and rolled across the pavement. "Stay there!" he commanded the girl in the car.

Patrick sprinted toward the bag and then dropped into a slide to snatch the bag.

Only to snatch empty air.

He swallowed and slowly glanced upward, his gaze following the contours of the gleaming red motor scooter and basket. A breath hitched in his throat.

Jabba loomed over him like a terrible giant from the darkest fairy tales. His four-hundred-pound frame—shoved into Spandex shorts and a tank small enough to be a bikini top—balanced precariously on his tiny scooter. He held his refried bean burrito between his teeth like a cigar, and the bag of PISA hardware between his hairy sausage fingers.

"I remember you," Jabba gurgled in a rattling groan.

Patrick scowled. "Here's something else to remember me by." He stomped his heel hard against the front tire of Jabba's scooter.

The force knocked Jabba off balance, and he toppled to the ground. The pavement trembled under him.

The bag bounced out of his grasp, and Patrick seized his chance. Jabba made another reach for the bag, and Patrick kicked it away. Jabba would need a minute to get to his feet, which left Patrick with enough of a lead. Patrick shot to his feet but staggered hard to the left when his vision went black. He shook it off, blinking through the fog.

He shuffled to the bag and then tried to scoop it up, only for his fingers to pass through as his solid mass flickered.

"Dammit." He tried again, and his fingers passed through. "Dammit, dammit, dammit!"

"I can help," the girl called. "I can help!"

Patrick dismissed her. Jabba had recovered and was back on his scooter. Hefting a PISA shelf, Patrick tried to push aside the screams of the living customers at the apparent floating board. Patrick dug deep for the last bursts of energy he had to hang on to the shelf and defend his turf. The shelf trembled in Patrick's grip, and he struggled to keep his hold on it.

The girl kicked the car door open and tumbled out end over end. She wobbled on her feet from the energy burst. Distracted, Patrick pursed his lips in confusion over her ability to manipulate reality. By all logic, as an Impression she couldn't, but Patrick welcomed any help he could get. Maybe there was something special about Impressions after all.

Concentrating on Jabba, Patrick took the offensive and swung the PISA shelf into Jabba's chest. The board shattered on impact, and the force flung Patrick against the girl. She squealed and rolled across the pavement.

He coughed and struggled to stand. "The bag…. Get the bag!"

The girl nodded and scurried on her hands and knees.

Jabba closed in at a snail's pace, and Patrick prepared to charge him again. Taking another PISA shelf, Patrick steadied himself. He couldn't hurt Jabba; he wasn't strong enough. But his scooter seemed to be an even match.

Patrick took another breath, and the girl squealed in excitement. "Got the bag!"

Patrick relaxed his muscles, letting the tension go. That day in the café filled his thoughts.

He pointed his fingers like a gun at Benji and smiled, full of smugness. "Don't tell me. Derrick, right?"

Benji smiled crookedly, confused by the question. "Sorry? I'm Benjami—Benji." He nodded. "Benji. Only my mother calls me Benjamin."

Patrick sucked in an overdramatic sigh and snapped his fingers. "Dammit. Swore you looked like a Derrick. I'm usually so good at that."

"So, you're psychic." Benji smirked.

"No." Patrick pulled a face of mock hurt. "I'm Patrick."

Shaking his head with a grunt, he focused on the weight of the board in his hands, the tang of sweat on his upper lip.

"Get in the car," he called to her. "Get in the car!"

Jabba closed in, and Patrick took one last breath as he let himself flicker out of existence and back in as Jabba passed through his essence. Patrick heaved from resuming his form, but he had one last shot. He spun on his heel, swinging the PISA shelf at the support bar of Jabba's seat. The support bar snapped, and Jabba crashed in a hard slam to the pavement. Patrick staggered from the rumbling quake of Jabba's energy.

"Remember *that*," he said and spat at Jabba's feet.

Shambling to the car, the girl waved frantically. "Get in, get in, get in!" she screeched and scrambled into the front seat.

Patrick yanked the back passenger door open and flopped across the backseat.

"What are you doing? How do we get out of here?" she asked, terror evident on her face as she looked back at him from the driver's seat.

"What's... your name?" Patrick mumbled, his consciousness fading.

"Angie." Her lip quivered. "How are we going to get away?"

Patrick shivered from the cold. Too cold. Much too cold.

"You've... driven go-carts... before, right?"

She nodded quickly.

He raised a shaking finger. "You're going to go backward.... Put the stick thing in the middle on the R and hit the gas. It's the skinny pedal. You know the difference between the gas and the brake, right?"

"Y-yeah. Like go-karts...."

"Good." He pointed a trembling finger. "You need to press on the gas pedal really hard... okay? Keep your... foot on it. Okay?"

"O-okay." Angie hunkered down in the driver's seat. "I'm not going to get in trouble, am I?"

Patrick chuckled. "Sweetie, you're with me... I am trouble."

Jabba crashed against the back windshield, flinging shards of glass. Angie screamed as Jabba clawed for Patrick.

"Hit the gas! *Hit the gas!*" Patrick roared.

The car jerked out of the space. "My foot slipped!" Angie called to him.

"Hit it!" he commanded as Jabba growled over him.

Angie obeyed, and the car bolted out of the parking space. Patrick shoved Jabba off him, and the car went airborne as they ran over his titan frame. The car wobbled on two wheels and then came down in a hard crash. Angie screamed.

"Keep going!" Patrick hollered over her crying.

The car wobbled on the uneven pavement and righted itself into a straight enough line.

Patrick had never been a praying man, but he whispered under his breath, "Please, Agnes, don't kill me. Please, Agnes, don't kill me...."

The car smashed full force into the CASA garage entrance and came to a stop in front of the empty escalator. Thank God for closing time.

"Did we do it? Did we do it?" Angie squeaked as she looked over her shoulder at him.

Patrick gave a trembling thumbs-up.

Karin and Agnes were over him in a white-hot second.

"What in God's name is the meaning of this?" Agnes raged as she ripped Patrick from the car.

Karin helped Angie from the car, but Angie broke away and hurried to Patrick's side.

"He's my friend. He saved the baby!" Angie hugged Patrick to her.

"Baby?" Agnes and Karin asked in unison.

Angie nodded, and reached in her pocket for the PISA hardware. "It's how I died. I punctured my throat with the screws, but the baby was going to swallow the dowels."

Patrick smirked. "You... did good...."

Angie smiled and seemed self-aware, older than her years. "It's time for me to go now, isn't it?"

"Y-yeah...." Patrick reached out and Agnes took his hand. She felt warm and he was like ice. "K-karin?"

"On it," she said and took Angie by the hand. "Come with me, sweetie. Would you like some dessert?"

Angie nodded quickly, bouncing on her heels. "Can I have a tiramisu?"

Patrick lay back and took slow shallow breaths. Agnes loomed over him as Karin led the little girl away.

"You know what I'm going to say," Agnes said in that calm, disapproving way.

"You're... dis... disappointed.... Got it."

Agnes hauled him upright. "No. Benjamin is going to kill you."

Chapter Nine: TARANTO

DESPITE LOOKING like someone's frail grandmother, Agnes had no trouble carrying Patrick's lifeless brawny body over one shoulder. Benji danced back as she slammed him across the counter and then primly straightened her glasses. Benji had spent the past twenty minutes desperate to get Patrick within reach, but now that he was here, sprawled inelegantly across the faux granite in front of him, he was so sick with anger that he could barely look at him.

"Now there's just the matter of dealing with the car," Agnes said as they looked at Patrick.

Patrick mumbled something unintelligible that was probably an attempt to explain his side of the situation, but Benji was past caring.

It seemed Agnes had had enough of Patrick's bullshit too. "Count yourself lucky that I didn't leave you out there, you miserable bastard."

Patrick flung an arm out and mumbled more gibberish that seemed to disagree.

That was what pissed Benji off the most. Patrick didn't seem to care about anything that wasn't whatever he was focused on in the moment. He didn't care who he hurt. He never stopped to consider how his actions affected others. Watching the Weople advance on Patrick had been the most frightening thing Benji had ever seen. The heart he knew didn't beat anymore had been racing, and he'd felt physically sick. There wasn't anything in his stomach to throw up, but that hadn't stopped the queasy, throbbing panic in his belly when Patrick had picked up that board and fought with the huge man on the scooter. Watching the fight had been torture. Logically he knew it hadn't taken more than a few minutes, but it had felt like hours.

And now Patrick was here in front of him, looking wrecked and half-dead, trying to play it off like it had been an afternoon of tackle football or something.

"What were you thinking? What? What could possibly have been important enough to risk your life like that?"

Patrick grumbled a response. Consonants and vowels slurred together and then echoed off the laminated countertop, and the effect was that of a drunk man speaking a foreign language.

Frankly, Benji was surprised Patrick was bothering to try to explain at all. Then again, there was no guarantee that the unintelligible words coming out of Patrick's mouth were actually an explanation. It was far more likely that Patrick was telling him off.

Patrick lifted an arm in a weak gesture to back up a particularly vehement point, and Benji winced when it smacked back against the counter with a thunk.

Agnes eyed them both with something that bordered on amusement, though with her it was hard to tell. There was the tiniest curve to her lips, which Benji was pretty sure indicated a smile. Hell, for Agnes it was practically a beaming grin.

She reached down and grabbed Patrick by the scruff of his neck to haul him upright, supporting him until his bone-white cheeks gained a little color. He still looked gaunt and weak, but Benji didn't think he was in imminent danger of winking out of existence. He knew Agnes could fully recharge Patrick if she wanted to, but he also knew that she wouldn't. The ball pit was an important ritual, especially to Patrick. The strict rules Patrick had concocted for purgatory were part of what kept him sane, and Benji wasn't going to be the one to interfere with that.

Agnes held on until Patrick was strong enough to brush her off. He leaned heavily against the counter but was able to support his own weight. His eyes blinked open to half-mast, and even that was clearly an exhaustive effort.

"I gave him a good ten minutes. Your touch will help," she said sotto voce as she edged by Benji. She wrapped her fingers around his wrist, and he felt the usual staticky zing that accompanied her touch. The boost was both physical and emotional—he felt less muddled and a bit stronger as well. She gave his wrist a squeeze before letting go. "And that was so he doesn't drain you the second you touch him."

She looked over at Patrick, who hadn't moved. "Benji, about Patrick—"

"Go easy on him, he's had a hard day?" Benji said sarcastically. He curled his upper lip into a sneer.

Agnes snorted. "Not at all. He's the most emotionally stunted, stubborn man I've ever met. Give him hell."

She surprised Benji by going up on her tiptoes and pressing a brief, feathery kiss against his cheek before disappearing, leaving only the faint scent of wet wool behind after she'd teleported.

He stared at the empty space she'd occupied for a second before turning back to Patrick. He wasn't sure if Patrick had registered Agnes's departure at all. He wasn't sure he wanted to share any of his aura with Patrick. Why should he, when Patrick clearly valued his own afterlife so little?

Patrick tried to push off the counter to move toward Benji, and Benji shot forward to grab him before he could collapse. Patrick looked about as strong as a newborn lamb. He was too heavy for Benji to carry, so he let himself sink slowly to the floor with Patrick in his arms. And since he'd never been good at holding an angry grudge, he rucked up the back of Patrick's T-shirt and let his fingers rest lightly just above the waistband of his jeans. Patrick had always felt almost feverishly hot to Benji, but today his skin was clammy and chilled. Benji spread his fingers out, concentrating on how much he wanted to help Patrick. His aura flowed out of him, his fingers prickling as Patrick's skin warmed under his touch.

Benji was glad they were already sitting because the energy transfer made his knees weak. Or maybe it was just relief that Patrick was okay. Either way, he didn't feel like he was in much better shape himself.

He pulled back and looked at Patrick. Really looked at him, taking in more than just his mussed hair and his gray, drawn face. There were lines on Patrick's forehead that he'd never noticed, either because he'd never been this close to him before or because the trauma had aged him.

"Trauma he brought on himself," Benji muttered. It was hard to think about how utterly helpless he'd felt watching Patrick fight off the Weople in the parking garage. He swallowed hard, trying to force the lump in his throat down. He'd really thought he might lose Patrick there for a few minutes, and it had been terrible.

This wasn't just a crush. He'd convinced himself that it was a proximity thing. Patrick was the only available guy in purgatory, since Benji definitely wasn't going to try to form any sort of relationship with one of the Impressions. Or moon around after a customer, though that would probably be more productive than trying to get an Impression to actually have a conversation that didn't revolve around its death.

But there was no way that the panicky terror he still felt coursing through him was due to a crush. He'd fallen head over heels for the prickliest, most sarcastic, most kindhearted and caring asshole he'd ever met. Dammit.

Benji stroked a finger down Patrick's cheek, and Patrick's eyes fluttered open at the contact. Each touch made Benji a little weaker, and each touch roused Patrick that much more. Without Agnes's power boost, Benji would have been in the ball pit by now. If he kept it up, he'd end up there yet.

He pulled his hand back, mindful of the fact that if he were in his right mind, Patrick wouldn't be nuzzling into Benji's palm like a newborn kitten seeking heat. This didn't have anything to do with Patrick's feelings for Benji, it was just an automatic reaction—

"Benji," Patrick croaked out, and Benji startled so hard he nearly bucked Patrick out of his lap.

Benji braced himself for an onslaught of accusations and abuse, but they didn't come. Patrick nestled closer and repeated his name, and Benji's stomach flipped when he realized that Patrick still wasn't quite himself.

That had to mean something. The physical attraction between them was undeniable, but with Patrick's hot-and-cold behavior, Benji had convinced himself that was all it was. But calling out for him in his semi-comatose state? That went beyond the realm of hookup. Benji felt like his heart was in his throat as he cupped Patrick's cheek, ghosting his thumb across cheekbones that didn't look quite so sunken anymore. Patrick's eyes shot open, and he scrambled out of Benji's lap, all elbows and uncoordinated knees.

Benji groaned as he took a flailing limb to the kidney. Not that he actually needed it anymore, but it still hurt.

"Are you fucking *kidding me?*" Patrick yelled, jumping to his feet with a grace and coordination that surprised Benji, given the pile of pathetic goo Patrick had been only moments before.

Benji struggled to his own feet, keeping his distance from Patrick, who was actively glaring at him now. "Why am I not in the ball pit? Where's Agnes?"

Benji took a careful step forward. He didn't know if the power boosts he and Agnes had given Patrick had left him confused and disoriented or if this was just plain old Patrick Defense Mode. It didn't matter. Either way, he and Patrick were going to have words.

"I've been feeding you some of my aura so you didn't dissipate before I had a chance to tell you what an absolute fucking moron you are," Benji snarled. His knees still felt weak with relief at seeing Patrick whole and mostly steady on his feet, but the tenderness he'd felt a second ago had vanished, leaving only the white-hot burn of anger and betrayal.

Confusion flitted across Patrick's face. "You shouldn't be able to—"

"I don't care," Benji interrupted. Patrick's confusion morphed into shock, his eyes going wide. Benji knew what he probably looked like. Benji's temper was almost nonexistent, until it exploded. Charles used to jokingly call it hulking out. And nothing got Benji there faster than someone he cared about taking stupid risks. "I want to know what the hell you were thinking going out there."

Patrick's expression changed again, coming closer to his usual aloof ennui but missing the mark a bit. He looked shaken and weak, and his eyes didn't seem to be focusing right. He leaned heavily back against the counter and waved his hand negligently. "I think you mean what in *Wallville* was I thinking," he said. Even his trademark smirk couldn't completely erase the exhaustion on his face. "Get it? Because Wallville is hell. Amirite?"

Benji clenched his fists at his sides, since his other option was to throttle Patrick, and he'd expended too much energy keeping him on this plane to banish him with an act of aggression.

"Can you be serious for one goddamn second so we can talk about this?"

Patrick's fake good humor dropped like a curtain. "No, because there's nothing to talk about."

He was still a bit wobbly on his feet, but Patrick managed to leave the counter and start stalking away. His movements were stiff, and Benji wondered if that meant fighting with the Weople had left actual physical injuries. The thought pissed him off even more.

"Well, too bad, because I'm not done," he bit out, his jaw clenched.

Patrick had made it an entire home mock-up away, out of the kitchen setups and into the children's furniture, but he was slowing down. Benji caught up with him without a problem.

"What if they'd taken you away? What was worth the risk to go out there?"

Patrick sighed wearily. "There wasn't any danger, Benji. There was a kid there. We had it under control."

If Benji hadn't been standing there with Agnes and Karin earlier, he might have believed that, but as it was, he knew it was a lie. Going to the outer edges of the parking garage by itself was a risky endeavor. But fighting with the Weople? That was a whole other level.

"You know that's not true." Benji's voice broke, and he swallowed hard. His panic and anger had taken a lot out of him, and he felt his own energy levels ebbing dangerously low. "There aren't second chances with the Weople. If they take you, you're gone for good."

Patrick laughed humorlessly. "And is that so bad? If we believe that they take people to hell, then it's just exchanging one consciousness for another, isn't it? The law of conservation of matter, and all that."

Benji stared at him in horror. "Is that so bad? Is that so *bad*? Are you fucking kidding me?"

Patrick shrugged. "Trading one unexplainable existence for another? Who can say? I can't. Apparently I wasted my life getting my doctorate in particle physics when I should have been studying theology instead."

"You were trying to get taken." Benji rushed forward and crashed into Patrick, sending both of them flying into the children's TARANTO wardrobe with enough force that the door cracked and splintered under the impact. "You absolute asshole. You're too scared to move on. You want someone else to make the choice for you because you can't believe that there's anything else out there. You're so goddamn scared of admitting there might be a higher power that you play chicken with wraiths for fun."

Patrick's wooden smile didn't come close to lighting his eyes. "It's more Russian Roulette than chicken."

A sob escaped Benji's throat, and he fisted his hands in Patrick's collar, slamming him back against the door. "You can't do that." His voice sounded pleading, and he cleared his throat, trying to get a handle on himself. "People count on you, Patrick. Have some respect for that, even if you don't have any for yourself or this place."

He let go of Patrick's shirt, all of his anger abruptly draining out of him. He felt tired and achy. Broken in a way that he hadn't experienced since Charles walked out. Why did he always have to fall for men who were so self-absorbed they couldn't see past their own noses?

He only made it two steps away before he felt Patrick grab him around the waist and reverse their positions. His breath was hot on Benji's forehead as he held him against the door. The splintered wood pushed against his back, stabbing through the thin cotton of his T-shirt.

"I don't want anyone to count on me. That's the point!"

Patrick glared down at him, but Benji refused to be cowed. He stared back, his jaw set and his expression angry.

"I was fine! Everything was fine until you came. I was *fine.*"

Benji didn't respond, not that Patrick waited for him to. Now that he was finally talking, it was like a dam had broken. Benji didn't think he'd be able to get a word in even if he'd wanted to.

"After Alec I realized that everything here is fleeting. Attachments are stupid. Everyone leaves. And it had been fine. Good, even. I liked my life here. My MILAN bed. My weekly crossword puzzle showdown with Henry. Scaring the ever-loving fuck out of Tommy. Helping people move on."

Patrick's expression was so vulnerable and bleak that Benji had to look away. He'd wanted Patrick to open up to him, but this was too much. All or nothing. Everything with Patrick seemed to follow those rules. There was no middle ground.

"But you—you were something else. Someone to hang out with, someone to talk to who actually could keep up. And I thought that would be enough, but you kept pushing." Patrick was the one pleading now, his voice hoarse. "Goddammit, Benji, why do you have to push?"

Patrick punctuated the last word with a hard push of his own. The sliver of wood punched through the back of Benji's T-shirt and punctured his skin, a pinprick of pain that was instantly forgotten when Patrick crashed their lips together. There wasn't anything gentle or teasing about the kiss—it was frantic and angry, all hard edges and barely contained hostility, just like Patrick. Benji gave as good as he got, kissing back with the same bruising force, like he could communicate all of his worry and relief that way.

Kissing someone new always came with a learning curve. A negotiation for dominance, a tentative exploration into what pleased the other person. This wasn't like that. Even though Patrick had been the one to instigate it, he immediately let Benji take control of the kiss. And Benji felt none of the usual hesitance, instead pouring everything he had into the bright-hot slide of Patrick's lips against his. He'd braced himself against the cabinet when Patrick had slammed him into it, and he brought his hands up from his sides now, gliding over hard muscle until he could slide his fingers into the soft hair at the nape of Patrick's neck. He used gentle pressure and tiny, teasing tugs to get Patrick to curve into him, wrapping Patrick's bigger body around his own as he stretched and strained to meet him in the middle. Every point of contact between them seemed to sing with energy, and if he'd been able to pry his eyes open Benji was half-sure he'd see actual sparks flying. The energy transfer that was usually a comforting warmth had kicked into overdrive, and Benji's skin felt electric, crackling with something that made his hairs stand on end.

Patrick reared back suddenly, and Benji instinctively dropped his hands, letting him go. He wasn't surprised when Patrick bolted, taking one step back and then teleporting away.

Benji knocked his head back against the broken door, his mind whirling as he fought to center himself. His breathing was abnormally loud in the otherwise empty room, and it echoed around him.

He gave himself a moment before leaning forward, wincing as the splinter of wood pulled against the tender skin of his back. He craned his neck trying to get a good look at the damage, but he couldn't see anything in the shadows of the room.

He pulled his shirt off, his mouth falling open when he saw the huge hole in the back of it. He bent an arm up behind himself, sweeping his fingers over his still-sore skin. They came away dry, which didn't make any sense. He'd felt the shard of cabinet go into his back, and his shirt was ruined. He hurried over to the long LUCENTE mirror mounted on the TRIGNO wardrobe and turned around, blinking in confusion at the smooth expanse of his back. The only thing that even hinted at an injury was the faintly pink skin where the puncture wound had been.

But if they healed that fast, why had Patrick still been limping so long after his fight with the Weople? Were the injuries the Weople inflicted more serious? Could Patrick die from them?

Benji started to toss the shirt aside but came up short when his gaze caught on the hole. With Patrick gone to who knew where, leaving even more questions in his wake, it was the only proof Benji had that what had just happened was real.

He looked at it for another long moment before smoothing out the wrinkles and slipping it back over his head.

Chapter Ten: FIORE

PATRICK SPLAYED out on his MILAN bed as the living customers shuffled around him. Lost in his own world, he tapped his pen on the crossword booklet. He had already done six of them. One more would get him just enough in the zone to face another day of the usual Impressions. The usual bullshit drama. The usual sameness of everything. And then check out, go to bed, and take it fresh in the morning.

He folded the book back on itself, cracking the spine.

"Ten across. Devoted." He read the clue out loud as he rolled to his back. He quickly scribbled in his answer. "Doggedness."

A customer crouched over the bed and flicked over the MILAN price tag. "Oh look," she said happily. "Won't it be perfect in the guest bedroom?"

Her bright-eyed girlfriend wandered over. "It'll be an adventure to get it through the front door."

The young woman frowned. "You're right…. Maybe we should keep looking?"

This time Patrick didn't even have to try to ward customers away from his bed. He personally saw to it that the MILAN line was the worst seller in their CASA. No matter what the managers had done, no one would buy any MILAN products. He smirked with the passing thought and crossed his legs.

He pondered the next clue. "Ekindu's Friend." A moment passed. "Gilgamesh."

Patrick ran his tongue over his bottom lip, and the prickle of a memory made his stomach clench. The feel of Benji's mouth on his invaded his thoughts before he could shut it out. Fucking idiot. Taking on Jabba didn't even get his head back in the game.

Patrick dropped the crossword booklet over his face to block out the overhead fluorescent lighting. He couldn't avoid Benji forever. That was rich. *Forever.* Even being around Benji ground his sharp wit into infantile putty.

Karin had teased him he was going soft. Who the fuck was he? This wasn't junior high. This wasn't passing love notes asking for confirmation of feelings by circling yes or no.

Patrick grunted as more customers muttered about buying his MILAN bed and deciding against it. Why couldn't he be a seventeen-year-old acne-ridden teenager secretly sneaking peeks into *Tiger Beat* at the grocery store again? He'd take his crush on Val Kilmer to his grave, but even that embarrassment was infinitely preferable to crushing on Benji.

He snorted against the crossword pages. This whole situation proved if there was a God, he was a comedian.

"I need your assistance in Kitchens." Karin said over him.

Patrick lifted one of the open halves of the book off his face and narrowed his eyes.

"I'm off the clock," he muttered.

Karin tossed her head. "You're dead. Time doesn't matter."

He answered her witty retort with a middle finger.

She tapped her foot. "We have a situation that I need your particular expertise for."

Patrick sighed and cast the puzzle book aside. He peeled himself off his bed just as a customer lay in his spot, testing the MODENA mattress.

He growled under his breath. "That's my fucking bed."

Karin clapped a hand on his shoulder. "Come on, big guy."

Patrick went along with Karin's nudging. "Fine. Show me the drama."

"Who said anything about drama?" Her flats made a soft shuffle across the tile thoroughfare. The customers were emptying out for the night, and the crowds thinned to a trickle and then nothing.

Patrick scratched at the scruff on the back of his neck. "You did say—"

"Expertise." Karin circled around him. "What's gotten into you? Are you feeling all right? You should have healed up from your scuffle by now."

Scuffle. Ha. It had been an all-out brawl. Trust Karin to underplay things.

"I'm fine," Patrick lied. He stood straighter, and a shock of pain stabbed into his ribs. He slapped his hand over his chest, trying to ease it away. "Fuck."

"Jabba took it out of you, didn't he?" Her tone was irritatingly casual.

"Nothing I couldn't handle. Nothing like saving an Impression from Wallville." He shot her a glare.

"And crashing a car into the lobby."

He smirked. "Cool, right?"

"You and I have different definitions of cool."

"Smile, Karin. It might warm that withered-up thing you call a va—"

He blinked and she was nose to nose with him. "What were you about to say?"

"Heart. Warm your *heart*."

She stepped back and fixed him with a dour look. "Uh-huh."

The lights dimmed around them as CASA officially closed for the night. CASA became his fortress of solitude when the customers left. But there hadn't been much solitude for him since Benji first walked through those doors and into Patrick's afterlife. Why did Benji have to be his type? He cursed himself. Why couldn't he have been an Impression that Patrick could guide into moving on? Then he'd have taken care of business in the shower like usual and gone about his hereafter. It was a puzzlement that they had to retrain themselves to engage the senses, but sex drive never faded, even in death. But the shower hadn't been as tempting—or fulfilling—of late. Damn Benji.

They slipped around the divider into one of the simulated kitchen layouts, and Patrick froze.

Benji stood across the kitchen with Agnes at his side.

Patrick clenched his jaw as Benji turned his gaze to the floor.

An opulent table spread of steaming meatballs, gnocchi, and sweet tomato jam sat between them on the butcher-block bar. The scent of espresso wafted up from the tiramisu that sat ready on dessert plates, and Coke bubbled in wine glasses. Overhead, the FIORE pendant lamp twinkled like a dandelion puff sprinkled with dew. Opulent was stretching it a bit. As opulent as one could be with budget-conscious dishes and flatware, at least.

He shook his head at the lamp. He'd dissuaded a perky coed from buying one earlier today. The Impression who'd told him it would end up killing her boyfriend had been ridiculously good-looking, but all Patrick had been able to think about was how his hair wasn't quite as shiny as Benji's.

"What the fuck is going on?" Patrick grunted. Benji was the last person he wanted to see. Which would be impossible given the close quarters.

"The situation," Karin said with a beaming smile that seemed to suck the joy out of him. "Handle it."

Benji ducked as Agnes whispered something in his ear—probably the same lame-ass pep talk he'd just gotten from Karin, but creepier and more cryptic—before she patted him on the back and promptly disappeared. Benji stepped forward hesitantly, like he wasn't sure of his welcome. And damn if that didn't send a twinge through the heart Patrick wished he didn't have. He didn't want Benji to be afraid of him.

Patrick came closer. He might as well have been stepping into a boxing ring. He followed Benji's lead, and they took their seats at the same time. Another bolt of pain sizzled through Patrick's nerves. It had never taken him this long to recover from his excursions to the garage, but he had never taken on Jabba on his own before. The guilty memory made him break out in a sickly shiver.

Benji pursed his lips and was about to speak when Patrick headed him off at the pass.

"Just getting old and feeble," he said with a grin.

"And senile," Benji said with a slight frown. "You lost your mind taking on the Weople."

"I was chasing my marbles." Patrick rubbed at his ribs before settling. He glanced at Benji, noting his soft smile. Patrick fought through the flustered feeling by clearing his throat.

He couldn't mistake the genuine concern that twisted Benji's adorable features. "How are you feeling?"

"Like death warmed over, thanks." Patrick chuckled humorlessly.

Benji furrowed his brows. "That's not even close to funny."

"Oh, and I'm sure you're hilarious." Patrick eyed the elegant meal between them, plated on cheap minimalist flatware.

"I'll have you know I'm quite funny."

"Looking," Patrick slipped in at just the right moment.

Benji snorted. "We're resorting to that?"

"Well, you are a kindergarten teacher." Patrick grabbed his fork and then scooted a meatball across his plate.

Benji looked down at his plate. "I was."

"You are," Patrick said firmly. "You are and you always will be."

Benji cracked a slow smile, and Patrick tightened his grip on his fork.

"That's possibly the nicest thing you've said to me," Benji said.

Patrick speared a meatball and took a bite. "What?" he said as he chewed. "I didn't say anything." He pointed with his fork over his shoulder. "There's an Impression over there mumbling to himself."

"H-how are you d-doing th-that?" Benji's voice cracked and his eyes rounded.

"Making words?" Patrick took another bite. "Come on, cupcake. They covered the five senses in kindergarten. Next to head, shoulders, knees, and toes."

"Eating." Benji pointed. "Can you even taste it?"

Patrick tilted his head and glanced at his fork. He then speared another savory meatball with a swirl of sweet tomato jam. He scrutinized Benji as he took another bite. "Of course I can."

Benji gaped at him and Patrick moaned around the mouthful of savory meatball, gnocchi, and sweet tomato jam. He reveled in Benji's cheeks burning a bright red and watched him squirm in his seat.

Patrick swallowed and put his fork down. He swished the Coke in the wine glass and then took a sip. "Ah. Refreshing." He set down the glass and resumed eating.

Karin and Agnes had spared nothing in the romantic setup, Patrick noted as he scanned the dimmed showroom. Trying to get Patrick in the mood for Bella Notte or some such level of BS. It wasn't going to work. He would see to that. He had broken too many rules with Benji, and he had to set his limits.

"I got a question for you," Patrick said, muffled by his meatball. "Do you think every store or restaurant has its own version of purgatory? What do you think is over in the Sacratomato Pizza Kitchen down the street? Man, I used to love that place. What would the demons be there? I mean, there's the Weople here. The SPKers have to be something, you know?" He swallowed and then sipped his Coke.

"Patrick."

Patrick nearly spat his Coke. He'd never heard his name sound like that before, infused with want and jealousy and a thousand other things he didn't have a name for. Benji sounded wrecked.

He quirked a brow at Benji, hoping against hope that his face was blank and didn't show how much Benji's voice had affected him.

"Teach me," Benji said, his eyes still wide and his gaze locked on Patrick's mouth.

Whoa. Hello, loaded comment. Patrick cleared his throat.

"Teach you what?" he asked.

Well. One loaded comment deserved another.

"How to eat."

Patrick's stomach clenched as his mind dive-bombed into the gutter. He fought for a smooth recovery. He ran a hand over his face, and took a breath.

They locked gazes, and Patrick stubbornly set his jaw. If he was going there, he was all in.

After taking a glistening meatball on his fork, he held it out across the table. "Open wide and say 'ah.'"

Benji wasn't going to take the bait. There was no way. Patrick was sure of it.

He wasn't prepared when Benji leaned forward and parted his lips in that perfect seductive pout.

Stop, Patrick mentally screamed, cursing himself instead of Benji.

He threw the fork aside and shot from the table. Benji sat back, his mellow expression making Patrick angry. Anger was good. It was a hell of a lot more familiar than the tenderness from a minute ago.

Benji thought he had him all figured out, did he? He thought he could predict Patrick's mood swings and hang on for the ride? Well, good for him. Because Patrick would be the first to admit that even he didn't have a backstage pass to whatever the fuck was going on with him right now, so fuck Benji very much if he thought he did.

"This is how it's going to be, huh?" Patrick growled as a jolt of hot pain raced down his spine. He gnashed his teeth and knitted his brows. In all of his bravado, his body cruelly reminded him he had gotten his ass kicked by a guy on a motor scooter.

"I don't know. You tell me," Benji said, unimpressed, and he crossed his arms. "You were the one going there."

"Fine," Patrick snapped and flung the dishes off the table with a vicious swing of the arm. "Let's go. Right now. Here."

Benji maintained his unimpressed expression. "Mmm-hmm."

"Oh come *on*." Patrick said, reaching for the waistband of his jeans. "Just two dudes fucking like jackrabbits in the middle of a CASA showroom. Takes fucking in public to a whole new level."

Benji frowned. "Fucking? Is that what you think this is?"

Patrick had his fingers at the button and fly of his jeans but hesitated. "That's exactly what this is."

"This?" Benji gestured between the two of them. "*This*? I'm stuck here for…." He fell silent and then shrugged. "All eternity or whatever, and you think this is a momentary thing?"

"Work with me, cupcake."

"Benji. My name is Benji." He glared at Patrick. "And I'm not going to be just another notch in your MILAN bed."

Patrick retreated to the kitchen counter and leaned back against the fake sink. Curling his fingers under the lip of the counter, Patrick clawed his fingernails into the particleboard. He couldn't win anymore. And he had never been the most gracious of losers.

Benji appeared in front of him, his energy radiating off his smaller form into Patrick's tense frame.

Patrick couldn't look at him. But it was no use when he felt Benji's warm fingers across his cheek. He swallowed, and Benji leaned closer. Benji had him powerless. All of his aggression, his taunts, his jabs, anything to push Benji away, were for nothing.

Benji pressed against him, his head to Patrick's chest.

They stood in silence. Patrick maintained his grip on the counter.

Benji pulled away and every part of Patrick screamed for him to come back. But when he did return, Benji tilted his chin up and placed the softest of kisses on Patrick's mouth.

Patrick froze and tightened his grip on the counter until his knuckles bleached white.

Benji kissed him again, encouraging Patrick to respond. But he remained still, his mind a muddle of primal need and emotional exposure.

Finally, when Benji looped his arms around his neck, Patrick fell into the tenderness. He returned the kiss with one of his own, leading Benji's chaste and timid kiss into a hungry one.

Patrick pulled him closer, their bodies meshing and singing with the energy transfer between them. It was never about the kiss. Kissing was an activity for the living. Sharing auras was the true pleasure between spirits. Benji shivered against him and moaned against his mouth. Patrick tilted his chin down and coaxed Benji to open for him. When Benji submitted, they tasted each other, and Patrick pulled away suddenly with the remembrance of sweetness.

His breath stuttered in his throat, and Benji mewled disapprovingly. Patrick answered in kind by returning the affection and claiming his mouth once again. Benji's hands trembled as he explored Patrick's frame and crept up his shirt to his taut stomach.

Patrick nestled one hand in Benji's hair and the other at the small of his back. When he felt Benji's knees quake, Patrick abruptly pushed Benji away and held him at arm's length.

"That's… enough," Patrick said as he fought to catch his breath. If he had taken any more of Benji's aura, they would have gone down a road there was no coming back from.

Benji's face was sheened with sweat, his mouth glossy and red from Patrick's attentions. "What… what happened? What was that?"

Patrick didn't answer and pulled away from Benji. He considered the plates scattered across the floor. If the car he had crashed into the downstairs entry hadn't already convinced them, the employees would start thinking the store was cursed.

"What did you do to me?" Benji insisted.

Patrick looked up to the FIORE light and took a steadying breath. He'd definitely need a moment in the employee showers later.

"I believe it's called kissing, cupcake." He grinned as Benji staggered to a seat. "You know about the birds and the bees, right? They're not literal birds and bees." He slipped behind the butcher block to hide the evidence of his arousal but maintained his unruffled attitude. "So. We're doing this."

"This?" Benji shook his head.

Patrick nodded slowly as if Benji were a small child. "You know. That thing where we sometimes stop talking and make out?"

"Dating?" Benji asked with a smirk.

Patrick reeled back, offended, and his stomach clenched. "I didn't say anything about dating. I said checking each other's dental work."

"Dating." Benji gave him a wolfish grin.

"No. Dating is when you suck my dick," Patrick said flatly.

"That's not how dating works!"

Patrick blinked. The blissful innocence act would only get him so far, but he was going to ride that pony to the end of the line. In the distance, an Impression groaned, calling out for her relative. Saved by the fucking bell again, and the perfect answer to a cold shower.

"Fuck. I'm off the clock," he muttered. He watched Benji, who still had that big smarmy grin on his face. "Gotta jet. Working overtime tonight." Benji's grin crawled up his skin, and he fumbled. It wasn't like him to fumble. Karin would have a fucking field day.

"Um. See you tomorrow?" Patrick asked, trying to save face and failing.

"It's a date."

Patrick scowled and answered Benji by flipping him off.

Chapter Eleven:
ORBA

BENJI HAD never been one of the popular kids growing up. He'd been too ordinary to stand out, which had never really bothered him. It had also meant he was rarely bullied. But his sister was his opposite, always going out of her way to be noticed, even if it wasn't in a positive light. Allyssa had hit a goth phase in middle school that had been painful for the entire family, especially when a few of the boys in a grade above her had started calling her Wednesday Addams. The teasing and pranks had escalated from there, though the details were fuzzy in Benji's mind twenty years later. What did stick out was his mother's speech—ostensibly to both of them, but he and Alyssa had known even then that it was just directed at her, since Benji got along with everyone—about how to fight back without fighting at all.

"Kill them with kindness," she'd told them.

It hadn't worked for Alyssa. The boys had kept on tormenting her until she left a dead mouse in one of their lockers. She bought it frozen at a pet store, but school lore was that she'd killed it with her bare hands.

But his mother's words had hit home for Benji, and they had become his modus operandi whenever things were rough. Hindsight showed him that it led to him letting people walk all over him, but it had also served him well when he needed to defuse awkward or difficult situations. He was using it in force now. He wasn't sure if he'd say he and Patrick were in a relationship, exactly, but they were at least relationship-adjacent. Patrick insisted they weren't, but he seemed to enjoy Benji's company to a point. Every time Benji pushed Patrick further out of his comfort zone, Patrick slammed on the brakes in the most peculiarly cute way.

It wasn't like Patrick to get flustered and fumble. But Benji's niceness and understanding noticeably messed with Patrick's sense of balance. Keeping Patrick even more off-kilter by being unrelentingly *nice* was all part of Benji's master plan.

Each time he kept his cool when Patrick invariably lost his own, Patrick became just the slightest bit more immune. Benji reasoned that within a few weeks, he'd actually be able to give Patrick a compliment without Patrick tearing it apart, looking for a hidden meaning. Maybe in a month Patrick would be able to stick around after a make-out session. Maybe they could even have sex.

Patrick was definitely willing on that count, but Benji was holding firm. But the clues were there even if Patrick hid them behind his usual air of confident bullshit. Benji recognized emotional fragility when he saw it, and he wasn't going to take advantage. Mess with Patrick to put him off guard? Yes. Sleep with him when his head wasn't entirely in the game? No.

Besides, cockblocking himself had some unintended benefits. Their astral energies were tied to high emotions. Anger sucked it out of them. And apparently lust—especially frustrated lust—gave them a bit of a power boost.

Patrick remained tight-lipped about what had happened between them in kitchens that night. Benji didn't have words for that kind of aura transference. There was so much he still had to learn. Like how to replicate *that* interesting party trick that had left him shuddering for days.

Benji wrapped his fingers around the Lego Yoda he'd fished out of the ball pit in Bambini Mondo a while ago. He liked to carry it with him because it was small and didn't take up much of his energy to hold, and it was also convenient when he wanted to practice manipulating objects. He held his palm out, pouring his focus into the small plastic toy until it hovered just above his skin. Patrick was wrong about CASA having limits. Anything was possible if you had enough energy to expend.

And boy, did he. Every time he thought he and Patrick were on the same page, Patrick threw a wrench in things, like he had at the romantic dinner Karin and Agnes had set up for them. They'd had a few tense make-outs since then, always with Patrick trying to push for something, like Benji wouldn't notice his trembling hands or the way his breath stuttered out of fear, not arousal.

It was hard to get to really know Patrick without all the conventional trappings of a regular romance. They couldn't go for long walks or weekends away at a seaside hotel. They couldn't have awkward barbecues to introduce their friends and family to each other, or wander around each other's apartments taking in all the knickknacks and other ephemera that really showed who someone was behind closed doors.

But Agnes and Karin's dinner had shown him that although they couldn't do it conventionally, they *could* date. It would just take a little more finagling and planning than the baseball games and concerts in the park that Benji had used as his fallback when he'd been dating in the mortal realm.

He'd been at a loss for what to do until he'd stumbled upon an Impression who had been killed by a television. She hadn't been in CASA long—not only was she completely unable to communicate with the man who'd been scoping out the television benches, she'd barely been able to communicate with Benji.

He smiled now, remembering how fierce the Impression had looked despite being clad only in an oversized NKOTB reunion tour T-shirt and a pair of fraying granny panties. Her attire hadn't stopped her from frantically trying to shove the customer away from the aesthetically pleasing and temptingly priced television storage solutions. Her hands had kept going through the man's chest, and she'd been getting increasingly desperate. When she realized Benji could see her, she started yelling something, but he hadn't been able to hear her. From the way she went practically apoplectic when the customer crouched to look at the price on the ORBA, Benji surmised that it was the offending piece of furniture. He couldn't understand her crude hand gestures, but when the man pulled out his cell phone and started googling fish tank dimensions, he got the general idea.

"Particleboard and water don't mix," he'd whispered in the man's ear. The customer squinted at the ORBA and shook his head as if trying to clear it before walking away.

The Impression went from faded to clear-as-a-bell as soon as the man left the aisle.

"The idiot was going to put a fifty-gallon fish tank on one of these," she shouted, still agitated. "And when it broke he was going to sever an artery trying to save the damn fish."

Benji smiled and reached for her, pushing a bit of his energy at her when she flickered. She went with him without question as he guided her toward the elevator so they could go down to the entrance.

"I take it you had a ORBA?" he asked, curious but not wanting to probe too deep in case she didn't know she was dead. Some of the Impressions didn't.

She snorted inelegantly. "I did. Stubbed my toe on it in the middle of the night when I got up for a glass of water, fell, and put both hands right through the flat-screen TV I'd saved three years to buy."

He wasn't quite sure what to say to that, but luckily they arrived at the entrance before he had to respond. She clung to his hand when he stopped a few feet from the door.

"I can't go any farther," he said apologetically. "But you go on. Great things are waiting out there for you."

She frowned at the doors. "I'm going to miss Netflix," she said before squaring her shoulders and marching off into the unknown.

Benji didn't stay to watch her go through. He never did. It freaked him out a bit, and it made him jealous too. It didn't seem fair that others could move on and he couldn't. But she'd reminded him of one of the benefits to being on the mortal plane—streaming movies.

How could he have forgotten about Netflix? And in that moment, his grand plan to start sweeping Patrick off his feet started to come together.

BENJI RAISED his head, listening carefully. Karin was coming down the hallway, her breathing more labored than usual. She was concentrating hard, carrying a laptop with several cords draped around her shoulders like scarves. He grazed his fingers over his Yoda one last time and tucked it into his pocket.

"On the table?" she asked as she passed him with the laptop. That close he could see that her brow was furrowed and she looked a little sweaty. He was glad he hadn't tried to transport the laptop himself, energy boost or no. It was precious, and he couldn't risk dropping it. Without it, his whole date night would be ruined.

"Yes, please. By the projector."

He'd been able to drag that over by himself, but it was lighter than the laptop and had a considerably shorter distance to go. Moving it from the cabinet to the table was nothing compared to Karin carrying a laptop up from the employee locker room.

Benji had been relieved when he'd snuck up to the administration wing a few days ago and found that his Netflix login still worked. It was technically Charles's account, but he hadn't changed his login after he'd moved out, and Benji had taken that as tacit permission to continue using it.

It had been hard, logging in and seeing his own profile had been deleted. Charles had always hated how the sappy romances and comedies that Benji favored ruined his own dull academic documentary recommendations, so he'd set the separate profile up for Benji when they moved in together. Benji assumed he'd just forgotten about it and that's why he'd never deleted it after their relationship ended, but now he realized Charles must have kept it active on purpose. The unexpected kindness of that act had hit him hard. As had logging in and seeing that it was gone. He wondered who had been the person to tell Charles he'd died. It wasn't like they shared any friends—Charles had taken them all with him when they'd split.

Benji fell over the table when he turned around and saw Agnes there with her arms full of candy from the registers and a big steaming bowl of popcorn. Or rather, he'd done the ghost version of falling over something—starting so hard he went incorporeal and actually fell through it.

The popcorn. There was no way to describe it. Benji's mouth would be watering right now if it were capable. It smelled amazing.

Agnes rolled her eyes and dumped her burden on the table Benji was currently sitting under. "Get up off the floor, and I'll teach you how to actually eat it instead of just pretending to drool over it," she said dryly.

It was tempting. God, was it ever tempting. But as much as he wanted that popcorn in his mouth, he wanted the lesson to come from Patrick more. Even if that meant he didn't actually get any of the hot, buttery ambrosia tonight. There would be other chances.

He manfully suppressed a pout as he stood up, brushing his clothes off out of habit. Dust didn't stick to him, not unless he willed it to. It was a neat trick, but took some getting used to. Just like everything else about CASA.

"No thanks, Agnes. You've done enough just bringing the food up for me."

She pinned him with her laser-like stare, and he knew he wasn't fooling her. Karin snickered from her spot near the laptop, making Benji's transparency complete. Maybe he could get Patrick to give him lessons in not letting every single thought show on his face. After he got him to teach him to eat because that was clearly more important. But it would be nice to go a day without getting mocked. Or at least a day with only Patrick mocking him.

Agnes's lips quirked into her slightly scary version of a smile. "Just might work," she murmured, nodding.

"We weren't subtle enough last time," Karin said in agreement. "Benji's plan is much better."

He sighed as he moved over to snag a VGA cable from around Karin's neck and start hooking the laptop up. She clearly hadn't known what he needed, since she brought several. He saw an HDMI and what he was pretty sure was an old ethernet cable, though he had no idea where she'd have gotten that.

Agnes craned her neck, watching him closely. "So you're going to show a movie using this?"

He wondered when Agnes had last actually watched a movie. Had they even had talkies then? He decided discretion was the better part of valor and bit back his joke.

"I'm streaming the movie and using the projector to put it up on the wall. Kind of like how movie theaters do it."

Agnes poked at the laptop. The screen flickered from the burst of electromagnetic energy. She drew her hand back quickly, and Benji almost laughed. It was the closest to chagrined he'd ever seen her.

Karin joined them, squinting at the laptop. "So there's a movie reel in there?"

Not for the first time, Benji wondered just exactly how old Karin and Agnes were.

"Uh, no. Nowadays movie theaters are all digital." He bit his lip when he looked up and saw two blank faces. "It's hard to explain. But no, there are no reels of film."

He'd had a hard time figuring out what to screen for Patrick on their movie date, but after an hour agonizing over his choices, he'd settled on *The Avengers*. It was the perfect mix of comic book geekery, fists meeting faces, and the three-way dilemma of Chris Evans, Chris Hemsworth, or Tom Hiddleston. Robert Downey Jr. went without saying. But Hemsworth and Hiddleston were always a difficult choice that usually settled in a tie. It was exactly the type of movie he bet Patrick would have lined up to see on opening night.

Benji was going to be kind of devastated if Patrick didn't love it. Which was ridiculous, all things considered. But he wanted to give Patrick something special, to do something for him that no one else could. He and Patrick were alike in that way. They were both prone to grand gestures. Benji's were just usually a little better planned out and a lot more well intentioned.

"You're doing a very nice thing here, Benji," Karin said, and there was no mistaking the wistful smile on her face. She was definitely a little jealous.

He grinned. "We could make it a weekly thing, you know. Movie night," he clarified when both Agnes and Karin gave him a confused look. "Not that I wouldn't like to have a weekly date with Patrick. I would. But we could have a movie night. For everyone, I mean."

It felt a bit silly now that he'd said it out loud. Could the Impressions even watch a movie? He wasn't sure. There was still so much he didn't understand about CASA. But Agnes and Karin definitely could, so it would at least be the four of them. Like a family night, since they were the only family he had now.

"I'd quite like that," Agnes said after a moment of consideration.

Karin clapped her hands together. "Me too! How many digital movies does this thing have on it?"

Benji smothered a laugh behind his hand, pretending to yawn. "Uh, they're not on the laptop, exactly. We're streaming them from a service that has a bunch of movies. Old television shows too."

If Karin was young enough, there might be an unfinished plotline out there that had been nagging at her for decades. Maybe she'd spent all this time wondering who shot J.R. He had to bite his lips together to keep from laughing at the thought of Karin with Farrah Fawcett hair and bell-bottoms.

Agnes shot the laptop a look of deep mistrust but grudgingly nodded. "Streaming. Laptops. Digital movies. What's next, cars that drive themselves?"

They all looked up when someone cleared his throat in the doorway. Patrick leaned against the frame, looking reluctantly amused.

"I figured the very vague note you left on my MILAN this morning to meet you here tonight meant you were reconsidering my blow-job offer. I didn't realize it was a meeting to talk about future cars. I'd have dressed with more care," he said wryly, gesturing at the stained *Despicable Me* shirt he'd plucked from Lost and Found a few days ago. Benji hadn't had the heart to tell him it was a minion and not a Twinkie with a face. Patrick had been absolutely delighted by it.

Agnes made a disgusted sound and wrinkled her nose at him. "If you cared about anything at all, you'd stop raiding that box and start materializing your clothes like the rest of us."

Patrick's eyes widened. "What's that I hear in your voice, Agnes? Concern? So you *do* like me!"

She fixed him with a withering stare and rolled her eyes. "I'd like you to be gone," she muttered before disappearing.

Karin shook her head and followed suit, leaving the two of them alone in the conference room.

Benji watched Patrick for a few seconds, sighing softly when he saw Patrick's easy posture tighten up when it was just the two of them. "Just so you know, cars that drive themselves actually exist. Or at least, the prototypes do. They've had several moderately successful tests."

Patrick gave him a thin-lipped smile. "Time does march on, doesn't it?"

Benji cleared his throat, uncomfortable with the maudlin turn things had taken. He knew life was moving on out there without him, but he didn't like to be reminded of it. And there was no better remedy for escaping reality than slipping into someone else's.

"Would you go to the movies with me?" he blurted, wincing at the abruptness of the subject change.

Patrick's brow furrowed. "Are you forgetting that pesky business of us not being able to leave the premises?"

There was definitely interest behind the snarky attitude, and Benji gave himself an internal high five. Operation Movie Date was cleared for takeoff.

"Welcome to the CASA Cineplex, sir," he said, bowing low. "We'll begin our screening momentarily. Please help yourself to concessions and find a seat."

Patrick was still looking at him like he was crazy, but his eyes were sparkling, a sure sign that Patrick was enjoying himself.

Benji fiddled with the light switches while Patrick roamed around the table, finally settling on one of the two seats at the end of the table farthest back from the projector.

"So we don't disturb any of the other customers in our movie theater if we get frisky during the imaginary movie," Patrick said with a conspiratorial wink. "I was always a back row kind of guy."

Benji snorted. He had no trouble seeing Patrick in the back row of a theater, though it had probably been to throw popcorn instead of get up to anything lewd. For all his bravado, Patrick was surprisingly prudish. Benji knew he'd been hurt by someone before, which accounted for a lot of his hesitancy to get intimate, but that didn't explain why Patrick flustered so easily when their hands brushed. It was endearing.

"It's not an imaginary movie," he said, pointedly refusing to engage in Patrick's childish innuendo. He brought up Netflix and logged into Charles's account.

His hand hovered over the projector button. "I have a really important question for you," he said, looking over at Patrick.

"Gee, Beaver, I don't know where babies come from. You'd better ask Pop," Patrick said, his eyes wide.

Benji's lips twitched. "Asshole. Seriously, this is life or death."

"Afterlife or death, you mean?"

Benji drew his hand back and crossed his arms. "Maybe I was wrong about you. I doubt you'd like this anyway. You're probably all Superman all the time."

Patrick gave him an offended tsk. "Earth isn't so badly off that it needs to import aliens as superheroes," he scoffed. "Marvel all the way."

Benji grinned and flicked on the projector. The title credits for *The Avengers* popped up on the large screen. "Right answer."

Patrick's mouth dropped open. "No. They did not make my favorite comic ever into a movie. Did they? Did they really make Avengers into a movie? Who played Thor? Val Kilmer, right? Had to be Val Kilmer."

Benji snorted a chuckle. "What?"

Patrick shrunk down in his seat a little bit. "Nothing."

Pure happiness bubbled through Benji. For the first time in a long time, he was exactly where he wanted to be. He could count the number of perfect moments he'd had during life on one hand, and he was thrilled beyond belief to realize he'd get to have them in the afterlife too. A lot more of them, too, if he had anything to say about it. He bet he could easily fill both hands and both feet with happy Patrick moments if he really set his mind to it.

"Oh my God, I can't tell you how happy I am to get to be the one to introduce you to the perfection that is Chris Hemsworth," he said, delighted.

"But first, we have a score to settle." Benji would have pulled on his handlebar mustache if he had one. It was the ultimate villain moment. "I believe you promised to teach me how to eat." He looked pointedly over at the popcorn and candy Agnes had arranged on the table.

"Come on! That could take forever! I'll teach you after, I promise." Patrick pouted and rubbed his face when Benji didn't unpause the movie. "Benji, it's *The Avengers*," he whined.

Benji raised his eyebrows, holding Patrick's gaze.

"Oh, fine," Patrick said. He didn't bother getting up. Instead, he just teleported over to the table, appearing on it sitting with his legs crossed underneath him. "I hope you choke on it," he said as he held a piece of popcorn up to Benji's lips.

"Now who's forgetting that we don't need to breathe?" Benji teased, the words muffled by the food.

Patrick's lips twitched and he withdrew the popcorn. "You don't get to be the funny one. That job is already taken, by me."

"I'll just settle for being the pretty one, then," Benji said, batting his eyelashes coquettishly.

Patrick choked on the Swedish Fish he'd just tossed into his mouth. "No arguments," he rasped when he finally managed to swallow it. "Basically, it's just like everything else here. Mind over matter. Be the change you want to see in the world and all that metaphysical jazz."

Benji smiled fondly. "That's a Gandhi quote."

"Whatever, it still fits. If you want to be able to eat, eat," Patrick said with a shrug. He ate another Swedish Fish.

"So that's it? I can eat because I want to eat?"

Patrick saluted him. "Make it so."

Benji eyed the popcorn with distrust but picked up a piece. It smelled amazing, and he could feel the salt crystals on the surface of the buttery kernel. "So I just go for it, Captain Picard?"

"It's hard to explain. Why don't you fall through the floor when you walk? It's not because you're corporeal, because you're not unless you concentrate and will it. But your feet hit the floor and you don't sink through because you expect to be able to walk on it. It's never occurred to you that you *couldn't*, so you can. Eating is the same basic principle. It takes a fair amount of energy, so we don't do it often, but some things are worth it, you know?"

Patrick shot him a wicked grin. He grabbed a handful of popcorn and stuffed it into his mouth with a decadent groan.

Benji took a breath and tried to center himself like he did when he was practicing object manipulation with his Yoda figure. He gingerly placed the popcorn kernel on his tongue and focused on the weight of it. He willed his taste buds to engage, but it was like having a piece of cardboard in his mouth. There was no salty zing or smooth, oily roll of butter across his tongue.

He spit it out into his palm with a grimace.

"Do you actually taste things or are you just fucking with me?" he asked, narrowing his eyes at Patrick, who was licking the salt off his fingers with exaggerated bliss.

"Oh, sweetheart, if I was fucking you, you'd know," he purred. Instead of continuing on with his teasing, though, he straightened up and took one of the chocolates off the pile. "Try this. It's easier with softer foods at first. Just put it in your mouth and remember what it was like to eat. Think about what you want it to taste like. Think about the feeling of chewing it, or how it feels to swallow."

Benji snickered at that, and Patrick flushed. Clearly the innuendo had been accidental that time. He really was adorable. Benji leaned forward and let Patrick put the chocolate in his mouth. It was cool on his tongue, and he thought about it melting and spreading sweet, thick chocolate across his taste buds.

He nearly choked when he realized he wasn't just remembering the taste of chocolate—he was *tasting it.*

A grin spread across Patrick's face. "Right? See? You're doing it, aren't you? Now chew it and swallow it."

Benji did, amazed to find his mouth flooded with saliva that definitely hadn't been there before. Tears pricked at his eyes, and he blinked quickly to dispel them. What a stupid thing to cry over.

He looked away, but Patrick slid his thumb across Benji's eyelids, gently collecting the unshed tears. "Hey, no. It's cool. I get it. It's a lot."

Benji took a breath and opened his eyes, grinning into Patrick's. He brought his hand up and caught Patrick's, twining their fingers together.

"Let's watch this movie," he said. He pulled himself up onto the table, settling in next to Patrick.

"Avengers assemble!" Patrick crowed, and Benji laughed, happiness spreading over him like a blanket.

IT WAS a good thing that Benji had the bowl full of popcorn to keep himself occupied, because otherwise he'd never have made it through the whole thing without cooing over the adorable furrow between Patrick's eyebrows that appeared while he craned his entire body toward the screen.

Benji had assumed Patrick would be the kind of guy who talked all the way through a movie, critiquing the acting and special effects or making predictions about what was going to happen next. And maybe he was that kind of guy—Benji would be amazed if he wasn't, because being a bit of an asshole just seemed to be part of Patrick's DNA—but Patrick didn't utter a word through the entire movie.

Patrick gasped when Thanos made his brief appearance in the first end credits, his excitement dancing across his face like a five-year-old at Christmas. He watched with rapt attention, like he was trying to memorize every cast and crew member's name, and then cracked up when the battle-weary team went for shawarma. He didn't let Benji speak at all until the entire thing ended and the Netflix menu came up.

"Let's watch it again."

That wasn't exactly what Benji had envisioned Patrick saying to him at the end of their first official date. He'd kind of hoped Patrick would be overcome with emotion and throw himself into Benji's arms, cursing himself for wasting so much of their time together by running away.

And while any excuse to spend time with Patrick was a good one, even if it didn't involve Patrick emoting, Benji was dead tired.

Ha. Dead tired. Because he was tired. And dead.

Benji bit back a grin at his unintentional pun. Normally he'd share it with Patrick, but he didn't want to break up the oddly charged mood with a bad joke.

"Tomorrow, maybe? We could have a movie marathon with the Avengers' back stories."

Patrick's eyes grew comically wide. "There are more Avengers movies?"

Benji rubbed the back of his neck. "Well, yeah. There are a couple Captain America movies, and there's the Hulk's movie. Oh, and Thor. And Iron Man, of course. There are a bunch of those."

Patrick held his hand out imperiously toward the laptop. "Let's watch them now."

Benji felt his aura flicker, which he'd learned was the ghostly equivalent of a yawn. He'd expended too much energy setting everything up, plus all the energy he'd used eating the popcorn. As much as he'd like to spend the night watching movies, he needed to sleep.

"I'm glad you liked it, but I'm beat."

"I can fix that," Patrick said with a heavy-lidded smirk. He slid across the table, and Benji nearly fell off the edge when Patrick wrapped his arms around him. His nose knocked against Patrick's collarbone, and he felt a zing of energy rush through him when the soft fabric got pushed aside. Benji couldn't help but nuzzle in closer, chasing the addictive charge.

Patrick curved around him, pressing open-mouthed kisses against Benji's neck. "So good like this. I'd forgotten," he muttered. "Orgasms for everyone, and then we'll watch more movies."

Benji tilted his head, giving Patrick better access to his neck. Then Patrick's words sank in, and Benji reared back, actually going over the edge of the table this time. He was still tangled up in Patrick, so he brought him over as well. They landed in a painful heap on the conference room floor.

"I didn't figure you for the sort who liked a little pain with your pleasure," Patrick muttered as he sat up and examined the rapidly healing rug burn on his elbow.

Benji licked at his lip where he'd bitten it in the fall and grimaced when he tasted blood. So much for the hope that he'd find the grace and coordination in death that he hadn't had in life.

"I'm not averse to it, but only with prior consent," he said, rubbing his jaw. He tested the sore spot on his lip again and was surprised to find it healed. The lingering taste of blood and the tenderness of the new skin were the only evidence it had happened.

Patrick shot him a lascivious grin and stood up. Benji took the hand he offered him, not surprised in the least when Patrick used it to pull him close as soon as Benji was on his feet. "Consent is fluid," he purred.

Maybe they'd have to screen *Fifty Shades of Grey* on one of their date nights. Though what Benji saw as a cautionary tale probably would come off as a how-to manual for someone with Patrick's dented moral compass.

"It's not," he said firmly. He didn't push Patrick away again, but he didn't give in to Patrick's kisses and caresses, either. "And we're not doing anything until we hash out the parameters."

Patrick pulled back with a choked laugh. "Are you asking me to make a sex contract?"

His eyes were creased with amusement, and Benji wanted to say screw informed consent and tackle him then and there, right on the conference room floor.

But the more logical part of him knew that Patrick was all talk. If he pushed him, Patrick would turn tail and run again, and Benji would have undone all the progress he'd made since Patrick's last flight.

So he tamped down his libido and settled in for an uncomfortable talk. "No, I'm asking you to be in a relationship with me." He didn't miss the way Patrick flinched at the word, but he didn't shut Benji down, and that was heartening. Baby steps. "And that involves knowing what you're comfortable with and moving at a pace that we can both be happy with."

Patrick's exaggerated grimace was almost enough to hide the flicker of vulnerability on his face, but Benji caught it. He didn't know what had happened to Patrick to make him so surprised by kindness and patience, but it made him want to put his fist through something. Benji had never been a violent guy, but he wanted to beat the crap out of whoever had put that furrow between Patrick's brows and the hesitation in Patrick's voice.

"I'd be more comfortable with you on top of me," Patrick said, but the deflection didn't have the same edge to it as his last one had.

"It's a place I'd really like to be," Benji said, grinning when Patrick's eyes widened in surprise. "But not until I've earned it."

"I'm not a quarterly bonus," Patrick snapped. "You don't have to earn me."

"But I do. And it's not you, exactly. It's your trust. You aren't going to really be able to let go and relax with me until you trust me, and I'm not going to push you past your comfort zone just because I'm spending my afterlife with blue balls."

Patrick snickered and made a grab for Benji's crotch. "Oh, I can let go with you," he said, his tone sultry.

Benji felt himself harden under Patrick's warm grip, and he didn't fight it. Sparks of pleasure shot up his spine just from the limited friction.

He had no doubt that when he and Patrick finally did have sex, it would be downright explosive.

"Okay," Benji said. He dragged his fingers through Patrick's hair, delighting in the zing of energy and arousal that resulted. "I'll drop my pants right here and let you give me a blow job if you answer one question for me."

Patrick flicked his heavy-lidded gaze from Benji's tented jeans to his face. "Anything."

Benji scraped his nails across Patrick's scalp, gentling him like a skittish animal. He knew Patrick would probably bolt, and he was okay with that. Patrick needed to understand that Benji was serious about this. His mother had been fond of the saying about breaking a few eggs to make an omelet, and he was about to upend the whole carton.

He stroked down over Patrick's neck, lightly caressing the soft skin and short hairs with the pads of his fingers. Patrick's gaze was glazed over, and Benji took a minute to appreciate that before bringing everything crashing down. That was probably what Patrick looked like when he was fucked out, and Benji sincerely hoped he'd get a chance to confirm that at some point.

But first, the omelet.

He took a breath.

"Who's Alec?"

Chapter Twelve: ROME

THE QUESTION hit Patrick like a silenced hollow-point to the back of the head. Quiet, unexpected, momentarily confusing, and painless. Patrick rumbled, holding Benji in hand, eager to find out if it was true that it was always the quiet ones who were the most filthy.

"Wait, wait," Benji said in a half-moan, trying to back away.

Patrick planted another hot kiss on Benji's neck, savoring the contact of skin on skin, aura on aura, and most of all, the salt of sweat of another human, his own hardness rising to the occasion. He had carefully orchestrated plans to lay Benji out in his MILAN and claim ownership over every inch of him, but the conference room would do in a pinch.

"Patrick, I said wait." Benji pressed his palms flat to Patrick's chest and eased him away.

He blinked, confused. "Wait, what? We're burning daylight here."

Benji knitted his brows in that adorable way, but his stern expression wasn't as cute. "I asked you a question."

Turning away, Patrick snorted dismissively. He scratched at the back of his neck, his hardness going limp with every passing second. "You said you were tired, right?"

Benji shook his head. "That's not what I asked."

Patrick nodded. "Yeah, anyway, I'm zonked. Big day tomorrow." He maintained his even expression. It was a piss-poor way of changing the subject, but he would march barefoot across miles of broken glass to avoid it.

"Hey," Benji snapped, clasping a hand on Patrick's shoulder. "If we're doing this, there's no secrets."

Patrick shrugged him off and headed for the door. "Look, it's going to be packed tomorrow. We should get some rest."

"Why won't you tell me?" Benji called after him. "Who's Alec?"

The name slammed into Patrick's gut. Benji might as well have kicked him while he was down. He didn't answer as he took three steps beyond the threshold and then teleported to the only place safe enough from prying eyes.

His feet hit the floor in the darkened warehouse, and he made a beeline for Scratch and Dent. It was the last place that exclusively belonged to him. Benji had taken over as steward of wayward children, but Patrick found solace among the misfit furniture corralled in Scratch and Dent.

He rolled his shoulders, shaking off the last pleasant shocks of aura exchange. Except there was nothing pleasant about it. Things were going well. Benji was ready and willing, and Patrick was ready to show Benji what it was like to fuck in a crowded CASA when no one could see them. But not physically. He shivered, remembering the feel of Benji's hands on him. He was no stranger to aura fucking, but the real deal? The real *human* deal? That was a different animal. Especially the emotional intimacy that came with it.

When it came to openness and expressing… feelings, that wasn't Patrick's scene. And he'd been a fuckwit to think Benji would be okay with keeping it casual. It could have been a utopia of opportunistic blow jobs and fucking in inappropriate places. But, alas.

Benji wanted honesty. Who the hell wanted honesty anymore?

What the fuck are you doing? Patrick cursed himself as he wandered aimlessly through the expansive scratch and dent department. *What the fuck are you doing?*

The ENZA bookcase was a pathetic sight: white veneer peeled off it in long thin strips like a weeping wound. Patrick stubbornly set his jaw and cracked his knuckles. He cupped his hands in front of his mouth, puffing a breath into them. Wisps of blue light trailed from his fingertips and danced down his knuckles, dripping like condensed vapor. He reached out, smoothing his fingertips over the wounded bookcase.

Wounded? Was that what he was calling it?

Patrick slowly mended the scratches with his caring hand, brushing in long strokes against the jagged strips.

He had never taught Benji how to mend, and in that moment, he resolved he never would. Mending took more energy than anger, but instead of sickness, it left tranquility behind.

Tranquility. Heh. Patrick hadn't known such a concept in... years? Could it have been years? Just how long had he been in CASA, anyway? He tracked to fifteen years. He was certain of fifteen years. He had his markers, his hard data. How many times the robins came to make the nest on the café windowsill. How many times the advertising changed over for the different holidays. How many times customers came in with shorts and flip-flops, sweating from the hot summer sun, and then in coats and scarves, shivering from the cold.

How much hard data had he kept track of since Benji? He shook his head, searching for the details. He knew he'd seen the robins. He had to.

"How many times?" he muttered under his breath. "How many times?"

He tried counting off on his fingers and only reached two. That wasn't right. He counted again.

Was it three? Four?

He'd lost track. Patrick never lost track.

There were rules. He prided himself on those rules as much as Karin and Agnes gave him shit about them.

The first rule was everything was temporary, but not him. Because CASA was a bitch like that.

Second rule was never under any circumstances get attached. If rule two ever needed clarification, he was to see rule one.

He'd gotten attached. Again.

Patrick took a long slow breath and pulled away from the ENZA bookcase, admiring his work. He ran his fingers over the edges and frowned at the dullness.

"You've been here a long time, haven't you?" he asked the bookcase. "You'll get to leave someday." He patted the piece of furniture like a child. "Someday."

He turned away, contemplating the darkness of the warehouse. Benji was around here somewhere. Moping at Karin, or whining at Agnes. Or worse, conspiring with them for another scheme.

"Movie night." He snorted in derision and then teleported to the top of a stack of torn boxes. He crouched like a gargoyle looking for his next victim.

Why did he have to ask? Benji opened his mouth, and there came the name, and the question Patrick never wanted to answer.

"Who's Alec?" Such a simple innocent question had turned a potential night of hard-won fucking into rolling in Gloom shit. The name poisoned Benji's lips and made Patrick's dick limp in less than three seconds.

Patrick slid down the stack of boxes. His new patient caught his eye: poor hapless string of TURIN lights with four shattered bulbs. He cradled the lights, feeling along the plastic covered wires. His fingers grew cold as he sent the mending currents through the cord.

Mending. Feh. What a joke.

"Excuse me...?" A young woman spoke up from the entryway.

Patrick jolted and dropped the lights, startled by a late-night appearance of an Impression.

"Yeah?" he asked instead of slapping on the happy CASA employee act.

"Um.... What are you doing?" she asked.

Patrick furrowed his brows. "Organizing my comics."

He scooped up the lights as she slipped into the scratch and dent area, brushing past his shoulder. He recoiled from her touch and bristled. This was his safe space, and now here she was drifting through the piles of CASA rejects.

She inspected a dinged DRAVA table and tapped a finger to her chin. "I don't see any comics."

Patrick blinked, losing his concentration on mending the lights. She responded to him? The little girl he had rescued in the parking garage could interact with her own independent ideas and could even affect the living world. But that was rare. Impressions were just echoes of a person's humanity. They only thought on the most basic needs, they didn't form new concepts. Not like this.

Putting the TURIN lights aside for now, he took a seat on a nearby stack of torn boxes.

"Who's your favorite superhero?" he asked. It was worth a shot.

"Hawkeye," she said with a dreamy smile. "Jeremy Renner is so hot!"

Patrick sat back, and his gut clenched with the sharp slap of a reminder of the catastrophic movie failure.

"No, really," she began as she poked at a dresser drawer. "What are you doing? Isn't it too late to be all alone?"

Whatever armchair philosophy was falling out of her mouth, she was becoming less and less entertaining.

"You know what they say," Patrick said, lying back on the boxes. "Married to the job."

"I was married. I think. Once, maybe?" she said, and he caught her troubled expression.

"Been in CASA long?" he asked. If she could interact with him, she had definitely aged a bit as far as Impressions went.

She nodded. "I've been in the warehouse, just wandering around. I'm looking for something. I wish I could remember."

Patrick sat up and put his fingers together. He had a decision. Should he run her through the song and dance routine of "good morning, you're dead" and ship her off to her final destination? Or should he actually—

"I wish I could remember a lot of things," he said, patting a spot next to him on the box.

—have a conversation with someone who wasn't Benji, Karin, or Agnes.

She took a seat next to him, and Patrick sized her up. Strappy sandals, skinny jeans, a blousy tank top, all grounding data of summer. Patrick committed it to memory. At least summer had come around.

She smiled and brushed her fingers through her long dark hair. "Do you remember being in love?"

Patrick slapped the box next to his thigh. "What kind of fucking question is that?"

She giggled. "I think dear sir doth protest too much."

He grumbled, planting his chin in his palm.

"You do, don't you?" she said, getting too damned close to his personal space for comfort.

He had nothing to lose and chomped on the verbal bait.

"I thought I was."

She nodded, seeming to ponder his answer. "You thought?"

Patrick shrugged. "You know what they say. You think you know someone until they show you their taxidermied babies collection."

She shook her head, horrified. "What? That's not how that goes."

After he slipped off the boxes, Patrick then drifted through Scratch and Dent. He rubbed his hands and puffed a breath onto his fingers, once again calling forth the mending energies. He ran his fingers over the cracked fragment of a mirror. The glass melted like ice on warm pavement, in a slow pooling puddle, and then solidified into a perfect product.

"I don't know what you've been told, but that's exactly how it goes," Patrick said, scowling at a CAGLIARI bedframe. He clapped his hands together, and the sparkling energies showered from his fingers like firecrackers.

He watched over the bed frame as it lay like a lazy, worn-out lover, dappled in scratches from a long night.

"Seems he was cute enough to tick off your boxes," he said to her, all the while watching the CAGLIARI frame mend. "You know boxes?"

Patrick slid his fingers over the frame like grazing an inner thigh in a slow, seductive touch. He flinched as the memory of Benji's skin on his own invaded his thoughts and took no prisoners. His mouth ran dry.

"Yeah," she said, slowly kicking her feet. "I know boxes. Mine are dark hair, *intense* eyes...." She hissed in delight. "Arms. I love arms."

Patrick nodded as the long scratch on the CAGLIARI pulled together like a healing scab.

"I notice eyes," he said with a smirk. "Always notice eyes first." He leaned back, squinting against the dim lighting the CASA management always left on after closing. "Windows to the soul and all that."

Souls. He snorted. That never stopped being ironic. That's all they were—souls wandering the same happy showrooms that reminded them of lives they never would have. He'd tried that once, just for the sense of normalcy. He had tried to comfort himself that if he could maintain a normal life, it wouldn't be so weird to think about how he could never leave. It had helped establish his precious hard data. Affirm his humanity.

"How Shakespearian," she said with a kind smile.

Her lucidity perplexed him. Patrick furrowed his brows and watched her. She smiled all the while, unflappable. She had to at least be college age. Her dark hair had been cut into a recent fashionable style with wavy layers. Her clothes read socialite fashionista. Not exactly the comfortable shoes and clothes one wears to CASA in prep for wandering the store for hours.

He'd have to consult with Agnes on the finer points of what Impressions could and couldn't do. Did they gain logical cognizance the longer they remained in CASA? Was that what had happened to him? He'd lingered too long?

He had so many questions for Agnes. But that would mean talking to her without her making a jibe about Benji. And that was a nope.

Fuck. What are you doing? he scolded himself.

The thought of Benji made him more of an idiot by the second.

He set his jaw and moved on to a torn box.

Boxes were easy to mend. Never had to fix what was inside.

"You a writer?" he asked, trying to make conversation.

"Psychology major," she said proudly.

"Going to save the world one day, huh?" he asked and drifted further back into Scratch and Dent. Away from her and her kindness.

"The human mind is a fantastic thing. If we could better understand it, we could better understand ourselves and each other." She tilted her head, watching him work. "Something tells me you didn't get a degree just to work the night shift in CASA."

He glanced away, not able to face her. "PhD. Particle physics. Fast track to CERN."

Patrick kept the details short. It was always easier that way. Less painful when someone's eyes glazed over at his nonsense dreams.

"Really boring, you know?" He smiled but only felt the emptiness inside. The reminder hit him in an odd, uncomfortable place when his "boring nonsense dreams" were his everything. "Now, what you see is what you get. Trapped in retail purgatory for all eternity and doing crossword puzzles to keep from going insane."

He wished he was kidding. It had to at least get a laugh.

"Wanted to discover the God particle, huh?" She got to her feet and then linked her hands behind her back.

Patrick didn't answer immediately as he searched for something else to mend. A frayed PERUGIA duvet seemed to be ideal.

"I think it was the only way I'd find God," he muttered. He never wanted to get too deep into it. Not in front of the others. It was a discussion he never wanted to have. He had a theory about Agnes and Karin, as well as what the ball pit really symbolized, but as long as he ignored it, life would seem… *sort* of normal.

"Man of science, huh?" she asked. "Man after my own heart."

He nodded, wiping his fingers over the loose duvet threads. "I only understand what's right in front of me. If I can touch it, I believe it."

After restoring the duvet, he began folding it into a proper square.

"And that's why you don't believe in love."

Her words were like a hot spike to his nonexistent heart. Patrick fixed her with a frigid glare. If only he had the power to banish Impressions with a thought.

"Where the fuck did you come from, Dear Abby?" he growled in warning.

She tilted her chin toward the rows of checkout lanes in the distance.

"I saw when they brought you in from the parking garage." She shook her head in pity. "The way he looked at you. And the way you panicked."

Patrick stalked past her. "You don't know what you're talking about."

"I read people," she said calmly. "How else can I know if they're lying?"

Fuck. She *was* psychoanalyzing him.

"Look, Abs. I have a lot of work to do, as you can see," Patrick said. He had to find something else to fix or he was going to start breaking shit by accident.

"Organizing your comics? Right. Of course." She smirked and thankfully kept her distance.

"I work here," he bit out, scowling.

"You live here." She never missed a beat.

He barked a laugh. He thought he'd get tired of living jokes.

He fucking despised them.

"So. Let's talk about you," he said in an attempt to turn the tables. "You said you were married?"

"I think," she said, and her face slowly went blank. "Not that I recall." She mentally drifted elsewhere.

Patrick thanked the silence as the Impression lost a small measure of her cognizance. She'd vanish soon enough. The thought smacked him in the back of his head. Thankful she'd vanish? That was kind of douchey.

"Interesting question," she said as she regained her clarity. "Why would you bring up marriage? Were you?"

"No," he said flatly. "Never."

She blinked. "A good-looking guy like you? I'm sure you'd have long settled down."

He glared at her. "The guy never asked, okay?"

She flashed a thumbs-up. "Got it."

Turning in a slow circle, she seemed to take in the massiveness of the warehouse floor. She gestured to the distant checkout lanes. "He wasn't asking you."

Patrick clenched his fists. "He's just a guy," he said. "It's proximity."

She nodded with a smirk. "Proximity. Right."

He rolled his shoulders, working out the ball of stress building in the back of his neck. "I can touch it. Therefore, I believe," he said.

It made sense to him, anyway.

"He's not an it."

"He *has* an it. And it is magnificent." He gave her a shit-eating grin.

"Has anyone ever told you how good you are at deflecting?"

"Might have come up a time or two." Patrick shrugged. "Putting those book smarts to use, huh, Abs?"

She crossed her arms, and he read the frustration in her stance. Good. Maybe she'd wander off soon.

"Why don't you see what's right in front of you?" she asked.

He straightened with a long exasperated sigh and then popped his neck. The pleasant pop and crunch sent a warming tingle down his spine.

"It's like milk," he said and then puffed a breath into his hands. The blue mending energies laced through his fingers.

She arched a brow and frowned dubiously. "It's like milk?"

He nodded. "It's like milk that's gone three days past its expiration date." He placed his palm over a sad, dinged-up TARANTO. "So, you're standing there having this deep philosophical crisis about whether you should chance having chunks in your cereal, or throw it out."

She shifted her weight, seeming to consider him.

"Why not try the milk?" she asked.

Patrick leaned back from his work on the TARANTO. He swallowed when he recognized it as the same one he had shoved Benji against when he stupidly let him know he was interested. More than interested. He would have fucked him right there if common sense hadn't prevailed. Well, if by common sense he meant complete terror.

He grunted in frustration, sexual and otherwise. "Because I'd have to throw it out anyway."

Her smile returned, bright and brilliant. He knew she was working her psychology prowess to gain his trust. Damned Impression. She was a smart one.

Calmness crept over him and sank into his pores, warming his skin. The mending side effects were kicking in, and he relaxed against a stack of boxes.

"Why don't you try it?" she asked as she joined him next to the stack of boxes. She felt along the edge of the one for a ROME wardrobe frame. The wayward box had been separated from its family of sixteen other boxes. Why the damned thing came in so many packages seemed obscene to Patrick. Packing a car with a ROME system was a special kind of hell. Turning to him, she nodded. "If it's still good, at least you'll have cereal for one more day."

He blinked at her, and then tilted his head like a confused corgi.

"Drink the milk," she said.

He smirked and then glanced from the box, to her, then black again. She hovered near it and maintained the contact.

"It's that one, isn't it?" Patrick asked with a nod. "The ROME?"

She sighed softly. "I couldn't get it out of the car. And...." Her face went momentarily blank before she resumed her thought. "I never thought this would be purgatory. Amanda fucking hated this place."

"Daughter?" he asked. It was a stab in the dark, but he noticed the mothers getting younger and younger.

"Wife." She hesitated, as if considering her answer. She nodded. "She was my wife."

"Is," Patrick corrected her.

She shook her head. "Is?"

"Is," he stated again. "She'll always be your wife."

She brightened. "See? You do believe in love."

Patrick waved her off with a dismissive flick of the wrist. "I believe in what I see. Your wife should be waiting for you beyond the doors. I'll page Karin to help you out."

She started off but only got a few steps away before she stopped. "I never caught your name?" she asked.

"Patrick," he said, standing a little taller.

"Drink the milk, Patrick. You have more than enough for one more bowl of cereal."

He watched her smile finally fade as her body dematerialized into trails of vapor, vanishing through the ethereal breeze.

Patrick remained in the silence and savored the solace.

His body tingled with the cooling tranquil salve of the mending energies on his soul. Spitting an infantile chuckle like a fourteen-year-old boy, he got the joke.

The Impression had been his lucky charm, reminding him Benji was magically delicious.

Chapter Thirteen: TRIGNO

KISSING PATRICK left Benji breathless, which was interesting in more ways than one. Most intriguingly, he didn't need to breathe, not really. So how could he be breathless? The same principle held for the way Patrick made Benji's heart race. A curiosity, to be sure, because his heart didn't actually beat in the first place. It could be a psychological thing, some remnant of his humanity so ingrained that he felt the sensations even though it wasn't actually happening, simply because he was used to his heart racing and his breath going funny when he was kissing someone.

Except he'd never felt anything quite like this. His lungs burned and his heart raced as he focused on the soft slide of Patrick's lips over his own. Patrick's tongue sweeping into his mouth felt far more intimate than any kiss had before. Even Charles hadn't been able to make Benji's knees weak and his breath catch with just a kiss, and he'd loved Charles more than he'd thought possible.

Patrick dipped his hand below Benji's waistband, and Benji's breath hitched again. As their make-out sessions grew more frequent, it was getting harder and harder—pun intended—to keep things strictly above the belt. Benji was starting to think he'd severely underestimated Patrick's stubbornness and his own willpower.

Patrick had told him a little bit about Alec since their movie date. Enough that Benji could see that Patrick was trying, but not enough to make Benji comfortable with playing out any of Patrick's increasingly filthy suggestions. It turned out that Patrick not only had a talent for dirty talk, he also had a lot of interesting and sometimes concerning ideas about the role different CASA furniture pieces could play in their lovemaking. Benji was only sure he was joking half the time.

Patrick teased his fingers lower, dipping under the edge of the Under Armour boxers Benji had chosen for today. He'd never actually worn any in life, but they'd looked comfortable and sexy in the ads he'd seen. He had no idea if that was actually true or not, but his mental approximation of them was plenty comfy.

He let his hand slip away from where it had been caressing the skin between Patrick's shoulder blades, trailing his fingertips down the warm, firm skin of Patrick's back and leaving goose bumps in their wake.

He closed his fingers around Patrick's wrist and tugged gently, dislodging his hand. Patrick groaned in frustration and let his head thunk against Benji's chest. His temple caught Benji's collarbone, sending a sharp-sore ripple of energy up Benji's shoulder and down his arm. He shivered. It was almost as good as an orgasm, and Patrick was wickedly good at inciting it.

"You have to stop doing that," Benji said when he'd gotten his breath back.

"Stop cockblocking me and I will," Patrick said, his signature smirk firmly in place.

It was quickly becoming an old argument, and Benji fell into the rhythm of it easily.

"Tell me all about Alec, then."

Patrick stuck his tongue out. "He was a guy. His name started with an *A* and ended with a *C*," he said flatly.

Benji watched as Patrick rolled off the GORZENTE they'd been lying on and starfished on the short-fibered SFOCATO rug underneath it. The store would be opening any minute, so even if Benji hadn't called their make-out session quits because of Patrick's wandering hands, they'd have had to stop soon anyway.

Patrick liked to tease him about his discomfort with fooling around in front of customers who couldn't see him anyway, but Benji didn't care how illogical it was. It just felt wrong. Besides, once the doors opened and the customers started pouring in, the Impressions would start materializing too. And they actually could see them, and that was some messed-up shit.

Benji heard the telltale squeak of a poorly oiled cart wheel making its way down the aisle. He rolled to his side and watched as Patrick blinked one eye open and glared in the direction of the noise.

"I love the smell of CASA in the morning," Patrick said as he sat up and rolled his neck, stretching.

Benji was starting to regret introducing Patrick to Netflix. In addition to burning through a good portion of the movies he'd missed out on, Patrick had started watching older favorites too. They were going to have to start torrenting things soon if Patrick didn't slow down. If Benji didn't kill him for his new propensity to speak in bad movie quotes, that was.

"Okay, Lieutenant Kilgore, let's go," he said, hauling himself up.

They didn't save a customer's life every day, but Benji liked to spend at least a few hours a day out with the crowds. It helped him remember what it was like to be alive, back when his biggest problem might be CASA not having enough PULITO boxes in stock in the color that coordinated with his classroom.

But between helping Impressions get their messages across to the living and helping lost children find their parents, Benji was able to keep himself pretty busy. But by far the best part of his day was hanging out with Patrick in their new morning ritual. They'd part ways in a bit and go about doing their own thing, but for the next hour or so, Patrick was his.

Patrick stood up and stretched again, revealing a sliver of belly that was deliciously sprinkled with hair. Benji couldn't tear his eyes away from Patrick's treasure trail, something that definitely didn't escape Patrick's notice from the way he winked at Benji.

"Anytime, sweetheart," Patrick said with a lascivious smile. "You just say the word."

Benji smiled sweetly. "Alec."

Patrick's nose wrinkled in annoyance. "Not that word. So I take it you don't want to join me for a shower before our date, then?"

God, did he. But the thought of Patrick naked and wet was more than Benji could handle this early in the morning.

"Coffee," he said, shaking his head.

"Spoilsport," Patrick teased. He pulled his borrowed CASA shirt up to his nose and sniffed. "I've got to hit up Lost and Found at the very least. This is rank."

"Why don't you just materialize something for yourself?"

He changed his own clothes to illustrate the point. The jeans were modeled after a pair he'd seen on a customer a few days ago, tight enough that they made Patrick's eyes linger on the man's ass as he'd walked by.

From the strangled sound Patrick made, he liked them just as much on Benji.

Patrick heaved a put-upon sigh and scrunched up his face again, with an expression too overdone to actually be taken for concentration. Nothing happened.

"Can't."

"Won't," Benji countered. He'd heard Patrick's reasoning for his inability to change his clothes at will, and it was bullshit. Patrick had a complicated explanation that involved conservation of matter and the frequency that particles vibrated at, but really it came down to belief. He didn't believe he could do it because it was counter to the laws of science. Laws that had been the most important thing in Patrick's life before, well, his death. "You can eat, and that doesn't make sense. You can teleport."

"Different things, darling," Patrick said, his voice singsong. "If you're not joining me for that shower, then I'll go help myself to some new clothes. Maybe Tommy finally washed his uniform shirts and restocked his locker. I like his stuff better than Lost and Found. He uses Tide. Meet you in ten."

He was gone before Benji could reply, leaving Benji standing alone and shaking his head.

The day was in full swing, CASA shoppers filtering through the store with rapidly filling carts and eager expressions. He'd seen three people in Santa hats and Ugg boots a few days ago, but today everyone was wearing tank tops and flip-flops. He looked down at his feet, frowning. He'd never tried to change his shoes. A blink later he was wearing the comfortable pair of Havaianas he'd last seen in his closet. They were molded to his feet perfectly from years of wear. Even though he knew they were just a manifestation of his ghostly energies, part of him still believed they were the real thing. He lifted his foot, grinning when he saw the splash of orange paint that had never fully worn off the bottom of the left sole.

Benji listened to the reassuring slap of the familiar shoes against the tile as he made his way to the employee lounge. He could teleport, but it was a room off the locker room, and he didn't want to chance popping in and seeing Patrick naked. Not with his blood still thrumming from their early morning make-out session and the teasing banter that felt a lot like foreplay these days.

The café was the obvious choice for their morning coffee dates, except for the fact that they couldn't actually drink coffee there. Not during business hours, anyway. The living could see objects they picked up, so it made sense that they'd probably be able to see coffee cups hanging in midair. And now that Benji could actually drink it, he wasn't content with just sitting there and smelling it like Patrick often did when he spent hours on end up in the cafeteria doing God only knew what with the strange old man who was there almost every day.

So that left the employee lounge, where a pot of burnt coffee was almost always on the warmer. They timed their dates for an hour or so after the morning shift started, too early for any employees to be on break or for the next shift to be milling around, killing time before hitting the floor.

And if anyone did happen to walk in while they were there—well, it wouldn't be the worst thing. Benji was starting to feel sorry for Tommy, who Patrick tormented mercilessly. Benji had overheard more than a few of the employees talking about how crazy he was, since Tommy insisted the CASA was haunted. Maybe someone else walking in and seeing two coffee cups floating in midair would help him. Despite being a nervous kid, HR sure did promote him quickly. It seemed just last week was his first week, now he was among management. It was a little sad that he was the manager *every* employee talked about for his… eccentricities.

"…but they only have it in the pine color, and everything else in her room is white."

Benji tripped over his flip-flop, startled by the sound of a voice he hadn't heard in months. A voice he'd assumed—hell, more like hoped—he'd never hear again, and that was before he'd died.

"Well, whose fault is that? I wanted the cherry crib, but you insisted on the white finish."

Benji didn't recognize the other voice, but he couldn't help himself, inching forward toward the children's furniture department. He doubted Charles had ever set foot in a CASA before, let alone the children's department. He'd hated all of Benji's CASA furniture, and he also hated kids.

"White is timeless. And the cherry was too heavy for her room. We agreed."

The defensive lilt to Charles's voice was so familiar that Benji didn't have to be close enough to see his face to know that Charles's lip was curling upward. Still, Benji sneaked closer, popping his head around a hanging display of puppets so he could peer over the aisle divider.

Charles looked tanned and healthy. Even with the unmistakable look of annoyance on his face, his classic features were gorgeous. He looked like he'd gained a little weight, and his glossy dark hair was flecked with gray, but the overall effect was distinguished. Benji snorted, wondering if Charles had dyed his hair to make himself look more professorial. It was definitely something his vain ex-boyfriend would do.

But shopping in a CASA? Out of character for the man who'd insisted on an $8,000 sofa that had been as ugly as it was uncomfortable. The same went for arguing in public. Charles was nothing if not obsessed with his image, which meant biting condescension in public, not fighting. That always came later, after they'd gotten into the car, when he'd unleash on Benji, criticizing him for whatever social faux pas or imagined misstep he thought Benji had made. So who was this guy he was with, and why were they arguing in the middle of a bunch of pint-sized dressers?

Benji nearly had a heart attack when Charles looked up. He ducked down, hiding behind the puppet castle before realizing that even if he looked directly at him, Charles wouldn't be able to see him. His slouching and covert creeping had been totally unnecessary. Though some habits, like assuming people could see you, were hard to break.

He straightened and walked into the aisle, coming as close as he dared to Charles and the other man. They were dressed almost alike, button-down shirts rolled up, exposing tanned and strong forearms, and tailored khakis with pristine boat shoes. No flip-flops or form-fitting jeans for them.

Benji studied the stranger curiously. He was about Charles's height but definitely younger. Probably closer to Benji's age than Charles's, which stung a bit. Charles had sworn up and down that he wasn't leaving Benji for one of his students, and apparently that had been true. Thinking Charles had left him for a younger man had hurt, but he'd been able to deal. It was so…. Charles. But finding out the other man he'd been thrown over for was a little older than himself? That was harder to digest. And shopping for furniture, which must mean they lived together. Or at least were going to be soon. That seemed insanely fast, unless they'd been seeing each other before Charles had left him.

"Are we really going to be one of those couples that fights in CASA?" the stranger asked, the anger that had been so apparent only moments before bleeding into amusement.

Charles laughed. Laughed. Benji nearly swallowed his tongue. Was this really the same man he'd dated for so long? Benji had never heard Charles make a sound like that, chagrined and self-effacing.

"Gay cliché," Charles said, and then the two of them were kissing, right there in the middle of CASA. Public displays of affection? Humor? It was like being in bizarro land.

Benji rounded the last aisle and came up short so quickly that a woman ran her cart right through him. She shivered and looked around wildly, the hair on her arms standing on end. He couldn't focus on her, though. His attention was fixed on the small pager tucked in the breast pocket of Charles's immaculately ironed shirt.

His gaze shot down to Charles's hands, which were unmarked. Benji let out a breath he hadn't known he'd been holding. Then the stranger raised his own hand to rub at his temples and Benji saw the thing he'd been terrified of seeing on Charles's skin—a hand stamp. It was faded on one edge and dark on the other from being unevenly applied, like most club stamps were. But this wasn't the remnant of a night out on the town. Somewhere down in Bambini Mondo was a tiny hand with a matching number.

Charles was dating someone with a kid. What the fuck.

Without conscious thought, Benji dissolved and reappeared in Bambini Mondo. It was a busy day, and there were tons of kids there, but Charles and his boyfriend had definitely said "she" when talking about the kid's crib, so Benji could rule out half of the kids toddling around by virtue of that. If she was in a crib, she'd be tiny, but that didn't make much sense, since Bambini Mondo had a minimum height requirement. Still, he started with the smallest ones first, scanning kid after kid until he found one who had the same sequence of numbers stamped on her hand.

When he saw her, everything stopped.

Literally. He was so surprised and distraught that his energy pulsed, overloading the circuits and sending Bambini Mondo crashing into darkness. Kids screamed and employees rushed around trying to reassure them and figure out what was happening, and Benji stood in the middle of the chaos, unable to feel guilty about the mess he'd caused because he was too busy feeling nothing at all.

She wasn't tiny. Or rather, she wasn't as tiny as Benji had expected. The mention of the crib had made him think baby, but this girl had to be at least four.

She was also unmistakably Charles's. From her patrician nose to the shape of her ears, she was Charles all over. His boyfriend might have been the one with the stamp, but there was no way this little girl wasn't Charles's biological child.

He could barely hear himself think over the cacophony of crying children. The lights blinked back on a few seconds later, dimmer because they were on a generator rather than the main circuit. Benji took a purposeful breath and closed his eyes, focusing on drawing into himself. Expending enough energy to short out CASA's electrical grid should have dissipated him instantly, but he felt stronger than ever. He was a little disappointed—if ever there had been a time he'd welcome the oblivion of wherever they went when their energies were expended, this was it. He could use a little calming nothingness just about now.

He didn't stick around to watch the aftermath of his tantrum down in Bambini Mondo. No kids had gotten out and things were under control, so he tamped down the hot tendril of guilt snaking its way up through his throat and turned on his heel, making his way toward the stopped escalator. He wasn't sure teleporting was a good idea right now. He'd probably end up stuck in a wall.

The escalator hummed to life when he was halfway up it, and a beat later the lights came back to full power. CASA was back on the grid.

None of the customers he passed looked panicked, only annoyed, so Benji figured the power had only been out for a minute or two, tops, not the eternity it had felt like to him. People were already back to stuffing their carts with plastic junk they'd never use, completely oblivious to the fact that Benji's energy had somehow attacked the store.

He could feel Agnes and Karin somewhere on the fringes of his consciousness, but he didn't take the time to look for them. He'd always had a vague pull that told him where they were, and Patrick, too, though the connection to him was stronger. He ignored them for the moment. Right now he couldn't think about anything other than getting answers from Charles about the little girl downstairs.

Even if his estimate was off by a year or two, which he doubted, there was no way this kid hadn't been conceived when he and Charles were together. He'd always suspected that Charles cheated, but this was still a shock. As far as he knew, Charles had never had any interest in women. Then again, as far as he knew Charles didn't have any children and wouldn't be caught dead shopping in a CASA, so clearly he was working with bad information.

Charles and his mystery boyfriend were still in the children's furniture section when Benji found them. His heart was racing from the run, and he felt a prickle of moisture at his temple. He wiped it away absently, and it wasn't until he rubbed his fingertips together a moment later that he realized it actually was sweat, not just the phantom feeling of it or the tiny misting of it he'd experienced before when he'd exerted himself. It was proper sweat, running down his face. He held his hand to his chest, his breath catching when he realized he could feel his heart beating. That was new too. Probably just another manifestation of extreme emotion. Finding out your ex-boyfriend had a child definitely qualified.

Feeling bold, he held his hand out in front of Charles's face. Nothing. Still invisible.

"Why are you here? Who is this? When did you have a daughter?" he shouted, his throat raw.

Still nothing. Charles didn't flinch or even cock his head like he used to when he'd hear something in the distance.

Benji swallowed down his disappointment and tried to center himself. Everything was going haywire, and he didn't want to accidentally hurt someone by knocking something over.

And that was when he saw the Impression. She was biting at her lip a few feet away, her hands wringing together. The look on her face was pure, unadulterated fear, but it wasn't directed at him. She was staring past him with a focused, laser-like gaze Benji had seen dozens of times before.

Shit.

Shit, shit, shit.

Was she here for Charles? Maybe his boyfriend?

Shit.

The Impression came closer, looking more anguished than she had a moment ago. Benji stepped closer, his eyes widening when he realized that they'd moved on from the tiny desks and two-tiered bookcases they'd been looking at earlier.

Charles ran his hand over the smooth white finish of the piece he and his boyfriend were examining. "It would match," he said, squinting thoughtfully. "I still don't see why we can't just use Josie's."

The other man snorted, not looking up from the product information card. TRIGNO, it said. Cabinet, white.

They were looking at changing tables.

"Because you insisted on getting her a convertible one and she's still using it as her dresser. Remember? We spent what, eight hundred on that thing?"

"Then let's get her a new dresser and keep the changing table with the crib," Charles said.

The man fisted his hands at his sides. "Great plan. She was already mad enough about the crib, and she wasn't even using that. Let's go ahead and take away furniture that's actually in her room. She's already feeling anxious, why not give her more of a reason to hate me?"

Charles moved toward him and rested his hands on the man's shoulders. "Kerry," he said softly, and the man's head dropped forward, all of the anger disappearing. "She doesn't hate you. Why would you say that?"

"Because she overheard my goddamned sister at the baby shower last night saying it was good that I'd have one of my own now," he muttered. "And I tried to explain that it wasn't like that, but Josie wouldn't talk to me this morning."

Charles's lips curved up into a heartbreakingly beautiful smile. Benji had forgotten he could look like that—compassionate, kind. Loving. It had been a long time since he'd had that megawatt smile aimed at him, and it made him remember all the good times they'd had together.

"Josie wouldn't talk to you this morning because she forgot Rainbow Dash at your sister's last night and you refused to go back and get it," he said, his voice soft and amused.

"We were five minutes from home when she realized! I told her to make sure she had everything before we left—"

Benji could feel the reverberation of Charles's quiet laughter in his own chest. "And what did she say? She said, 'I hate you, you're the worst dad ever.'"

Kerry scowled at him. "I'm glad that's funny to you."

Charles slid a hand down Kerry's arm and wrapped it around his fist, bringing it up to his mouth to kiss it lightly. "Yeah, because it cements my status as best dad. Because she only has two, so if you're the worst...." He grinned when Kerry's lips quirked into a reluctant smile. "You are her dad. We have adoption papers that prove it. And I'll be the

Blob's dad, as soon as he's born and I've adopted him. Josie knows she's ours. It doesn't matter who her biological dad is."

Kerry tapped him on the shoulder with a closed fist. "Don't call him the Blob. We already picked out his name."

Charles's smile was incandescent. It blew every memory of Charles he had out of the water—he was positive Charles had never been this happy with him. It made his chest ache, both with inadequacy and undeniable jealousy. Who was this guy? Why was he able to make Charles smile like that? Why did he get to have a family with Charles when Benji hadn't been able to? Why had he been so adamant that he didn't want kids when he already had one? And why was he so happy to be a dad now?

The pager in Charles's pocket lit up and started vibrating. He and Kerry both looked at it and burst out laughing. "Time's up," Kerry said ruefully. "It hasn't been an hour yet. I wonder what she's done?"

"Organized an army of tiny minions and tried to overthrow Bambini Mondo, probably," Charles said with a shrug. He was so laid-back and comfortable in his own skin. It was almost unbearably attractive. "God, they're going to totally walk all over us, aren't they? It's hard enough saying no to her—I can't imagine we'll have better luck when there are two of them."

Kerry wrinkled his nose. "I can say no. You're the pushover."

Charles smirked triumphantly, and Kerry seemed to realize his misstep a beat too late. "Well, maybe you should be the one to go dole out her punishment, then," Charles said, pushing the still-buzzing pager into Kerry's hands. "I'm going to get this one. I'll meet you down in the warehouse? I wanted to pick up a changing pad."

"Get a couple new covers too. I don't think we kept any of Josie's," Kerry said. He leaned in and pressed an easy, proprietary kiss at the edge of Charles's mouth and walked off.

Benji was still standing stock-still in the middle of the aisle. People veered around him, the crowd parting like water around a large rock, flowing back together as soon as they'd gotten past him. No one seemed to notice how strange that was.

Benji was spurred into action when the Impression crept closer, gesturing wildly at Charles when he started writing down the warehouse information on the TRIGNO.

"Is it him?" Benji asked her, his heart caught in his throat.

She shook her head, and relief coursed through Benji's veins. But if it wasn't Charles—

He looked down the aisle in the direction Kerry had disappeared. "The other one?"

She was still wringing her hands, nodding.

Benji studied the changing table cabinet. It was tall—maybe it fell on him? Or maybe he was killed before it was even assembled. The Impression wasn't forthcoming with information, which was frustrating. Some of them were too new to talk, and he desperately hoped that wasn't the case here.

Though, would it be the end of the world if Kerry died?

Shame and revulsion fell over him like a blanket. What the fuck was his problem? He was hoping this guy died? Jesus.

Benji ran a hand over his face roughly. His skin was dry, even though he still felt sweaty. Back to normal, then. Apparently actively wishing for a guy to die wasn't a strong enough emotion to physically manifest. Good to know, just in case he wanted a future as a serial killer.

"So the TRIGNO kills Kerry?"

The Impression hesitated and then shook her head. Her eyes practically bulged out of her head as she shook it violently, urgently gesturing toward Charles, who had finished writing the ticket information and was tucking the sheet and tiny stub of a pencil into his breast pocket.

If it didn't kill Kerry or Charles, that left what?

His stomach dropped.

"The baby?" he asked, his voice breaking.

She nodded, her expression as horrified as Benji felt. He couldn't let that happen.

"What do they need, anchors?"

That was pretty common, people cutting corners and not bothering to anchor heavier furniture. It would be a simple fix too.

She shook her head and mimed something he didn't understand. The sense of urgency increased when Charles wandered out of the aisle, presumably headed toward the changing pads.

"Can you talk? What happens? I need details!" He hadn't meant to shout, since that usually stressed the Impressions out and made them even more useless, but he couldn't help it. He wasn't going to let a baby die.

She shook her head and ran over to the TRIGNO display. It looked like a fancy bookshelf with a fold-down tray that Benji assumed held the baby. It seemed unstable, but anchoring it to the wall would fix that. It wasn't like the table-like models next to it, and Benji could see how its aesthetic would appeal to Charles. The rest of them were pretty ugly, but this one looked like a real piece of furniture.

The Impression knelt down underneath the piece and then stood quickly. She didn't have enough energy to be corporeal so her head went through the changing table piece, but she fell to the ground and clutched at her temple.

A chill went through Benji. She was miming her own death. "You hit your head on it after bending down and died?" She nodded. "But the baby won't be tall enough—"

She shook her head hard and placed a palm on the flat surface of the changing table, then swung it away in an arc that landed on the floor.

"Oh God," Benji said, swallowing hard against the acrid bile that crept up his throat. "Kerry hits his head on the changing table and knocks the baby out of it?"

He hoped he was wrong. Because as terrible as the baby dying would be, it would be worse if his father was the one who caused the accident.

But the Impression nodded, her lip quivering and her eyes shining with tears he knew she wouldn't be able to shed.

"Did you—"

She nodded.

"Both of you?" he asked, his voice cracking.

She nodded again.

How awful. And the baby wasn't here, so it must be on the other side. Waiting, motherless. Jesus Christ. He had to get her over there. She must be in agony.

This wasn't an easy fix, though. He wasn't going to be able to just throw anchors into their cart or nudge Charles toward a different model, since there wasn't anything else that looked remotely like it. With his aversion to CASA products in general, there was no way Charles would go for a cheaper model that looked, well, cheaper.

Kerry had said the old changing table had cost some exorbitant amount, which meant it was probably from the fancy furniture store Charles had loved to shop at when they'd been together. Why weren't they getting the new one there? Benji caught up to Charles, who was tossing several changing pad covers in bright colors into his cart. His clothes were designer, as usual, and immaculately turned out. So money couldn't be that much of a problem.

They were probably using a surrogate, which was pretty expensive. Benji had looked into it himself, before he and Charles had gotten into their final blowout over Charles not wanting kids. Maybe that was why they were cutting costs on furniture.

Still, it was hard to envision Charles allowing particleboard furniture in his home. He'd made Benji put most of his things in storage when they'd moved in together, after the leg had fallen off Benji's LECCE coffee table.

Inspiration struck. He just had to convince Charles that the thing would fall apart. Charles was already predisposed to thinking CASA furniture was poorly made—which it wasn't, but Benji figured it was okay to exaggerate this once—so all he had to do was make Charles remember that. Give him proof that he'd been right.

Benji stepped in front of Charles's cart, and predictably, Charles swerved around him without hesitation. Benji kept leaping in front of him, leading him back to the TRIGNO display. When he finally got him there, Benji concentrated harder than he ever had before, pouring all of his energy into making Charles hear him.

"Take another look," he whispered in Charles's ear. He was close enough to feel the way the short hairs at the back of Charles's neck prickled up. "Maybe it's too wobbly."

Charles hesitated but then moved toward the display.

"Should make sure this will hold the Blob when he's bigger," he muttered to himself, shaking his head slightly.

Benji pumped his fist. Victory. He darted over to the TRIGNO and grabbed on to the edge of the changing table lip. He waited until Charles's long fingers were feeling over the joint and then placed his hands next to his, close enough that Charles shivered.

Benji clenched his teeth and pulled hard, his biceps shaking with the effort of trying to dislodge the piece. Floor models took a lot of abuse, and this was no exception. It was worn from people jiggling the table part, probably trying to see if it was solid or not.

Benji fell on his ass, skidding across the floor and knocking into the display behind him. His hands were empty, but a long crack had formed in the lip of the changing table. Charles was staring at it openmouthed.

"Piece of crap," he said, shaking his head. "Everything here is junk." He let go of the table with a huff of disgust. "God, Benji, how could you stand shopping here? You had decent taste in everything else."

Benji started but relaxed when he realized Charles was just talking to himself. He didn't see Benji sitting a foot in front of him.

He followed Charles down to the warehouse, unable to leave him alone. Did Charles still think about him? Did he miss him?

Not that it mattered. Charles had obviously moved on, and quickly. Or maybe he'd been with Kerry all along. Maybe Benji had been the affair. But how would that have worked? They'd lived together, for God's sake.

Josie and Kerry were waiting at the door to the warehouse. She had sparkly light-up sneakers on and was dancing in circles around Kerry, who had a hold of one of her hands and was twirling her around.

Kerry looked into the cart. "Those will do nicely," he said, nodding approvingly at the changing pad covers.

"Yeah," Charles said, distracted. "Listen, I changed my mind. The tables up there were rickety. I'm not going to trust them to hold the Blob, especially if he's half as squirmy as this one was," he said, reaching down and tickling Josie.

She shrieked with laughter, and he snatched her up and swung her onto his shoulders. She promptly grabbed him by the ears. "Let's go!" she giggled, tugging on them.

He moved obediently, not even looking back to make sure Kerry followed him. Which he did, grabbing the cart and moving after him seamlessly, like it was something they'd done countless times before. They were obviously a close-knit family.

Kerry and Charles moved around each with an ease that suggested years, not months.

Which was impossible.

"What do you mean, you changed your mind? We talked about this, Charlie. Benji doesn't need expensive furniture that will just get scuffed up and ruined. CASA is fine for the nursery."

Benji started at hearing Kerry say his name, but Charles didn't look surprised at all. It was even more surprising than the fact that Charles was allowing the nickname. God knew he'd given Benji enough trouble about his own. He'd called him Benjamin most of the time, even though Benji thought it sounded pretentious.

"It fell apart in my hands! What if that happened when Benji's on it? We can afford something nicer. It'll be fine," he said, leaning in to press a kiss on a visibly exasperated Kerry's cheek.

Josie laughed again, relinquishing Charles's ears so she could pat his cheeks. "Kiss Daddy again, Dad," she demanded.

Charles obeyed, ducking in again and placing a smacking kiss against Kerry's cheek this time. Kerry laughed and swatted him away.

"Fine, you can have your hoity-toity furniture. But we're still getting these, right? I like them." He rifled through the cart and pulled out one of the colorful changing pads.

"Yeah, of course," Charles said. He ran a finger across the soft fabric, a small smile on his face. "His namesake would have loved this. Garishly colorful and from CASA. This was Benji's idea of heaven."

Benji choked. They were naming their son after him? The last conversation he'd had with Charles had involved him calling Charles pedantic. But it was like that had all been forgotten—Charles sounded fond when he talked about him.

It was like Benji was a distant memory for him, with all the hard edges and imperfections sanded down. Like he'd been gone long enough that Charles could be generous and remember only the good. The happy times. Like the way he'd teased Benji about his CASA addiction before things between them had degenerated and the barbs had become real instead of jokes.

Kerry wound his fingers through Charles's and squeezed, his expression soft and sympathetic. "You're sure naming the Blob Benjamin won't be too painful for you?"

Charles smiled and shook his head. "If this had been five years ago, when we were pregnant with Josie? Yes. If Josie had been a boy, I couldn't have. But now it feels right. It's been almost eight years." He raised their joined hands and kissed Kerry's hand. "Thanks for letting me. Not every guy would be okay with naming their only son after their husband's ex-boyfriend."

Kerry wrinkled his nose. "I'm not most husbands," he sniffed. His expression softened again. "And Benji isn't any ex. He was important to you, and you lost him, even though you weren't together at the time. And from what I've heard about him, he was a great person. The Blob could do a lot worse for a namesake than someone as kindhearted as your Benji."

Benji didn't bother trying to follow them as they made their way to the checkout. He felt rooted to the spot—he probably couldn't have moved even if he'd wanted to. He felt like he had ice water for blood, burning its way through his veins as his heart pumped it through his body.

But that was impossible because he didn't have a heartbeat. Not really. Or blood. He didn't exist. He'd died. He'd died, and Charles had moved on.

Five years ago, he'd said.

Five years ago he couldn't have named Josie after Benji, but now he could.

Because Benji had been gone for *eight years*, and now he was healed enough to hear his name again. Eight years.

Benji closed his eyes and took a breath, drawing air into lungs that didn't need to breathe. He searched the store for the familiar tug of Patrick's energy and pulled on it, popping into the café in a blink. Patrick was sitting there at his usual table, a wary expression on his face.

"Hey," he said, drawing the word out. There was a half-finished crossword puzzle on the table in front of him, but the boxes weren't filled in with Patrick's chicken scratch. A prop, then. Something to make it look like he hadn't been sitting there just waiting for Benji.

"How long have I been here?"

Patrick winced and tried to cover it with a smile. "Uh, about three seconds? Four, now."

Benji slammed his hand against the table. A couple at the table next to them jumped when the salt and pepper shakers rattled.

"In this CASA. How long have I been here, Patrick?"

Patrick shrugged. "Karin's the one who keeps employment records."

Benji clenched his fists and swept one arm out, sending the crossword puzzle to the floor. The couple next to them stood up and left, abandoning their meal with a nervous glance back.

"Don't fuck with me. Not about this," Benji bit out. "How long have I been here? It feels like a couple months, but it's not, is it?"

Patrick hesitated and then shook his head. "No," he said carefully. "Not exactly."

Benji blew out a breath through his nose, a bit surprised it didn't come out as fire. "What does that mean?"

"I don't know how much time has passed," Patrick said plainly. "Time does pass differently. I don't know why, I think it has something to do with the plane we're on. It intersects with the mortal one, but it's set apart. Different. A day for us could be a month or more for humans."

Benji swallowed. So Charles hadn't been hiding Josie from him. She hadn't been born when he'd been alive.

Patrick reached out but flinched away before he could make contact with Benji's arm. Smoke rose from his fingers, and he flexed them like he was trying to shake off a sting.

"Benji—"

The lights flickered in the café, and the chair Benji had been sitting in fell to the floor with a clatter when he stood up. "Don't," he spat.

Patrick held his hands up and stayed in his seat. "Go talk to Karin. She can answer your questions. She would have earlier, but I asked her not to."

That baffled Benji. "You asked her not to? Why?"

"I—"

Understanding crashed over Benji as he looked at Patrick's stricken face. "You didn't want me to know because you thought I'd leave," he said flatly.

Patrick's eyes slid closed, and he looked more vulnerable than Benji had ever seen him. It tugged at Benji's heart, but he was too incandescent with rage to succumb to it.

"Was I ever more than just a game to you? You might be determined to waste your future here, but I'm not. I'm not, Patrick. And you knew that. You knew I'd want to move on, and you lied to me so I wouldn't."

Patrick hung his head miserably. "Listen, I can explain—"

An hour ago, Benji would have been ecstatic to hear those words. But now? It felt like getting handed the keys to a house that had just been blown down by a hurricane. Meaningless. Empty.

He shook his head, snarling in disgust.

Benji's energy flickered, the tickle-flutter of it pushing against his skin like jumpy muscles. He usually kept his concentration centered on being. Existing. Staying corporeal. But right now that was the last thing he wanted. He let go of his control, let his energy dissipate and scatter.

He held Patrick's gaze until the last second. As his vision grayed out and his limbs faded into weightlessness, he shook his head again.

"No."

Chapter Fourteen: MODENA

PATRICK PLOPPED into the café chair across from Henry. The legs shrieked across the tile flooring. He buried his face in his hands, heaving long, groaning breaths.

Henry sat across from him and kept his blithe smile as he pushed a meatball around his plate.

Patrick wouldn't cry. He had been done with tears years ago. Tears were weakness, an admission that the offensive won. His shoulders shook, and a breath stuttered in his throat. Fuck that. He wasn't going there. Admitting defeat was for the man he used to be.

As much as he'd denied it, that man he used to be had come to the surface the moment Benji walked through those CASA doors.

He slapped the table and bellowed like a cornered wolf. Henry didn't blink when his glass rocked and his fork fell from his hand and then clattered to the floor. Frowning, Henry shifted awkwardly to retrieve his fork.

Patrick took a slow breath through his nose and out his mouth as he watched Henry consider whether his fork was still usable. Henry hummed a little tune as he wiped it off with his napkin and then inspected it again.

"Sorry," Patrick said and hung his head. It was useless thinking that Henry could hear him, and he knew that. "I've really done it now."

Henry sipped his tea, and Patrick followed his line of sight as he looked out the windows. The robins were gone, as were any remnants of the nest. How many generations had gone by, Patrick asked himself. Such a simple thing had steadied him and brought him comfort, like Henry's constant companionship. Henry wasn't much of a companion.

Over the years Patrick had stopped thinking of him as a person, another CASA regular, but a puzzle, a *thing* to figure out.

There was nothing to figure out. There was no great twist to the little old man who came on his own every day. Henry was just a guy that liked the ambiance. Patrick had set up in his head that Henry brought the crossword books for him, as if communicating, acknowledging his existence. He probably just left them behind out of forgetfulness.

As if in synchronization with his thoughts, Henry shifted in his seat and then reached into the interior pocket of his coat. He pulled out a crossword puzzle book and then placed it on the table between them. After a moment, he ceremoniously laid a new pen across the colorful cardstock cover.

Henry slid the book to Patrick's side of the table, and Patrick swallowed hard. Was it an offering? Was there something? Henry said nothing and sipped his tea, staring off into space.

Patrick shook his head in a slow, confused swivel.

Puzzles like Henry fascinated him. In all of his hunting for something to focus on instead of Benji, it was with Henry he could find the patience to sort out where he and Benji were going.

It was too late to turn back now. He and Benji had done things, said things, and all of them could never be forgotten. Patrick palmed his face.

"There are so many things I could do to him," Patrick muttered as he watched Henry. "You know that, right? Somewhere in there, you know."

Henry sipped his tea.

Patrick laced his fingers as he rested his elbows on the table.

"How long have we been doing this, Henry?" he asked. "How long have I been staring at you, and how long have you not blinked?" He leaned back, sighing. He knew. "Since Alec, right?"

Patrick blinked back the sting of regret welling in his eyes. That man's name was like poison. Alec's influence hung around CASA like a sickly film that could never wash off. He was everywhere. On every piece of furniture and on every inch of Patrick's skin.

He shivered with revulsion.

"That asshole doesn't deserve to be here anymore," Patrick said as if giving Henry a pep talk through his own crisis. "He got what he deserved. He left us."

Henry's silverware clinked across his plate in response.

Patrick scratched the back of his neck. He frowned. "Yeah. No one deserves that." He then forced a smile. "Do you remember him? Did you leave crosswords for him too?"

Henry took a bite of his gnocchi.

"Do you remember when I came here?" Patrick asked, knowing full well he wouldn't get so much as a grunt. "I was so… green." He clenched his fists, and turned to look out over the café.

"Alec." He snorted. "God. Alec. He was everything I wasn't." He spread his hands, trying to indicate Alec's magnitude. "He was magnetic. He made this place safe. We… we made it a home." Patrick swallowed, caught off guard by his confession. "I…."

Don't say it, he warned himself. He gritted his teeth. He wouldn't admit defeat. Alec didn't deserve that power over him anymore.

"He *used* me," he told Henry and then cleared his throat. "I was certain I was in love with him." Patrick scoffed. "Love? Here? What the fuck was I even thinking? What the fuck was I expecting? A house on a tree-lined street? A two-car garage? A dog and a cat? Maybe adopting a kid?" He coughed, holding in the urge to fall apart.

He balled his fingers into tight, angry fists. "He twisted all of that," Patrick growled out the words. "He twisted me into this. Into *him*."

Patrick leaned into Henry's space as he licked sweet tomato jam from his fork. "I've become him. And Benji had no idea."

He traced his fingers along the table, outlining Henry's food tray.

"There are rules," Patrick said. "Not to get close. Not to get involved. Not to…." He grunted, disgusted with himself. "Not to *feel*."

He nodded at Henry. "I bet you know how to feel. Or you knew once. Dancing with Raquel at the USO show? Germany, right? You were there?"

No answer. Just as well.

Patrick forced himself to swallow the lump in his throat. "I fucked up, Henry. I knew what I was doing. I knew damned well what I was doing. An Impression told me to drink the milk. What a fucking joke." He tossed up his hands. "Was I stupid? What the fuck is this? Love?" He spat the word like a curse. "Love is useless here."

He shuddered as his spiritual energy drained from him.

"But Alec. God. Dammit." Patrick growled. "He made me believe it."

"He betrayed you, didn't he?" Benji asked softly from the café entrance.

Patrick wished he had imagined it, but when he looked up, he saw Benji's adorable face marred with hurt and regret. Patrick's concrete attitude cracked.

"Yeah," Patrick said. He ran his fingers through his hair. Fuck. This was really happening. "Come on." He beckoned Benji forward.

Timidly, Benji stepped into the café, and Patrick moved to a different table from Henry. Benji joined him, remaining silent. Patrick had the floor, and he clenched his jaw. The terror of what he would say—what he had to say—would make or break them. Patrick's money was on break them.

"I was once an Impression," Patrick said slowly, waiting for the words to sink in. "Like you, though. Stronger. More cognizant. Not everyone that comes through here is like that. Most are the weak Impressions we see every day. We try to make the Impressions move on as quickly as possible, heal that missing piece of their soul by helping someone else, and then let CASA pass judgment on them." He held out his hand, gesturing to the showrooms beyond. "When they first arrive, Impressions are disoriented, confused. But the longer they stay, they become cognizant, they understand why they're here. Some of them realize they're dead. Some of them don't care that they are."

He met Benji's dark eyes and took a stuttering breath. Benji nodded, encouraging him to go on.

"But I lingered, and the more I lingered, the stronger I got. I became cognizant, formed logic, routines. I called it *hard data*. Things to ground me, to keep me from being—" He looked away from Benji as his lip trembled. He bit into it, trying to keep his expression even. "—afraid of going insane. I became tied to CASA. This had become my home."

"But you didn't linger just for fun…," Benji said.

Patrick shook his head. "I met Alec."

Benji filled in the blanks. "He was a Guide."

Patrick nodded and looked back at Benji. "He was much more than a Guide."

It was Benji's turn to look away. He fidgeted in his seat. "You loved him."

Taking a long sigh through his nose, Patrick waited as he tried to sort out what he was going to say. He settled on, "He had me convinced I did."

Benji snapped back, his eyes narrowed, brewing with an angry storm. Patrick leaned back, sensing the energy crackling off his body.

"He didn't convince you of anything," Benji growled as he rose from his seat.

This was it. The breaking point.

"You loved him," Benji snarled. "And you're too fucking afraid to admit it. You're too fucking afraid to admit you're terrified of what's out there. You don't even want to try to leave. You'd rather rant and rave that this is it, that CASA is your home, that CASA chose you. I have news for you."

"Benji...," Patrick whispered.

"This place?" Benji threw out a hand. "CASA is just a fucking store. It doesn't choose anyone. There's no magic to it. It's you. You choose to stay here. You don't want to take a chance because you're still just as scared as the day you came."

Patrick shot from his seat, and the lights flickered from his wrath. "I'm fucking scared because you're moving on without me," he bellowed.

Benji jerked back, his eyes wide.

Silence fell between the two of them. Patrick damned himself for saying it. But the truth was going to come out eventually. This would have all happened one day. It was best to do it now, when everything was so fresh, before it became unbearable. Benji would hate him for only a fleeting moment when he stepped out of the front doors into his new charmed life. He would forget him in an instant.

Patrick hung his head, cussing himself. "Dammit. It's for the be—"

"When... when did you know?" Benji said, his voice low, a cross between a whisper and a horrified accusation. "When did you know?"

"A while." Patrick threaded his fingers behind his head, trying to get his bearings.

"A while?" Benji repeated hatefully, his own energy making the lights flicker and fizzle. Around them, customers shook their heads in confusion at the faulty wiring. "And you thought keeping me here was a good idea?"

Patrick let out a frustrated groan. "Why do you need to make this so complicated?"

Benji was in front of him in an instant. "Why do you keep blaming others for your screw-ups? Is that how you work? So you can absolve yourself of guilt?" He gestured in the vague direction of the parking garage. "So you can just throw yourself at the Weople and have us blame *them* for killing you?"

The tables trembled around them as their mutual fury rose. Static sparked through the florescent lighting, and the bulbs hissed and popped inside their plastic housing.

"Benji…," Patrick bit out. "Please."

"What?" he snapped. "What could you possibly have to say? Some other excuse?"

Patrick spun away. He couldn't look at him. Instead, he looked to the window where the robins once were. They would never be back.

"I thought it could work," he told the window. "I thought we could be happy here. And we were. You know we were." Slowly, he turned to face Benji. "I had no one to go back to when I came here, so I didn't give it a second thought. And then you realized how differently time moves here. That what felt like a whirlwind love affair between us was really eight years. I saw that panic in your eyes. And when you wouldn't let me explain, I knew I'd fucked up. I knew we were over." He sighed, the fight sucked out of him. "You want the truth. You want me to stop blaming others. You're right. I loved Alec. I stayed for him. I never loved someone so damned much, and when he left he took a fucking piece of me that I could never get back."

He paced a slow circle around Benji, sensing his cooling aura. "Agnes and Karin tried. Fuck they tried. All that shit with CASA making you feel happy inside. I never felt happy inside. Impressions came and went. My life became the job." He nodded to Benji. "And then there was you."

Benji's lip quivered, and Patrick caught him nibbling at it to make it stop.

"And I was such a fucking idiot." Patrick looked to the burned out lights overhead. "I was the same douche bag that preyed on a doe-eyed Impression. First, it was out of boredom. But then…."

Benji nodded. "And then?"

Patrick smiled. "And then you woke up. And I felt… happy inside." He snorted. "Fuck, that sounds so stupid."

"Not really." Benji cast his gaze to the floor.

"Okay, then." Patrick puffed a steadying sigh. Clapping his hands once, he cleared his throat. "Well. I guess Karin will show you the way out from here."

He would leave it at that. He wouldn't say good-bye because the damned word would get stuck in his throat, and he'd already made it harder than it was. Patrick pressed his lips into a tight line that was an attempt at a smile but got nowhere close. He gave Benji a small nod and then slipped past him, making his way back into the showrooms.

There would be other Impressions. There would always be someone to help. And Patrick would always be the employee of the decade. Maybe he'd get employee of the century. Maybe finally get benefits.

He managed two steps before Benji clasped his wrist.

The thundering force of their combined energies sent Patrick crashing to his knees, but Benji remained on his feet. Arcs of lightning crackled through the café; the living patrons ran for cover as the fire alarm screeched through the store. Customers stampeded around them, racing for the doors and leaving their purchases behind.

Patrick struggled for breath, an instinct of the living, but his all the same. He searched for Henry in the commotion, but found his usual chair empty. At least he'd gotten away from Benji's fury.

Benji stood over him like an angry angel, but it was too late for Patrick to ask for forgiveness. He hauled Patrick to his feet and then shoved him back into a café chair.

Patrick stuttered, breathing hard. Benji flickered from existence and then materialized, straddling Patrick's lap. He clawed his fingers into Patrick's hard jaw, his eyes dark and gleaming.

"Why do you have to push?" Benji demanded in a hissing growl, throwing Patrick's words back at him.

Before Patrick could answer, Benji leaned in and slammed his mouth over Patrick's. Their energies warred with each other for dominance, every light in the café shattering as mass casualties.

Patrick growled against Benji's mouth, demanding he bow to him. But Benji refused and sank his nails into Patrick's scalp, holding him captive as their auras clashed together. Patrick had no choice but to comply as Benji forced his lips apart and tasted him in a long sensuous lick of tongue against tongue.

Patrick's breath quickened as Benji set out to conquer him. In a long roll of the hips, Benji didn't so much invite as demand, but one way or another, they were finally crossing the point of no return.

Cupping Benji's rear, Patrick answered by bucking against his hips. Benji pulled back, letting Patrick collect his wits. Benji balanced himself on Patrick's lap as they frotted against each other. Their auras sang, the pitch growing, screaming for a crescendo. Benji's lashes fluttered, and then finally he closed his eyes. He braced himself on Patrick's shoulders and bowed his head as Patrick worked him.

Patrick smirked. Benji had no clue what was happening to him. For such a simple act that at most would earn an awkward chuckle at a dance club, Patrick had Benji right where he wanted him as their auras thrashed.

"What are you…," Benji whispered, swallowing heavy breaths. "How are you doing that?"

Patrick slapped his hand around the back of Benji's neck. "Come. Here," he commanded and yanked him close. Possessing Benji's mouth, Patrick unleashed the pent-up lust fueling his spiritual energies into one perfect kiss.

The ceiling squealed and buckled, and water surged from the sprinkler system. The rush of water flooded the café and soaked them through. Water ran over Benji in rushing trails, down his shoulders, arms, over the back of his neck, and washed over Patrick, pooling between them.

Benji seized, all of his muscles contracting at once as he clung to Patrick. They rode the combustion of aura to aura together. Rain droplets sizzled on contact with their charged bodies. Patrick snaked one hand up Benji's shirt, dragging his nails down his back in burning lines. Benji shivered against him, unable to form words, his breath hitching against their kiss.

It wasn't enough.

Patrick needed him closer, against him, skin to skin, spirit to spirit.

He broke the kiss just long enough to pull his wet tee over his head, and then helped Benji do the same. There was no hesitation to behold each other, no ceremonial savoring the moment, just the primal hunger to spiritually fuck.

Their mouths met, and Benji tried to form words in between each point of contact. But it came out like mewling gibberish.

Patrick pulled away. "Shh, shh, shh…." he whispered and then kissed him again. "You liked that?"

Benji shakily nodded and his teeth chattered. Not from the cold, but from the shock to his system. "What the fuck was that?"

Patrick hooked two fingers under Benji's chin, guiding him to meet his gaze. Patrick rumbled his approval of Benji's blown pupils and slightly parted lips, high on taking an aura charge down the throat. Living blow jobs seemed mundane in comparison. He ran his thumb over Benji's bottom lip, and Benji sucked the digit into his mouth.

"Is that a suggestion?" Patrick asked as he appraised Benji's bravado. The poor guy still retained his humanity, and it was admirable. Perhaps a blow job wouldn't be out of the question. As much as he'd goaded Benji about them, he had forgotten what they could be like.

Benji leaned into Patrick and tucked his face against the crook of his neck and shoulder, his voice a raspy whisper. "Did you just fuck me?"

Patrick chuckled deep in his throat. He rewarded Benji with a firm pat on the rise of his ass. "Gold star for you."

Pulling away, Benji gave Patrick a scrutinizing look that he did not appreciate. "Do you even remember how to have sex like the living?" he asked.

Patrick snorted, spitting water from his mouth. "Of course I do."

"Well, we are dead. Can you even get it up?"

"What kind of fucking question is that?" Patrick snapped.

Benji grazed his fingers across the crotch of Patrick's wet jeans and gave a purposeful, grinding rub with his palm. He hummed in delight. "Seems you can," he coyly whispered.

"Shit," Patrick hissed as Benji took the initiative with fondling him. "You're a damned kindergarten teacher."

Benji tilted his head and watched Patrick under his heavy-lidded gaze. "No, I'm not," he purred, his voice almost getting lost in the hiss of the water. He boldly went for the button and fly of Patrick's jeans, and Patrick's thighs tightened in anticipation.

Patrick slipped his fingers under the waistband of Benji's jeans and sunk his fingernails into the supple flesh of his rear. He clenched his jaw as Benji took control. He couldn't help the harsh growl of release when Benji took his cock in hand and gave a long languorous stroke. Screw aura charges. Patrick shook at the memory of physical contact.

Benji pressed forward against him, and Patrick's lashes fluttered. Shit. He was losing it already.

"I'm not a kindergarten teacher," Benji whispered into the shell of Patrick's ear, his voice deep inside Patrick's head like a demonic warning. "Not anymore." He caught his earlobe in his teeth and dragged them across the flesh. "*I'm a Guide.*"

Patrick flailed under Benji's touch. Benji's confession rocked him. Had he finally given up his humanity, the idea of passing on, so they could stay here? Benji couldn't understand what it meant. It was the passion talking, and Patrick would let it ride to the end. He clung onto Benji by the neck and waist, desperate for something to hold while he fell into the needs he had long denied. He angled Benji for a crushing kiss to avoid screaming from the agony and ecstasy of remembering what it was like to be alive. He had been all talk when it came to offering below-the-belt pleasures. He never expected he'd be the first. Out of defense, need, and reciprocation, Patrick channeled another aura charge through the kiss.

Benji pulled back, howling in heat as he shuddered hard. Patrick held him tight, watching him ride it out. That perfect arch of the back was enough to drive out the final scraps of logic he had left.

Touching, making out, expressing passion was secondary.

The second Benjamin Goss walked into his café, Patrick came alive.

Benji blinked, and Patrick grinned as he noticed him struggle for focus. He was too blitzed out on repeated charges. Patrick had more experience with them; he could keep going for a while yet. Benji slapped his hands over Patrick's jaw and their foreheads met. Benji glared in determination, his pupils blown wide enough to resemble a shark in frenzy.

"Are you going to fuck me like a man, or are you going to keep fucking me like the shell you once were?" Benji snarled.

There were no words for Patrick, all his rationalizing, analyzing, and hard data gone in an instant. Who knew if the robins would ever return. Who knew when the CASA would be repaired. How many cycles of customers wearing shorts and flip-flops and then winter coats and boots. The need, the hunger, the very ache to take what Benji had long offered consumed him.

He gripped Benji by the wrists, tearing his touch off his person. Benji protested and tried to jerk free.

"Stop," Patrick warned him.

With a measure of his will, he flickered them both out of existence and materialized on his waterlogged MILAN bed.

The sprinklers streamed throughout CASA, ruining the particleboard and fabrics. None of Patrick's mending ability could fix any of it. He had to learn to accept he was never in control. He could never fix anything. Not even himself.

In this moment, as he pinned Benji to the mattress, hands around his wrists, straddling his waist, Patrick realized he had become so irreparably broken that he had fallen in love with a man he'd already said good-bye to in his mind.

If he lied to himself long enough that Alec had tricked him into loving him, he could believe it. He also thought if he could perpetuate the same lie that he didn't love Benji, he could believe that too.

But fuck it all. He couldn't make himself believe either.

As Benji shifted and struggled under him, Patrick watched him as if inspecting him for flaws, imperfections. Like he was nothing more than a piece of particleboard furniture. But he wasn't furniture. He was never ornamental.

Patrick eased his grip on Benji's wrists, and Benji drew his eyebrows upward in question. He went still, seeming to sense Patrick's change in dominance. Reaching out, Patrick slipped his fingers over Benji's cheek, finding his hard data to bring him back from his lapse in humanity.

He swallowed down the lump in his throat. Charles was an asshole to let Benji go. Patrick was a douche bag to think himself worthy.

Patrick had taught Benji how to eat, and the catharsis on Benji's face made him believe for once life in CASA wasn't so bad after all.

"Hey," Benji said softly, barely audible over the shower of water. He cupped Patrick's cheek, running his thumb over one of his eyelids. "You're going to be okay."

Patrick chuckled but couldn't hide his vulnerability under an impenetrable wall of bullshit this time. He bent forward over Benji, kissing him with the care and gentleness that they hadn't had until now.

"Take off your pants," he whispered against Benji's mouth.

With a nod, Benji obeyed, and his soggy jeans and boxers dispersed in trails of smoke and then were smothered by the sprinklers.

Patrick followed suit, his jeans gone and nothing but the open air of CASA between them. Patrick kissed him again, giving in to the human contact. He reminded himself that this was what it was like once, and experiencing it with Benji would change him forever after he was gone.

Patrick shifted to plant a hot trail of kisses down Benji's jugular, over the ridge of his collarbone, and then paid special attention to his breastbone. Benji tilted his head back, pressing it into the ruined MODENA mattress. He threaded his fingers through Patrick's wet hair as Patrick moved lower, licking over Benji's taut abdomen with the flat of his tongue.

"Fuck…," Benji let out in a slow sigh.

Patrick said nothing as he took Benji in hand. Benji clenched his fingers, pulling at Patrick's hair. Heh, right where he wanted him. He'd show Benji he definitely remembered what it was like to fuck like he was human.

It was like riding a bike.

Or so he assumed.

After a series of strokes to coax Benji into readiness, Patrick then made a long savoring lick up the base of Benji's length to the glistening head.

"You're doing *what*?" Benji squealed. It didn't come out as a question, instead a squeal of surprise.

"Relax," Patrick cooed. "Just go with it."

He caught Benji knitting his brows in that adorable way and added biting his lip to the mix. It took every ounce of Patrick's will not to cut the foreplay short and get on to screwing Benji senseless. Oh, he'd give him something to remember him by, wherever he ended up.

Patrick took Benji in his mouth, and his lashes fluttered with the silken skin against his tongue. He had forgotten how good it could be. Benji's grip on his hair faltered and then tightened as Patrick settled into the rhythm. Not needing to breathe had definite advantages.

Benji probably thought he was being sneaky about it when he started to rock his hips just slightly with Patrick's ministrations. Before long, Benji was guiding the pace on his own with his grip in Patrick's hair.

Patrick welcomed his brazenness. What started out as an appreciative blow job turned into a wanton face fuck. He surrendered to Benji's control. Sex was always about the other, or it was supposed to be, anyhow. What tricks he learned from one partner wouldn't work the same with another. He let Benji set the pace, let him know what he liked, how he wanted it, and who was truly in control of the situation.

"Shit!" Benji cried out as he spent himself into Patrick's throat.

Patrick blinked, surprised at the salty sweetness. It wasn't revulsion, or asking if he had a preference. Moaning around Benji's cock, he gladly swallowed.

Benji hissed a string of breathless cussing as he relaxed his grip and went limp.

Patrick could have been a jackass and channeled a charge from his mouth straight to Benji's cock, but he didn't want to overdose the guy and risk him dissipating into the ball pit. He released Benji and took care to suck him clean.

Benji watched him with a pleasure-drunk expression, his cheeks ruddy, looking ready for a nap.

Patrick laid his head on Benji's stomach, listening to the silence inside his body and the hiss of the water overhead. "I see someone enjoyed themselves," he said as he licked his bottom lip.

"Mmm-hmm," Benji murmured. "Sorry about... uh... you know...."

"Coming in my mouth?" Patrick asked with a devious grin. "Don't worry. Swallowing is one of the things I've missed."

"So...?" Benji asked, his tone hesitant. "You haven't done this in a while?"

Instead of running from the question, Patrick gave honesty a shot. "We only fucked via aura charges," he said as he watched Benji's expression become concerned. "Alec and I, and later me and any Impression who was down for it. Didn't even need to take our clothes off. Just a casual tap in passing would do it."

"Did you even kiss him?" Benji reached out and petted Patrick's wet hair.

"I haven't kissed anyone since I came here, until you."

Benji maintained his gentle touch, and the kindness steadied Patrick's potential for anxiety.

"He really dehumanized you," Benji said, and his mouth drew into a deep frown.

Patrick patted Benji's flat stomach. "Well, I have you now."

Benji laughed. "This lovey-dovey thing is definitely a new thing for you."

"I thought I'd try it on for size," Patrick said as he sat up. "Until the next time you piss me off."

They laughed together. But Patrick understood the irony of the phrase. There wouldn't be a next time. Dammit. He had been doing well until he reminded himself.

He had thought it would be easier to tear them apart while it was all still new and fresh. Easier to heal in time. But it was excruciating to feel the newness of deep possessive love only to let it go. He would have welcomed the years of falling out of love and anticipating the day he'd be rid of Benji.

But even the latter wasn't true. Patrick wanted Benji with him forever, and he would have done anything to keep him. He did do anything. But he couldn't hide from the truth.

And now, with Benji lying next to him, naked and honest, Patrick understood what it meant to let himself be open.

Better to have loved and lost than to have never loved at all.

Patrick was not one for the arts; logic was his speed. He only believed what was in front of him.

But as Benji watched him and seemed to wait for him to sort through it all, Patrick decided things like love are best left unexplained.

He leaned down to kiss Benji with a gentle chasteness.

Benji blinked, confused by the gesture.

"I want you on top of me, now," Patrick whispered and waited for Benji to understand. "Please."

Benji smiled and wrapped his arms around Patrick's neck. "You have no idea how long I've been waiting for that."

Chapter Fifteen:
TRIGNO

SEX WITH Patrick was a revelation. And not in a biblical way, though the screaming of the fire alarms and the cold, wet mist from the sprinklers did give it an air of the end of times. As did the obvious resignation that seemed to weigh Patrick down. This was good-bye for Patrick. It was hard to castigate him for being so selfish when giving himself to Benji like this was such a selfless act.

Benji had lost count of the number of Impressions he'd helped. So many lives saved, but none of them had been his ticket to moving on.

He took a minute to collect himself, gentling Patrick with soft caresses over his wet torso. No goose bumps, despite the chill from the water. Another benefit of being dead, he supposed. Patrick's skin seemed to glow from the inside. The golden hue conjured thoughts of lazy island vacations and hot summer nights. The kinds of things they'd never be able to share.

It wasn't just the energy transfer. Benji's skin was still as marble-pale as always, bluish in the cast of the shadows from the weak emergency lights.

So this was how Impressions knew who they had to help. It wasn't a question—Benji instinctively knew. The magnetic pull he'd always felt, tugging him insistently toward Patrick, suddenly made sense. It was more than just the attraction that had thrummed through him from their first meeting. It was CASA.

Benji had been a doormat all his life. He put himself last. He catered to others' needs while ignoring his own. It had gotten him killed. The DEL TORO bookcase had been the instrument, but his own lack of self-worth had been the real cause.

And now he had the chance to save Patrick from the same fate. Even though he was already dead, he couldn't move on if he was missing that important piece. Patrick's fear of the unknown kept him here, sure. But so did his belief that he wasn't good enough to move on. He wasn't worthy.

Benji felt warmth coalesce in his chest. This was the right path.

And it wasn't a hardship by a long shot. He already loved and respected Patrick. Now he just had to convince Patrick to love and respect himself, and he knew exactly how to do it. He'd worship him the way Alec should have. The way Patrick should have demanded that anyone who had the fortune to take him to bed did. He'd show Patrick how much he was worth, and how treasured he was.

Patrick threw himself into carnal pleasures the same way he did into everything else—wholly and with no thought to the consequences.

That wasn't a surprise. Anyone who spent any time at all with Patrick could tell he was a fallout-be-damned kind of guy. All action and no forethought. And Benji probably knew that better than most, given that he'd spent the last eight years with him.

Benji drew in a breath, reveling in the way he could feel his lungs expand. He felt more alive than he had in a long time. Ironic, since he'd never been so certain he was dead.

Patrick's kisses were insistent. He went in with hard edges and no finesse. Benji nipped at his lip to slow him down, showing him how he wanted to be kissed. Softly, slowly, with no urgency. Like they had all the time in the world. Like there was no one else anywhere on any plane of existence who deserved Benji's time and focus more.

Patrick tensed, and Benji shifted until he was straddling him, holding his hips back so Patrick didn't rush into more frottage. Benji deepened the kiss, delving languorously into Patrick's mouth, stroking over the sharp points of his teeth and the tongue that was just as sharp in its own way. It didn't take long for Patrick to catch on, and Benji relaxed against him when Patrick gave himself over to the kiss, all of the tension flowing out of his body as Benji settled on top of him.

He brought a hand up to card through Patrick's hair, scratching his nails against Patrick's scalp. Patrick groaned softly, melting into Benji's gentle touch.

"No energy exchanges," Benji murmured. He tucked his face against Patrick's neck and licked at the skin, disappointed that it didn't have the salty tang of sweat. It wouldn't, of course, but he missed it all the same. "I'm going to make love to you in a very—" He nipped at the supple skin under his teeth, making Patrick squirm and laugh. "mortal—" He nosed up the column of Patrick's throat, pressing a kiss to where his pulse should be thrumming. "—way," he finished, and he punctuated it with a nuzzle against his jaw and a quick kiss on his swollen lips.

Patrick rolled his eyes but didn't protest. Benji lowered his head and pressed a row of kisses down his chest, paying special attention to each of Patrick's nipples, which reddened and stood up pertly after being laved by Benji's tongue.

He continued down, sucking what he hoped would be a hickey at the hard ridge of Patrick's hip. The sprinklers had stopped at some point, and the quality of light was different. Brighter. The emergency lights had been replaced by the soft glow of the overhead fixtures that stayed on even at night. How could he not have noticed how time passed here? It was so glaringly obvious now.

Benji laughed inwardly at the thought that he'd been kissing Patrick for days. He'd said that to a lover once, caught up in the poetry of promising to worship someone for days on end. It had been melodramatic and overdone at the time, but now it was just a truth. He could easily spend weeks, months, years tangled up with Patrick here in this corner of CASA where no one existed but them.

But he wouldn't. It wasn't fair to either of them. They needed to move on so Benji could make similar promises to Patrick wherever the next plane of existence took them.

He kissed his way down the crease of Patrick's hip, carefully skirting around the hot flesh that waited there and continuing his thorough adulation down Patrick's muscled thigh instead.

Patrick had been up on his elbows, watching Benji's slow descent, but he flopped down onto the mattress with a sorrowful moan. "You're killing me."

Benji grinned but didn't stop kissing him until he reached Patrick's foot. He licked the instep, making Patrick's leg jerk as he shrieked in delighted surprise.

"You're already dead," Benji said with a shrug. He met Patrick's sparkling gaze and then ducked down to continue, starting with the other foot.

Patrick was ready for him this time and didn't start when Benji swept his tongue over the tender bottom of his foot. He shivered when Benji moved up to press a soft kiss against the inside of his ankle, skating his lips over the thin skin like a whisper.

Or maybe more like a prayer. Benji believed in God, and that belief helped reassure him that there would be something even better waiting for him on the other side of those CASA doors. But Patrick didn't, and that was okay. He just had to believe in Benji. And himself. That would be enough.

Benji had outlawed energy exchanges, but that didn't stop him from pouring all of his love and trust into each kiss as he made his way up Patrick's leg. It wasn't the same zing as the way they could shift their auras to each other, but he could tell from the way Patrick was mumbling and writhing that it was more than just a normal touch. Maybe he really was able to put his intentions and feelings into his kisses. Why not? He had no idea what was possible here, but that hardly seemed far-fetched. And he really liked the idea of Patrick seeing himself through Benji's eyes, or through his emotions, at least. What better way to show Patrick how special he was and how much Benji believed in him?

Patrick was back up on his elbows by the time Benji looked up again. He held eye contact with him when he let his questing fingers softly catch against the skin of Patrick's scrotum. Patrick lurched like he'd been struck by lightning, his hips coming up off the bed at the unexpected caress.

"Easy there," Benji said, his lips curved into a self-satisfied smile. "Wouldn't want to pull a muscle. Since you're so out of practice, you know."

Patrick swatted at him. His breath came in heavy gasps, which Benji took as a compliment since neither of them actually needed to breathe. If he'd managed to make Patrick forget that, then he was on the right track.

Emboldened by Patrick's reaction, he slipped between Patrick's thighs and nudged his legs up, making a space for himself between them. Before Patrick could question it, he leaned in and licked a firm stripe down his perineum. Patrick's hips bucked up again, and this time Benji curled his fingers around Patrick's cock, stroking him slowly as he licked his way along until he could circle his entrance with his tongue.

"Christ on a motherfucking crutch," Patrick bit out, the words slurred and at least an octave higher than his usual.

Benji flicked his wrist on the next upstroke, the way eased by the precome that had been steadily leaking down Patrick's shaft during Benji's slow journey down one side of his body and up the other.

"Okay?" he asked, lifting his head so he could see Patrick. Rimming wasn't something everyone was comfortable with, though Benji had found that was more true on the giving end than the receiving end. But he didn't know where Patrick stood on it, and he didn't want to do anything that made him uncomfortable.

From the heavy-lidded look Patrick was giving him, though, Benji was fairly certain he wasn't going to object.

"Mmm," Patrick hummed. He let his head fall back onto the pillows but pulled his legs in tighter, giving Benji better access. It was all the answer he needed.

Benji wasn't coordinated enough to give a decent hand job while rimming. He gave Patrick another hard stroke and then slid his hand down to help spread his cheeks apart, giving himself unfettered access to Patrick's hole. A few broad strokes of his tongue against the sensitive flesh had Patrick's thighs trembling and his voice breaking as he said Benji's name.

Benji took his time, opening Patrick up with his tongue before adding his fingers into the mix. He couldn't fuck him, not without lube, and that wasn't the type of thing they stocked at CASA. It was a pity, but there wasn't anything they could do about it.

Benji pressed one last sucking kiss to the swollen skin and leaned up on his own elbows, bracing himself so he could swallow Patrick's length down and still have a finger buried inside him. Patrick hissed out a breath and came before Benji managed to open his throat enough to take him all the way in.

Benji tightened his lips around Patrick's cock and worked him through his orgasm. Patrick clenched down around his finger so tightly that he couldn't have moved it if he'd wanted to. So he didn't. From Patrick's shuddery breaths and half-voiced sobs, he was already at the brink of too much sensation—that might send it over into pain instead of pleasure, and that was the last thing Benji wanted.

"You're going to be okay," he said softly, unsure whether Patrick was awake or not.

Patrick snorted. Awake, then.

"Don't sell yourself short. I'm a hell of a lot better than okay," he said with a snicker.

Benji sighed. The walls were already going back up. Patrick was building up his defenses.

"I can't stay," Benji said.

"No, of course not," he said, and all traces of good humor fled from Patrick's tone. He rolled over, but Benji didn't let him get far. He pressed a kiss between Patrick's tense shoulder blades and scooted forward so he could spoon him. They fit together perfectly like this too.

"This isn't a place we're supposed to linger," Benji said quietly. "You feel it too, don't you? You talk about CASA like it's an entity, but it's not. It's just a place. The uneasiness, the energy coiling under your skin sometimes? That's not the CASA. That's you. It's your essence trying to get you to pass through those doors."

Patrick made a tight sound, like air hissing through clenched teeth. "And you're suddenly the expert on the afterlife, are you? Where were you all those years ago? Back when your advice might actually have made a difference?"

Benji bit his lip to keep from responding. Where had he been all those years ago, when Patrick was a fresh-faced newbie in awe of an all-powerful Guide named Alec?

He'd been a baby. If he'd even been born. And he knew that was what Patrick wanted him to say. He wanted to keep it light, to keep it easy between them tonight. "No strings attached" wasn't possible, but he could tell from the way Patrick was holding himself taut, angling himself away from Benji, that he was trying to sever them as neatly as possible.

Well, fuck that.

"You're a good person, Patrick Bryant."

Patrick choked, his body going from tense to ramrod straight in a millisecond.

"You deserve good things. You deserve a second chance, and a third one. You deserve all the chances you need to get it right, because you are kind and compassionate. You're a beautiful person inside and out, and I'm so sorry that Alec shook your confidence in yourself. If you could see what I see, Patrick, you'd have moved on years ago."

Patrick rubbed his face against the RIMINI pillow, but not fast enough to hide his tears. He didn't pull away when Benji tucked his face against the back of his neck, tears prickling in his own eyes as well. He'd watched Patrick slip a similar pillow out of someone's cart awhile back, replacing it with a firmer MESSINA model because the man was an alcoholic who frequently went to bed so smashed that he passed out from it. Like the Impression that had saved him, he would have suffocated with his face pressed into the too-soft pillow one night if Patrick hadn't intervened.

How could a man who spent his life saving others think he wasn't worth anything?

"If there's only one thing you take away from our time together, I want it to be this," he said quietly. He could feel Patrick's chest rise under his hand and stay that way—he was holding his breath. "You don't exist because of CASA. And I know that's hard to accept because we don't know why we're here, not really. But CASA isn't the thing that's tethering you here. That void you feel inside your chest? It isn't being filled by CASA any more than it could be filled by me. It's you, Patrick. It's a space inside you for you, and you need to fill it before you can move on. That's the secret. That's why we see Impressions smiling as they step out of those doors. They're at peace."

Patrick had started breathing again, ragged, soft snuffles that he tried to drown out by pressing his face against the pillow.

"You know why? It's not because whatever they see past those doors is so awesome. I mean, don't get me wrong. I hope it is awesome. I hope it's the most amazing thing I've ever seen. But it wouldn't matter, because once you're at peace, anywhere is utopia."

He kissed Patrick's bare shoulder and pulled the coverlet up around them. It was dry, but the mattress underneath them was still soggy, though it hardly mattered. They were both out in seconds.

Chapter Sixteen: SACCO

HAND IN hand, they walked the aisles of CASA one last time. Instead of a hurried pace, they took every second of time they could squeeze out of a leisurely stroll. They occasionally paused to admire various ruined home furnishings and pretended they too were shopping for an apartment they'd never share. A crew had appeared earlier that morning to start hauling things away, presumably to a gigantic fleet of Dumpsters outside.

"That's the best sofa," Benji said as he patted the SACCO's upholstery. "It would go awesome in the den."

Patrick nodded and played along. The wet carpet squished under his feet. "And those throw pillows would add just the right pop of color."

Benji leaned into him, and Patrick wrapped an arm around his waist. They hummed thoughtfully, and Patrick treasured the tenderness. He rested his chin on the top of Benji's head. "If we're going to pick out window treatments, there better be a goddamn ring on my finger."

Benji stiffened in his grasp. Patrick tensed as well. In all of his fight to make it a positive farewell, he'd just dicked it up.

Benji wiped at his nose and sniffed. "I didn't think you were the marrying kind," he said softly.

Patrick arched a brow as Benji looked up at him. He was smiling brightly despite the tears that glazed his eyes. Patrick tried to collect his thoughts. "This isn't about me," he said, urging him on through the showrooms. "This is your day."

Benji nodded and smudged away the water collecting in his lashes.

"Come on, now. You said so yourself. I'm going to be okay." He would hold on to those words for years to come. Benji's laughter and love would remain in his nonexistent heart. His kindness would be his persistent memory that he would persevere.

The future was a long line of unknowns for Patrick. What would happen the day the CASA closed for good? The day it was demolished? Where would he go then? What about Agnes and Karin? They were the only family he had known.

The unknowns were there, the reminders that things in life were never fair, nor were things in death. He smiled upon Benji, and when Benji returned the affection, he quickly looked away, trying to collect himself.

As they reached the long row of cash registers, the morning light slowly crept across the floor in long, flat golden pools.

Patrick shivered. He patted his chest, trying to slow his pounding heart. It was so stupid. He didn't have a heart. Or any other internal organs, for that matter. He believed he had them because of the psychological sense he needed them.

Benji tightened his grip on his hand, and Patrick made a slight nod.

They reached the final steps next to the corralled shopping carts and stopped by the cheerful blue-and-yellow umbrella stands. Patrick laid his hands on Benji's shoulders and then rubbed down the length of his arms. He said nothing as Benji watched him. All the while, Patrick silently committed him to memory.

Benji pressed closer, their bodies meshing one last time and their energies singing to each other. He reached out and grazed his fingers through the short scruff at the back of Patrick's neck. Benji's smile would be the one thing he'd miss most. That and his relentless optimism that CASA can indeed be a place of happiness.

The store would be a little emptier without him, but as Patrick lost himself in those big brown eyes, he knew Benji's influence would live on. He looped his arms around Benji's waist, pulling him tighter as their auras transferred back and forth. He savored the love between them.

Benji gave him an impish grin. "Are you going to kiss me, or are you planning to give me an aura charge for the road?"

Patrick puffed out his bottom lip in a mimicry of undue hardship. "How dare you make such an unseemly accusation. I've been nothing but a gentleman to you, cupcake."

Benji curled his lip, chuckling. "Do you ever listen to yourself?"

Patrick leaned in and planted a kiss on Benji's forehead. He inhaled his spicy scent. "Nope. And never will," he mumbled against Benji's skin.

As he pulled away to regard him, Benji got the drop on him by yanking him close to possess his mouth. Patrick tensed in surprise at Benji's newfound forwardness, but then he relaxed into it. He cupped Benji's cheek with one hand and held him by the waist with the other. Benji parted his lips, and Patrick answered the invitation, tasting his sweetness.

The nostalgia of their dinner date swept across his mind. He had been surprised then in the moment of passion in a human form. Now, he would treasure their last kiss together. His knees buckled with the shock of intense pleasure darting through every nerve. Benji held fast to him; despite his slight stature, he managed to keep Patrick from toppling.

They pulled away, panting for breath, and their foreheads beaded with a slight sheen of sweat fresh from spiritual climax.

Patrick croaked with a ragged laugh. "Jackass."

Benji winked. "It's your fault. You suggested it."

"Ah. Blaming others for your actions?"

"I have this asshole boyfriend that does it all the time. So annoying."

Sucking in a contented sigh, Patrick gave Benji's rear a firm pat. "There will be other asshole boyfriends," he said.

Benji nestled his head under Patrick's chin and hummed. "Why do you think there would be others?"

"I don't know." Patrick snorted. "Are you done with assholes?"

Benji gave him a wink. Patrick had no idea what it meant. "I didn't say I was done, did I?"

"Okay. Sure. Uh-huh, Yoda."

"Everything happens for a reason," Benji said and sighed sleepily.

Patrick swallowed. If he said any more, he'd lose his mettle. The words Benji had uttered while their heads shared the same pillow echoed through his head. Knowing he was loved like that, that someone thought he was worthy of that kind of devotion and fervent belief—it lightened something in him he hadn't known was burdensome, even though it had been hard to hear. He glanced at the pneumatic doors and then back at Benji. He smiled as his chest expanded with a deep calming breath. Rubbing at his eye again with his thumb, he couldn't fake that it was just something in his eye anymore. He cleared his throat and nodded with a smile that didn't reach his eyes.

"Do you want Karin to walk you out? She's better at this," Patrick said as his voice embarrassingly cracked. Dammit. He had to keep it together. He couldn't stand for Benji to pass on feeling guilty for leaving.

Benji took his hand, lacing their fingers together. He gently kissed Patrick's knuckles. "I'm sure you're just as good at it."

Patrick snorted, trying to choke down the building lump in his throat. He nodded to avoid fucking up anything with useless words.

Benji turned to the doors, the sunlight on his face banishing the deathly cast they all had. His eyes seemed to catch a spark of something, losing their murkiness and becoming brilliant with life.

Patrick pressed his fingers to his lips. Once he would have faked yawning to save face. Now it was to keep from outward gasping. So this was what it was like for Karin? Watching Impressions come back to life right in front of her? Seeing them off as they gained clarity that CASA wasn't the end—it was just an errand on the way to something bigger?

The rays filtered through Benji's dark hair, and Patrick would have made a joke about it, but Benji looked like an angel come to Earth.

Stay. Patrick wished inside his mind.

Stay.

Stay.

Stay. Stay. *Stay!*

He couldn't keep Benji anymore. He had been selfish, arrogant, and outright malicious. Patrick cleared his throat, and Benji startled.

"You okay?" Benji asked and took Patrick by the hand.

Patrick nodded and had to clear his throat again before he could speak. "Yeah." He smiled weakly. "You should go. I'm pulling a double today and got a fuckton of prep to do."

Benji knitted his brows in that adorable way that was like a punch to the gut. It was at that first expression Patrick knew he was done for, even if he didn't realize it at the time. Benji nibbled at his bottom lip. "You'll remember what we talked about, right?"

Patrick smiled. "Absolutely," he lied. "Make sure to tell all your new angel buddies about me."

"Angels?" Benji snorted. "Since when do you believe in angels?"

"Since I met yo—"

Benji whacked him on the arm. "Are you getting all Hallmark on me?"

Patrick reeled back and feigned grave injury. "How could you accuse me of such a thing?" He playfully checked over his arm for broken bones. "I think I'll live."

They blinked at each other and then shook their heads.

"Living jokes really do get old," Benji said as he glanced to the doors.

"You know what gets old?" Patrick said, crossing his arms. "Coffee. Coffee gets old. So go on. Get. Before Karin hogs all the creamer."

Benji turned his back to Patrick, fully facing the doors. Patrick gnashed his teeth but forced himself to relax. He had to watch. He would have to watch this happen for many more years to come.

He took one slow breath and then another, his chest rising and falling, trying to steady his hammering heart. He closed his eyes and let himself accept the moment.

His yellow employee shirt, the very symbol of his purgatorial prison bled away into a soft, faded black Nine Inch Nails T-shirt, the white screen-printing of the distinct NIN logo cracked and ragged from the many years of wear and tear. The fabric of his skinny jeans shifted and shortened into baggy camouflage cargo shorts, the frayed hem brushing like spider webs against his knees. His toes curled and then eased into his well-loved black and red Air Jordans.

They were the last set of clothes he had wanted to see when he had first come to CASA. The reminder that he was once human. The reminder he had a heart.

Now he never wanted to take them off.

"Hey," he said as Benji kept his attention fully on the doors.

Benji spun on his heel and then stumbled back. He tilted his head and pursed his lips.

"That's you?" Benji asked softly. He arched a brow, and Patrick watched him puzzle through it.

Patrick nodded and stuffed his hands in his pockets. He blinked as a piece of crumpled cardstock brushed his fingers. Pulling out the piece of trash, he smirked and held it up for Benji's examination. "*Aeon Flux*," he said, reading the print on the ticket stub. He chuckled. "That was such a shit movie."

Benji latched on to his worn-out T-shirt and hauled him close. Their mouths met. Patrick scrabbled for a handhold on Benji. Crushing him close, Patrick would force them to be one person if he could. Benji had coaxed him into being gentle last night, but there was nothing gentle about how they clung to each other. Shivering from their auras igniting, and the deep love that would endure, they breathed the same breath. Overhead, the electrical systems hummed to life around them. The auxiliary lights flicked on in marching rows, and the ventilation hissed and sucked the airflow.

The doors parted, flooding them with the blazing morning light. Construction crews flowed through the doors and around them like water over stones. Men clicked on their flashlights and gathered by the umbrella stands as they considered the floor plans. Fire marshals confirmed orders into their walkie-talkies. Harried employees followed next, leading work crews to the most affected areas. Patrick caught a glimpse of Tommy out of the corner of his eye. The poor kid seemed to notice him too. Patrick winked at him, and Tommy jolted like he was about to swallow his tongue.

Sighing, Patrick pressed his forehead to Benji's, and they listened to the chattering wave flow around them. He ran his thumb over Benji's bottom lip. "You're making me late for work, cupcake," he whispered. "We're going to stop playing this 'I love you, I love you more' shit."

Benji took Patrick's thumb in his mouth and nodded. He let go of Patrick and then took a hesitant step toward the entrance as repair crews slid past them.

"It's beautiful," Benji said in awe.

Patrick blinked through the spots in his eyes. When his vision adjusted to the consuming light, he choked. "Would you look at that?"

Benji turned to him, his brows drawn in question. "You've seen it all along, haven't you?"

Patrick shrugged. "It was faint, but yeah. I couldn't make out what it was, exactly. But it hasn't opened onto the abyss for me in a very long time."

Benji looked out the doors and turned back to Patrick questioningly. "And now?"

Puffy white clouds drifted across the crystalline blue skies. The manicured trees lining the sidewalks seemed to glow green from within. Birds cooed to one another as they fluttered along. Patrick's beloved robins zipped across his line of sight, heading away from CASA, across the shiny black parking lot leading into the horizon. A resplendent big box store monolith rose in the distance. The iconic red circular signage called them forth like a heavenly voice.

Patrick smiled faintly. "It's a Scope."

Benji beamed. "Not just any Scope. It's a Super Scope. Bet it has a Queequeg Coffee inside."

"Is that the frou-frou coffee place thing where people order shit with too many words and you pay six bucks for it?"

Benji gasped in mock affront. "Heathen." He tilted his head and flicked a glance over Patrick's outdated clothes. "Holy shit, you've actually never been to a Queequeg Coffee, have you?"

Patrick shook his head.

"Oh, man. I can't wait to see your face the first time you take a sip."

"I am not paying fucking six bucks for coffee with a name I can't pronounce."

It was a joke, but Patrick's stomach lurched. Benji was talking like they had a future together. Like he'd be there with him. Like they'd be there together.

For the first time ever, standing in front of the doors didn't make Patrick's heart race and his palms sweat. He felt peaceful. At home. Right. He looked down at his outfit and snorted. At least at Scope he wouldn't need to rely on Lost and Found.

Benji reached out for his hand. He nodded toward Scope. "Coffee date?"

There were a thousand reasons to say no. Maybe more. The unknown wasn't any more defined today than it had been yesterday. But somehow it didn't look as bleak with Benji by his side.

Slapping his hand into Benji's, Patrick took the lead. "Race you."

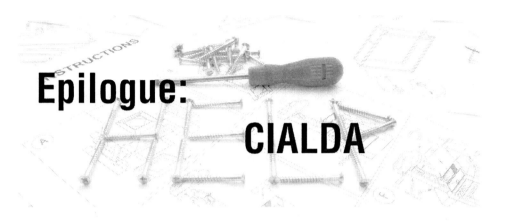

Epilogue: CIALDA

AGNES STEPPED lightly through the empty aisles. Silent serenity reigned over the affordable furniture.

She smiled, full of such pride the lighting flickered over her head. Patrick had finally taken the chance to leave. All it took was Benji's gentle coaxing and infectious innocence to make Patrick realize he could breathe again.

Agnes wrinkled her nose. Gentle coaxing couldn't be further from the truth. They had all dragged Patrick kicking and screaming like a child throwing the most irrational of tantrums in the middle of a department store.

She glanced around her. The store hummed with sleeping energy. She snorted at the irony. Stubborn shit though he was, Agnes understood the torture he had hidden in the deepest parts of himself. At last he knew peace.

Wherever he and Benji had gone—Scope, or even that cute new bistro on the corner—Agnes knew they'd found their little slice of heaven.

Patrick would finally experience fatherhood with Benji. They'd have the white picket fence, two cats and a dog, and the love Patrick was convinced he never deserved.

Agnes loved him like a son, and now she regretted not telling him more.

As she stood in the silence, she didn't realize the void Patrick and Benji had left behind. Their laugher was a fleeting memory, as were their stolen kisses in inappropriate places. Patrick had said he never cared as a defense mechanism against ever getting attached. But with Benji at his side, he didn't have a care in the world.

Drifting into the bedding showroom, she found Patrick's beloved MILAN bed. It had been remade with a new MODENA mattress and colorful feminine sheets with a coordinating duvet. The shiny plastic price tag proclaimed the bed was on final clearance.

Agnes chuckled and slowly passed her hand over the tag, altering the lettering to read:

For Display Only

It was the least she could do in his memory. Patrick would have been over the moon if he knew the best-selling line in all of the CASA corporation was the worst seller in their store. He had been adamant about protecting his sacred space, and it was a duty that Agnes would proudly uphold.

"I thought they'd never leave," Karin said from behind Agnes. There was a smile in her tone. "I hate to say it, but I'm going to miss them."

Agnes turned toward her and frowned with firm disapproval. "If I had to listen to Patrick's incessant whining for one more day, I would have fed him to Jabba myself." She straightened her cardigan primly.

Karin smirked, and reached out to pat her shoulder. "It's okay to miss them." Her lips pulled into a hungry grin. "How about some meatballs? Henry is pitching one hell of a fit."

Agnes pinched the bridge of her nose, trying to ease away a headache. "I owe that man everything. He has the patience of a saint."

"Look who's talking," Karin said as she stood straighter, beaming with pride.

Agnes took the lead to the café, only walking two steps away from Patrick's MILAN and then dispersing into sparks of light. She winked back into existence in the darkened café at the head of the lunch counter. The various dishes and desserts were prepped and ready for service once CASA opened for the day. The frozen tiramisu slowly thawed in the refrigeration case. A sheen of condensation glistened across the dusting of cocoa powder.

Agnes wrinkled her nose in amusement. Tiramisu. Patrick's favorite thing. As much as he insisted he couldn't eat them anymore, Agnes knew he must have snuck a few once in a while. She laughed behind her fingers. That boy.

She went through the motions of preparing herself a plate. Agnes gave a shifty glance around the café as Henry chowed down on his meatballs with a broody frown. She took her chance and pilfered extra POLPETTA meatballs, but went light on the gnocchi, yet heavy on the sweet tomato jam. No one ever knew of her vices.

She said nothing as she joined Henry at his usual table. He chewed angrily on his meatballs as he glared at his crossword puzzle like the page had called him a string of profanities.

"It's not going to run away, dearest," Agnes cooed as she gently speared a steaming meatball.

Henry grumbled and then took another mouthful of gnocchi. "You know how long I've been starving?" he mumbled around a full mouth.

"Long enough," Karin said as she materialized in the chair next to him. She rubbed her hands and smiled gleefully at her plate of CIALDA waffles topped with an overload of whipped cream.

"There was only so much pushing a meatball around my plate and meaningfully staring off into space I could take before I wanted to smack the shit out of that arrogant man," Henry rumbled and then shoved another meatball in his mouth. "He took my crosswords. They were *mine*."

Agnes gave him a comforting pat on the back of his hand. "You made a noble sacrifice, my love."

"You try next time and see how long you last," Henry pouted. His distinguished brow furrowed in that petulant way. "You couldn't go a minute without correcting them."

Agnes huffed. Henry had a way of getting under her skin. "Everyone has their own methods," she said and then adjusted her glasses. "But mine are better."

They laughed together, the CASA filling with a new kind of joy. Patrick and Benji were gone, and they wouldn't remember their time as spirits here.

Henry laced his fingers with hers, and Agnes blushed.

Karin blinked owlishly. "All right, you lovebirds," she warned them as she wiped a dab of whipped cream from the corner of her mouth.

Agnes snorted. "One day, you will learn the joy of finding your missing piece."

Karin crunched on one of her waffles and glowered at Agnes. It was her attempt at silencing her jabs, but Agnes reveled in the fact that she'd won.

"Um…. Excuse me…?" A young man's voice carried over the café.

The three of them were shocked to attention and turned toward the sound.

With a carefree smile, the young man brushed away the dark curly mop of hair hanging in his eyes. He shuffled his feet, his cowboy boots clicking across the floor. He wore the trendy worn jeans that all of the modern young men seemed to favor these days, and a slim-fitting tee printed with the words I'm A Pepper Too!

Agnes narrowed her eyes, perplexed by the oddity that somehow this new Impression seemed to be a perfect mix of Benji and Patrick's traits in one man. She glanced at Karin and then back at the young man. Karin held her fork to her lips, but her cheeks flushed an impossible-to-miss pink.

Henry smirked at Agnes and gave a conspiratorial nod. He ruffled his crossword puzzle page and pretended to ponder the next clue. "Looks like someone has a new job to do," he muttered out of the corner of his mouth.

Karin puffed out her cheeks in annoyance. She glared at Henry like a teenager humiliated for gawking at a rock star. Agnes held her tongue and fought every urge not to burst into cackles.

The young man stepped further into the café, and Karin shot to her feet.

"I didn't think they let customers in before opening," he said somewhat sheepishly. He smiled apologetically to them. "I'm really not sure how I got here, come to think of it."

"I can help with that," Karin said with a polite nod.

Agnes pretended to make herself busy as she stole a glance at Karin wringing her hands behind her back.

Standing straighter, Karin held her head high like a proper young lady. "What's your name?"

The Impression rubbed at the back of his head, his dark curls fluffing around his face. He seemed at a loss for words as he tried to recall.

Henry glanced at Agnes, and Agnes waved him off. Together they waited for the Impression to gain clarity.

"Adam," he said and nodded as if it had just come to him. "It's Adam."

Karin sucked in a slow breath, seeming bewildered.

"I'm Karin," she said extending a hand and casting a radiating smile. "Welcome to CASA."

Agnes smiled broadly as Karin excitedly elaborated on the finer points of employment. She giggled to herself.

Henry arched a brow. "You old meddler."

She winked at Henry. "Life is a lot like CASA furniture. It comes in pieces, and some assembly is required."

LEX CHASE once heard Stephen King say in a commercial, "We're all going to die, I'm just trying to make it a little more interesting." Now she's on a mission to make the world a hell of a lot more interesting.

Weaving tales of sweeping cinematic adventure—depending on how she feels that day—Lex sprinkles in high-speed chases, shower scenes, and more explosions than a Hollywood blockbuster. Her pride is in telling stories of men who kiss as much as they kick ass. If you're going to march into the depths of hell, it better be beside the one you love.

Lex is a pop culture diva, her DVR is constantly backlogged, and she unapologetically loved the ending of *Lost*. She wouldn't last five minutes without technology in the event of the apocalypse and has nightmares about refusing to leave her cats behind.

She is grateful for and humbled by all the readers. She knows very well she wouldn't be here if it wasn't for them and welcomes feedback.

Facebook: www.facebook.com/LXChase
Twitter: @Lex_Chase
Tumblr: lexiconofkittens.tumblr.com
Instagram: instagram.com/lexachase
Blog: lexchase.com
E-mail: lex.a.chase@gmail.com

BRU BAKER got her first taste of life as a writer at the tender age of four, when she started publishing a weekly newspaper for her family. What they called nosiness she called a nose for news, and no one was surprised when she ended up with degrees in journalism and political science and started a career in journalism.

Bru spent more than a decade writing for newspapers before making the jump to fiction. She now works in reference and readers' advisory in a Midwestern library, though she still finds it hard to believe someone's willing to pay her to talk about books all day. Most evenings you can find her curled up with a mug of tea, some fuzzy socks, and a book or her laptop. Whether it's creating her own characters or getting caught up in someone else's, there's no denying that Bru is happiest when she's engrossed in a story. She and her husband have two children, which means a lot of her books get written from the sidelines of various sports practices.

Website: www.bru-baker.com
Blog: www.bru-baker.blogspot.com
Twitter: @bru_baker
Facebook: www.facebook.com/bru.baker79
Goodreads: www.goodreads.com/author/show/6608093.Bru_Baker
E-mail: bru@bru-baker.com

Screw-up Princess and Skillful Huntsman Trilogy: Book One
A Fairy Tales of the Open Road Novel

Modern fairy-tale princess Taylor Hatfield has problems. One: he's a guy. Two: his perfect brother Atticus is the reincarnation of Snow White. Three: Taylor has no idea which princess he is supposed to be. Four: Taylor just left his prince (a girl) at the altar. Despite his enchanted lineage, Taylor is desperate to find his Happily Ever After away from magic, witches, and stuffy traditions. Regrettably, destiny has other plans for him. Dammit.

When word reaches Taylor that Idi the Witchking has captured Atticus, Taylor is determined to save his brother. He enlists the help of rakish and insufferable Corentin Devereaux, likewise of enchanted lineage. A malicious spell sends Taylor and Corentin on a road trip through the kitschy nostalgia of roadside Americana. To save Atticus, they must solve the puzzles put forth by Idi the Witchking. As they struggle, Taylor and Corentin's volatile partnership sparks a flash of something more. But princesses have many enemies, and Taylor must keep his wits about him because there's nothing worse than losing your heart… or your head.

www.dreamspinnerpress.com

Screw-up Princess and Skillful Huntsman Trilogy: Book Two
A Fairy Tales of the Open Road Novel

Modern day fairy-tale princess Taylor Hatfield has problems. One: he's a guy. Two: he's Sleeping Beauty, the most useless princess in existence. Throw in his true love, Corentin Devereaux, a huntsman descended from child-eating witches, and Taylor's younger brother, Atticus—this generation's Snow White—who tried to kill him. That didn't go so hot.

For two years, Taylor and Corentin live their Happily Ever After. But Corentin is cursed to lose his memory every seven days, including his life with Taylor—a painful reminder that he can't provide for the man he loves. Taylor insists Corentin has the strength to succeed, and when Taylor discovers a way to break the curse, he is more than willing to pay the cost.

When an enchanted blizzard devastates Corentin's hometown of New Orleans, Taylor is convinced Atticus is to blame and grows desperate to find him amid the Big Easy turned frozen wasteland. Corentin believes Taylor is chasing a ghost while he chases the ghosts of his own past. Old tensions scratch open scars, leaving both to wonder if they have each other's best interests at heart. The clock is ticking until Corentin loses his memory and the rabbit hole goes so deep they may never come out.

www.dreamspinnerpress.com

Carson is a California transplant settling into life in the Windy City. On his first Christmas away from home, he assures his worried family he'll be having a real Christmas dinner.

Recent culinary school graduate Tom Stockton earns some extra money giving out cooking advice at the Talk Turkey hotline. Tom's honeyed voice and sharp sense of humor are attractive to the lonely Carson, and Carson finds reasons to call the hotline again and again. But on Christmas Eve, Carson's call is less playful and more panicked with the big meal looming. Carson is just looking for advice, but Tom has a surprise in store that might lead to much more.

www.dreamspinnerpress.com

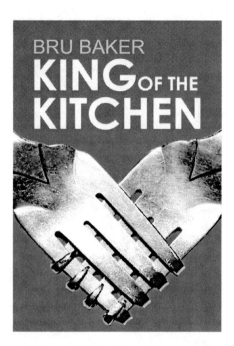

Rising kitchen talents Beck Douglas and Duncan Walters have been on the foodie paparazzi radar for years, since their status as heirs to two of the biggest celebrity chef empires around makes them culinary royalty. Beck is known for his charm and traditional food as cohost of his uncle's popular TV cooking show, while Duncan earned himself a reputation as a culinary bad boy, both for his refusal to work in his father's restaurants and his avant-garde approach to cooking.

They're also heirs to a food rivalry that could put the Hatfields and McCoys to shame, and when they're photographed in the middle of a heated argument, the press goes wild with speculation. Damage control ensues, with a fake friendship engineered by PR cronies that leaves both of them secretly pining for more.

Beck chafes under his uncle's micromanagement, and Duncan's relationship with his homophobic father becomes even more tenuous when Beck and Duncan start getting closer. It's hard to hide their chemistry on national television when Duncan joins Beck's cooking show, but they won't be able to take their relationship—or their careers—to the next level without breaking a few eggs.

www.dreamspinnerpress.com

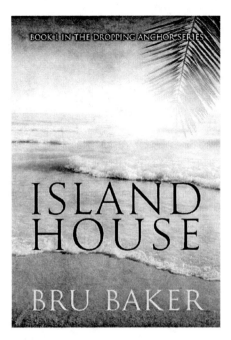

Dropping Anchor: Book One

Unable to move on after the death of his lover, British expat Niall Ahern clings to Nolan's dream of living in the Caribbean by moving to Tortola. Once there, he finds that not even the beauty of the island can fill the hole in his heart. Broke and spent in nearly every way imaginable, Niall wants out of the lonely, miserable, guilt-ridden life he's carved out for himself.

When Ethan Bettencourt, a wealthy tech guru, shows up in British Virgin Islands looking to purchase a second home, he gives Niall hope that he can move on. Both men fall hard and fast, but Niall finds piloting his yacht in the midst of a hurricane is nothing compared to weathering life's simple misunderstandings. As their troubles come between them, Niall is left to wonder if he and Ethan are over before they've begun.

www.dreamspinnerpress.com

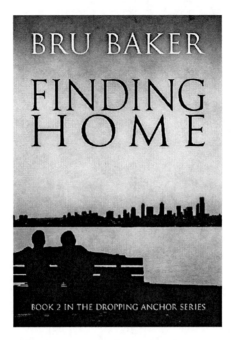

Dropping Anchor: Book Two

When an inheritance fell in Ian Mackay's lap, he fled the high-pressure banking industry and didn't look back. Since then, he's spent four years living carefree on the island of Tortola, his life a series of hookups and hanging out with friends.

After his best friend moves to Seattle and gets married, Ian finds himself lost. His unapologetic existence doesn't hold the same appeal, and he wonders if he's throwing his life away. After visiting Niall in Seattle, Ian decides to stay, but that means taking his life off hold and finding a real job. Meeting Luke Keys, who is about as far from a player as possible, isn't the plan but might be just what Ian needs. Luke and his values intrigue Ian, and he pursues Luke ruthlessly until Luke agrees to a date.

Their courtship sweeps Ian off his feet, and when the relationship gets complicated, Ian has the chance to cut and run. Habits born from years of being on his own are hard to shake, and self-proclaimed playboy Ian must decide if love is worth fighting for.

www.dreamspinnerpress.com

Dropping Anchor: Book Three

College sweethearts Frank and Warner have been together for sixteen years, married for eleven. Having grown up in a freewheeling hippie environment, Frank thinks their structured life is great, although lately he and Warner have fallen into a rut. Frank isn't concerned; it's what happens to old marrieds. Frank's blindsided, though, when he finds Warner looking into adopting, and Frank realizes just how not okay things really are.

Frank doesn't want kids. They bring chaos and unpredictability. He had enough of that growing up. Trying to salvage their relationship, Frank and Warner reach out for help. In the process of marriage counseling and working through their differences, Frank discovers his rigid adherence to schedules, anxiety attacks, and host of personality quirks are actually markers for Asperger Syndrome. With the help of a psychologist, Frank's life gets easier, and he realizes a future with children isn't as unfathomable as he once thought.

Through it all, Frank is stunned by how much making a family with Warner has boosted the intimacy between them. It's taken thirty-five years, but he's finally got a handle on life, and the future looks even better.

www.dreamspinnerpress.com

The Magic of Weihnachten

BRU BAKER

American Walsh Brandt is happy when a promotion lands him his dream job and a quiet new life in Germany. Until December rolls around, when he realizes it's almost impossible to hide from the holiday season in Germany.

Dierck Reiniger is fascinated by Walsh's hatred of Christmas and makes it his personal mission to help Walsh enjoy Weihnachten and the German traditions he grew up with. Walsh has a great time getting to know Dierck—but he still isn't sold on Christmas, despite Dierck's efforts. Dierck's on the rebound, and he's determined to develop their physical relationship slowly, much to Walsh's frustration. It isn't until they're alone in a secluded cabin—hiding from the traditional trappings—that Walsh finally recognizes what the magic of the season can bring when spent with someone special.

www.dreamspinnerpress.com

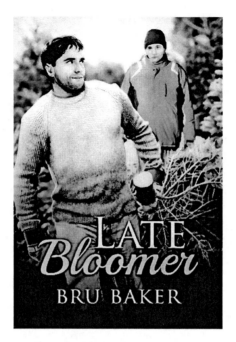

If not for his family and his Christmas tree farm, David Rochester would be a recluse. And Erik Shriver wouldn't know a quiet moment if it smacked him in the face. But now David's farm has brought them together. When Erik's flurry of bad jokes and frenetic energy sets David off kilter, his family notices and begins conspiring. They push David and a very willing Erik together again and again until David stops denying his attraction. But an almost-hermit and a soon-to-be-former club boy each bring baggage into a relationship. They'll have to take things slowly to find the middle ground between David's taciturn silence and Eric's boundless chatter.

www.dreamspinnerpress.com

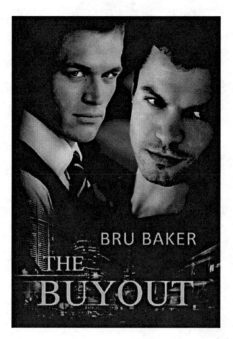

BRU BAKER

THE

BUYOUT

All Parker Anderson has ever wanted is to take over as CEO of Anderson Industries when his father retires. But when his father is ready to leave the company, he doesn't plan to pass the reins to Parker. Instead, he plans to sell the company, jeopardizing not only Parker's job but hundreds of others.

Parker finds an unlikely ally in Mason Pike, the company's resident IT guru. What starts as a flirtation takes them from coworkers to coconspirators in a plan to forcibly buy Anderson Industries out from under Parker's father. While they focus on the buyout, their budding romance has to be put on hold, but that doesn't stop them from flirting and teasing each other to distraction—and once their master plan comes to fruition, nothing and no one can keep them apart.

CPSIA information can be obtained
at www.ICGtesting.com
Printed in the USA
FSOW02n1724160517
34123FS